A crackling noise made Crysta whirl to look behind her

Footsteps? Frustrated by the low rushing sound of the river, she strained to hear, eyes scanning the woods for movement, heart racing, senses bombarded.

One word bounced off the walls of her mind. *Bears.* Still, if there was anything as big as a grizzly out there, surely she would see it. Or hear it. Wouldn't she?

She listened for a few seconds, flinching when leaves, caught by the wind, rustled overhead. Nothing. Whatever she had heard, it was gone now. She hoped. She ran across a stretch of marshy grass and back into the brush, darting right and left through the maze of undergrowth. Finally, she was safe.

Then a towering dark form loomed above her, like a predator coming in for the kill. . . .

ABOUT THE AUTHOR

Alaska has always been a dream destination for Catherine Anderson and her family. Although she hasn't achieved her dream yet, her brother-in-law provided reams of videotape that proved to be inspiration for *Cry of the Wild*. She also had behind-the-scenes help from her son John, an Alaska fanatic. Catherine lives with her husband and two sons in Roseburg, Oregon.

Books by Catherine Anderson

HARLEQUIN INTRIGUE
  92–REASONABLE DOUBT
114–WITHOUT A TRACE
135–SWITCHBACK

Don't miss any of our special offers. Write to us at the following address for information on our newest releases.

Harlequin Reader Service
P.O. Box 1397, Buffalo, NY 14240
Canadian address: P.O. Box 603,
Fort Erie, Ont. L2A 5X3

Cry of
the Wild

Catherine Anderson

Harlequin Books

TORONTO • NEW YORK • LONDON
AMSTERDAM • PARIS • SYDNEY • HAMBURG
STOCKHOLM • ATHENS • TOKYO • MILAN
MADRID • WARSAW • BUDAPEST • AUCKLAND

In memory of Barton Eugene Gatewood.
With special thanks to Gerald Christean.

Harlequin Intrigue edition published December 1992

ISBN 0-373-22206-8

CRY OF THE WILD

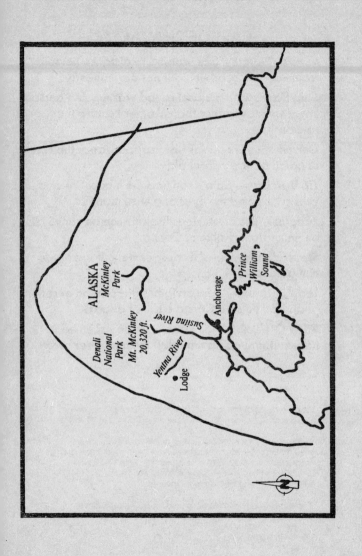

CAST OF CHARACTERS

Crysta Meyers—She wanted to distance herself from her twin brother—but not permanently.

Sam Barrister—His best friend was missing and he knew someone other than Mother Nature was responsible.

Derrick Meyers—Was his disappearance the result of harsh nature or foul play?

Tip Barrister—Sam's son had the innocence of a young boy and the eyes of a wise man.

Jangles—The mysterious Indian woman conveyed an immediate dislike of Crysta.

Steve Henderson—His desperately ill son made him a desperate man.

Todd Shriver—An incorrigible flirt and an excellent pilot, had he sold Crysta a bill of goods?

Riley O'Keefe—This good-time boy seemed to have nothing on his mind but the next beer run.

Chapter One

A midnight-black wind swirled around Crysta Meyers, drawing her toward a point of light that grew steadily larger. When she reached it, she found herself walking along a brightly lit corridor. Alarmed without knowing why, she examined the walls and saw that they were actually tall stacks of sturdy packing boxes, each about two feet long and over a foot deep. A storage building of some kind? Dust particles stung her nostrils. Fluorescent light fixtures, blue-white and eerie, hung from lofty steel ceiling beams.

Her boots echoed on the concrete floor as she moved along the narrow aisle. She paused to make a quick inventory of the boxes and came up with over a hundred. What was inside them? And why this sense of urgency?

She took another step, then glanced down at herself. The top three buttons of her blue chambray shirt were unfastened, the neckline gaping. Each time she moved, corded muscle flexed in her thighs beneath the faded denim of her jeans. She wore a wide leather belt with a large silver-dollar buckle. She studied the buckle a moment and then realized it was her twin brother Derrick's, personalized with his initials. She had had it made for him five years ago as a twenty-fifth-birthday gift.

Crysta turned a corner and found herself in still another aisle. Something sticky swept across her face. A cobweb. She sputtered and wiped her lips. Ahead of her, she saw a row of wooden crates. Diablo Building Supplies, Inc. was printed in black on the side of each. She wanted to hurry forward to see what was inside them, but her body froze midstride. She could hear her heart slamming, feel sweat popping out on her forehead. Fear.

Was someone coming? Yes, she heard them now, men talking, somewhere off to the left. She shrank back and immediately wondered what had prompted her to hide. Who were the men? And why did they frighten her so?

Crysta heard the men drawing closer. The more distinct their voices became, the more frightened she felt. A shadow shifted in the aisle up ahead. Crysta stared, then whirled and ran. Up one aisle, down another, left, then right, like a terrified mouse in a maze. The jogging loosened her belt. She heard a clatter. She whirled and spied Derrick's buckle lying on the floor several feet behind her. The silver dollar had been jarred loose and was rolling to disappear beneath a wooden pallet. She shouldn't leave it behind, not with Derrick's initials on it. Before she could go back for it, though, the shadow ahead took on the distinct outline of a man.

Hurry, hurry, before he sees you. She had no idea who the man might be, but her sense of urgency to escape undetected was too strong to be ignored. She threw a wild glance around her, looking for anything that would earmark this aisle so she could come back for the buckle later. On the floor, near the pallet, she saw a splotch of green paint. Satisfied, she turned to flee.

Suddenly, inexplicably, Crysta's surroundings changed. Momentarily disoriented, she faltered, a different kind of fear swamping her as she tried to recognize where she was and figure out how she had gotten there.

Cottonwood trees stood all around her, their billowy tops silhouetted against a powder-blue sky. Numbing coldness shot up her legs. She looked down and saw she was no longer on concrete but slogging through ankle-deep water in the shallows of a river. She could hear the stream rushing, the wind whistling.

The shirt she now wore was red flannel, western-style with pearl snaps. Icy water seeped through her jeans and heavy boots. She wore a different belt now, narrow with an ordinary prong buckle. Exhaustion made her legs quiver. Tired, so tired.

Sunshine glinted off the water. By the weariness in her legs, she knew she had been running a long while. To her right, up on the riverbank, was a stunted spruce, its trunk wind-twisted from years of harsh exposure.

Crysta's lungs whined for breath. Defeat and exhaustion dragged her feet to a stop. There was a thrashing sound in the water behind her, then low curses. Apprehension tingled up her spine. She was afraid to turn around.

"You can't get away, Meyers!"

The voice rent the air, deep and booming. Was it one of the voices she had heard inside the storage building? She couldn't be certain. Something silver arced over her shoulder and splashed at her feet. Through the distortion of the ripples, she recognized Derrick's personalized belt buckle, minus the silver dollar, the one she had lost in the storage building.

Another man spoke. "You dropped that the other night. We thought you might like it back. Pretty expensive mistake, leaving it behind. Sorry, chum, but the game's up."

Her movements sluggish, Crysta stooped and picked up the buckle. As she dropped it into her left breast pocket, her arm trembled. Still gasping for breath, she managed to reply, in a voice that sounded unlike her own, "Don't be worse fools than you already are. I've passed on the information."

"You're bluffing. Who could you have told?"

"Any number of people. For all you know, I could have used your mobile phone to call the police in Anchorage."

From the corner of her eye, Crysta spotted one man's rubber boots, military-green with yellow bands at the tops and soles. A quick movement flashed. Pain exploded inside her head. She reeled, unable to see. The next instant, she sprawled in the water. She willed herself to move, to run, but was too dazed.

The shocking coldness of the water soaked her shirt and lapped against her jaw, perilously close to her mouth and nose. A metallic taste shriveled her tongue. Blood. She stirred and moaned. When she opened her eyes, the world spun. Disoriented, she stared at her outflung hand. Her little finger came into focus, familiar yet somehow not. A sickening smell wafted to her, thick and rotten, like spoiled fish.

"You idiot! Why did you hit him?" someone cried.

"You heard what he said. Someone else knows. We have to get rid of him. We don't have a choice."

"No! Are you crazy? What do you mean, get rid of him?"

A funnel cloud sucked at Crysta, ink-black and swirling. She clung desperately to the shrinking microcosm of reality, struggling to make sense of the words ricocheting around her. *Him?* Rolling weakly onto her side, she tried to focus on the men's faces, but her vision was badly blurred. Something gleamed in the sunlight. She guessed what it was and tried to scream. She felt herself doing a free-fall through blackness, the men's voices fading decibels a second.

"You can't kill him!"

"Watch me."

She heard an ominous little click. The next instant, an explosive noise rent the air.

CRYSTA JERKED AWAKE, eyes bulging, the sound of gunfire still ringing in her ears, her chest banded by a crushing pain. She didn't know where she was. Someone or something was holding her down. With a quick glance, she saw that the sheet and blankets were entwined around her. She must have been thrashing in her sleep.

A parched sob tore up her throat. Her head ached fiercely. She worked one arm loose from the sweat-soaked sheets and ran her fingers along her temple, half expecting to feel swelling. Nothing. She stared at her little finger, so similar to the one she had studied in her dream. She knew of only one person with hands so much like her own: her twin, Derrick.

With that realization came a surge of panic. Crysta rolled from the bed and onto her feet, so dizzy she could scarcely stand, fear washing over her in icy waves. "Derrick?"

The sound of her voice bounced off the walls, quavery and raw with emotion. She swallowed and turned a half circle.

"Derrick?"

There was no answer, just a resounding silence broken only by the wild thrumming of her heart. Crysta stopped breathing so she might hear better, her pulse accelerating with each passing second. Within her, for the very first time in her life, she heard only silence . . . an awful silence.

The horrible smell of rotting fish still clung to her. Her stomach plunged. Sick—she was going to be sick. She spun and headed for the bathroom. Minutes later, she clung to the porcelain toilet bowl, limbs trembling. The silence inside her head had magnified.

She just had the flu, she assured herself. Yes, that was all it was, a simple case of flu, she assured herself. Yes, that was all it was, a simple case of flu and a bad dream.

Her nightgown skimmed her body like wet gauze. Cinnamon-colored strands of hair hung in a curtain around her face, sticky with sweat and hair spray. She must have had a fever, and it had broken in her sleep. No wonder she had dreamed something so crazy. Delirium. So real, it had seemed so real.

Pressing a hand to her chest, she rested a few more minutes, trying to ignore the feeling of impending doom that still hovered around her. Struggling to get herself back on track, she shifted her gaze to the everyday things around her: the crimson dish of scented soap on the sink, her ratty pink slippers by the tub, her terry robe on the door hook, the rack of magazines by the toilet. Derrick. She couldn't rid herself of the feeling that something was wrong. She didn't have dreams like this about him unless he needed her.

Tempted to call Blanchette Construction to find out where Derrick was working this week, she glanced at her clock. Six a.m. Derrick's boss wouldn't appreciate a phone call this early in the morning, and neither would Derrick. Besides, what would she say? Sorry for bothering you, brother dear, but I dreamed you were in trouble? She couldn't start making frantic phone calls. She wouldn't allow herself to. After three years of weekly therapy to distance herself from Derrick, she should be well equipped to handle a frightening dream about him without panicking. If she couldn't, then she had spent all that time and money for nothing.

Remembering her analyst's advice, Crysta closed her eyes and took a deep breath, repeating one sentence over and over in her mind. *It was only a dream.* She tried desperately to believe the words, but it wasn't that easy, not when her past was littered with dozens of similar dreams that had proven almost prophetic in their accuracy.

Childhood memories pelted Crysta. The time Derrick had been stricken with appendicitis while he was away at summer camp, and she had awakened in the dead of night screaming with abdominal pain. The time Derrick had been hit in the temple with a bat at baseball practice, and Crysta, miles away, had fallen to her knees, momentarily blinded with pain. Coincidences, the family physician had insisted, but Crysta and Derrick had known better. Over the years, Derrick had been treated to similar experiences, aware that Crysta was in trouble or ill when they were physically separated. In some indefinable, inexplicable way that even they couldn't understand, they were connected, emotionally and mentally, as other people were not.

As it always did after one of her dreams, a feeling of urgency filled Crysta, a compulsive need to find Derrick and assure herself he was okay. It was a compulsion she refused to gratify, for her sake and Derrick's.

Crysta forced herself to stand up, continuing to deep breathe. Only a dream, only a dream. It wasn't real. The litany provided little comfort. Even so, Crysta embraced the thought, determined not to let her dreams control her.

Not this time.

She would get started with her day and keep busy, just as her analyst had told her she should, until the dream lost its hold on her. It was what Derrick would insist she do if he were here. He was a grown man and perfectly capable of taking care of himself. If he was in trouble, he'd find a way to extricate himself from it.

A cup of tea would help settle her stomach, soothe her nerves and clear her mind. Groping her way from the bathroom, Crysta grabbed her robe from the hook and draped it around her shoulders. Still unsteady on her feet, she made her way through the living room and into the adjoining kitchen. After putting some water on to boil, she sat at the breakfast bar and dropped her head into her hands, fighting off another wave of nausea. Only a dream. She had to believe that.

FOUR HOURS LATER, Crysta still had a nagging sense of unease but otherwise felt fine. Her dream that morning had been just that: a scary dream.

She sat at her desk in the back room of her dress shop, tallying yesterday's receipts, the adding machine keys clacking rhythmically beneath her quick fingers. The height of her spike heels prevented her from crossing her legs without colliding with the underside of the desk, and an ache inched up her thigh from sitting so long in the same position. She squirmed, tugging on her white skirt so it wouldn't be hopelessly crunched and wrinkled beneath her.

The boutique's entrance bell chimed. Crysta glanced out the office doorway at Rosanne, her partner, who was restocking the cashier stand with mauve shopping bags. "Is that Mrs. Grimes?"

"No, just a browser." Rosanne straightened the last stack of bags, then looked over her shoulder and grinned. "Since when did old Grimy ever come on time? Maybe something wonderful will happen and she won't show for her appointment. You don't look quite up to her today. What's her fantasy this month? To look like Twiggy?"

"No, Farrah, I think. She's gone blond."

Rosanne groaned. "Give me a break. Who does she think we are, miracle workers? That woman's built like a sumo wrestler."

Crysta bit back a grin. It was, after all, her business to design dresses to camouflage the problem figure. Mrs. Grimes just happened to have more problems than most—

about a hundred of them, if Crysta was any judge of poundage. "I'll think of something."

"What, a tent dress? Or maybe a starvation diet?"

"Bite your tongue."

"Hey, I hate diets, too, but I detest fat more."

Crysta scanned Rosanne's stringy figure, quite certain the other woman had never dieted a day in her life. "The imperfect figure is what keeps us in business."

"Is that my cue to say thank goodness for Mrs. Grimes?"

"At least she makes a constant effort to look her best. She's very stylish, always does her hair and wears make—" A sudden pain in Crysta's chest made her break off and clamp a hand over her heart. She jackknifed forward over her desk, her head swimming with dizziness. "Oh..."

"Crysta!" Rosanne came running, her eyes round with concern. "What is it? What's wrong? Crysta, for heaven's sake, answer me."

A picture of treetops and blue sky flashed through Crysta's head. Then a horrifying sensation of falling came over her. She grabbed the desk, completely disoriented. When at last she got her bearings again, the pain had abated.

"Oh, God, do you think it's your heart? It happens sometimes, you know, even at our age."

"No—no, I'm fine," Crysta whispered shakily. "I'm fine. It was probably just a gas pain or something. It's gone now."

"You're sure? You look awfully pale. You shouldn't ignore chest pain. Maybe you should take the afternoon off and drop by the doctor's office. I can reschedule Grimy for another day."

The idea of an afternoon off appealed to Crysta, though she had absolutely no intention of using the time to see her doctor. Therapy or no, she was frightened now. Really frightened. "Do you really think you can handle everything alone? We've got a busy day scheduled."

"With my eyes closed."

CRYSTA LEANED BACK in her kitchen bar stool and tapped her fingernails on the Formica countertop, gazing at the wall phone. After an hour and a half of placing phone calls, one to Derrick's boss, one to Aunt Eva, and several others to his friends, she had no more idea where her brother was than when she had begun. Derrick was on vacation, his boss had said, but he didn't know where. Her aunt and Derrick's friends had said the same.

Given the fact that Crysta and Derrick had been trying to wean themselves from one another, it didn't strike Crysta as odd that her brother had taken a vacation without notifying her. But it did seem odd that he hadn't specified where he was going. With their mother's heart the way it was, both Crysta and Derrick made it a point to be accessible by phone whenever possible. Even when Derrick went on his wilderness treks, he left word at his departure point of what area he expected to be in on any given day.

Crysta resisted the temptation to call her mother. Her mom might know where Derrick was, and then again, she might not. The only certainty was that Ellen Meyers would become alarmed if Crysta revealed that she was trying to locate Derrick. After several years of watching her children deliberately drift apart, Ellen would sense something was wrong. And Crysta couldn't risk that. Not over a dream that might or might not have had special meaning.

With another weary sigh, Crysta glanced at her watch, disgusted with herself for regressing to the point that she had taken off work in the middle of the day to stare at her telephone. Normal people didn't do things like this, and above all else, Crysta longed for normalcy.

"I can't go on like this," she whispered.

The words echoed in her mind long after they were spoken. During the long evening, Crysta repeated them many times, until they took on the solemnity of a vow. Would she never learn? She had to get Derrick out of her head, once and for all, or live the remainder of her life alone. That discouraging thought accompanied Crysta to bed and followed her into a restless sleep.

TWO MORNINGS LATER, shortly after dawn, Crysta's ringing telephone jarred her from the depths of slumber. She shoved herself to a sitting position, threw a glance at the anemic light spilling in her bedroom window and reached for the receiver. Who would be calling at this hour? That question was answered when Crysta heard her mother babbling over the wire.

"Mom, what's wrong? Whoa, slow down. Derrick's what?"

"The police just called. He's missing!"

For an instant, Crysta felt as if the bed had dropped out from under her. "Missing?"

"Lost along the river. I knew he shouldn't go trekking off alone in that godawful country."

Crysta's head spun. She braced an arm behind her to keep her balance, trying to make sense of what her mother was saying. Derrick's job in quality control for Blanchette Construction took him up and down the West Coast doing random inspections at building sites. He could have chosen almost anywhere to spend his vacation. Godawful country, according to Ellen Meyers, was anyplace outside the reaches of Los Angeles.

"Mom, can you start at the beginning? Where was Derrick last seen?"

A little hard of hearing, especially when rattled, her mom rushed on. "Oh, Crysta, there are grizzlies in that place. And thousands of miles of wilderness. You have to go up there! You'd be able to find him. I just know it."

"So he was in Alaska?"

"Of course. People don't drop off the face of the earth here in the States."

"Mother, Alaska *is* a state. Try to calm down. I know you must be frightened, but getting so upset isn't good for you."

"But if he isn't found soon, he could die of exposure."

"Don't think the worst. I'm sure that won't happen."

Crysta wished she was as certain of that as she sounded. Her gaze flew to a snapshot on the nightstand. In it Derrick had an arm slung over her shoulders, head bent to press his cheek against hers. Reddish-brown hair, wide-set hazel eyes, fine features. They were a matched set except for gender. She couldn't imagine life without him.

Licking her lips, Crysta said, "Derrick's a competent woodsman. He'll find shelter. Have you called that Sam Barrister, the lodge owner? He and Derrick spend so much time together, he might know where Derrick went."

"I called him right away. He kept trying to reassure me, but I could tell he was worried. Derrick was staying at his lodge, like he always does when he goes up that way. He called from the lodge to check on me last week, in fact, right before he went on the hike. He disappeared along the Yentna River."

"How long has he been missing?"

"They can't be sure. It's been a whole day since he was due back, but he could have been lost earlier and no one would have known. When he didn't come back, Sam Barrister formed a search party. After they found Derrick's gear, he notified the authorities. He said that he tried to contact you, but he couldn't get your number through information."

"I see." Crysta's clammy skin turned icy. Images from her dream swept through her mind. Did the Yentna River have a wind-twisted spruce somewhere along its banks? And lots of cottonwood? Stop it, Crysta. Stop it. You can't let yourself begin believing in the dreams again, not if you value your sanity.

Wrapping the phone cord around her index finger, she watched her fingernail turn purple, then took a deep breath and exhaled very slowly. "Are they still searching for him?"

A jagged sob came over the line. "Yes, but for how long? After a certain period, they're bound to give up. Crysta, you can take a few days off. That woman—what's her name?— she can run the shop."

"Oh, Mom..." Crysta wished she was with her mother so she could comfort her. Being upset like this was bad for her health. "Derrick's all right. I'm certain of it. Don't cry, please."

After a moment, Ellen seemed to regain control. She heaved a teary sigh. "Crysta, you haven't, um, been in touch with Derrick or anything, have you?"

"Mother, of course not. Don't you think I'd tell you?"

"No, I don't mean like that—not a phone call or anything. I mean the other way. When you said you were certain he was all right, I thought—I know you two have been trying to distance yourselves from each other, but..." Ellen's voice trailed off. "I knew no good would come from all that counseling. Look what's happened. You're brother's in trouble, and you haven't sensed a thing! This is the first time, the first time, Crysta. What does that tell you?"

Crysta closed her eyes and wondered if a person's head could actually explode from tension. She must guard her every word, her every inflection, or her mother would guess the truth: that she had dreamed of Derrick, over two days ago. Ellen was already far more upset than was good for her, and Crysta knew from experience that her mother would believe the dream had significance.

"Are you still there?"

"Yes. I'm getting a terrific headache, and it's hard to concentrate, that's all."

Ellen's voice became sharp. "Is it coming on suddenly? Oh, Crysta, you have to go up there. I know this thing between you and Derrick has been a source of heartache for you, but, darling, he may need you."

While talking with her mother, Crysta knew better than to deny her telepathic link with her twin. Ellen would only become more agitated. "I understand that, Mom. I haven't turned my back on Derrick—you know that. He and I have just been trying to get things into perspective."

"Then you'll go? The closer you are, the better chance you have of contacting him! You know—sensing where he is."

Crysta yearned to scream or hang up the phone, neither of which was an acceptable course of action. It wasn't that she didn't care. She cared far too much. The dreams were bunk; she had to believe that. And yet...

"Listen, Mom, why don't I call Barrister and the police, then get back to you? Let me see what I can find out. What's the name of Sam's lodge? I've forgotten it."

"Cottonwood Bend."

With a trembling hand, Crysta quickly jotted down the name, the report of a gun echoing in her mind. What if something had happened to Derrick, something terrible, and she had wasted precious time? "I'll call you right back, okay? Try to stay calm."

"Crysta, don't hang up! You will fly up there, won't you? I'll pay for your ticket. Promise me you'll go."

"Of course I'll go. And I'll pay for my own ticket. I love Derrick, Mom. I know it may not seem that way sometimes, but I do love him, just as much as ever."

As soon as she broke the connection, Crysta flopped back onto her pillow. Cottonwood Bend? Then there *were* cottonwoods along the Yentna. Uncertainty swamped her. Two entire days had passed since her dream. What if, against all the laws of logic, Derrick had been trying to send her a distress signal?

Sitting up, she quickly dialed her aunt Eva, not caring if she rousted the older woman from bed at so early an hour.

"Mom just phoned," Crysta explained hastily when her aunt finally answered. "The authorities in Alaska contacted her. Derrick's missing."

"Oh, dear God."

"I was wondering if you could go stay with her, Aunt Eva. She's awfully upset."

"You're not going up there, are you?" Eva's gravelly voice went taut. "Crysta, you've no idea what most of Alaska's like. Those lodges aren't located next door to shopping malls and bus stops. I went up there once with your uncle Fred, remember, and I know what I'm talking about. You love your brother, and I understand that, but in this instance, letting the authorities handle it would be the wiser choice."

Crysta glanced at her brother's photograph. As competent as the Alaskan authorities probably were, they didn't know and love Derrick the way she did. "I really feel that I should."

"Your mother?"

Crysta ran a hand into her hair. She could always count on Aunt Eva to understand. "She's terribly upset. If my being up there eases her mind, it's a small thing to do."

"Flying to Frisco, maybe. But Alaska? A woman, all alone?"

"I'm pretty adaptable, Aunt Eva. Besides, Derrick's best friend, Sam, owns the lodge. He'll watch out for me. I have to look at this practically. Staying here, I won't be much comfort to Mom. She'll feel better if she knows I've gone up there. And I'll feel better, too. At least that way I can assure myself that everything possible is being done to find Derrick." Crysta reached for the phone book. "I need to make some calls and try to find out all I can. Meanwhile, Mom shouldn't be alone, not when she's so upset."

"I'll go right over."

"Try to calm her down, Aunt Eva. Stress the fact that Derrick's familiar with the area and a good woodsman. Remind her of who has been organizing the search. Derrick told me there's no better guide in all Alaska than Sam Barrister. I'll contact the authorities up there and divert their calls to me—either here or up there at Barrister's lodge. I'll get back to you with any news."

The moment Crysta hung up, she opened the phone book. After finding the area code for Alaska, which she could never seem to remember, she dialed information for the number to Cottonwood Bend and then placed a call to its owner. Seconds later, Barrister's deep voice crackled over the line. Was it similar to one of those she had heard in her dream? No, that was crazy.

She quickly introduced herself. "Are you having a storm up there, Mr. Barrister? We have a terrible connection."

"It's the mobile phone. I took it in for repairs, but it's still on the fritz. I'm trying to limp by with it until the end of the season."

The nape of Crysta's neck prickled. So the lodge wasn't serviced with phone lines. *"Your mobile phone,"* Derrick had said in her dream. Sam Barrister's?

"I'm thinking of coming up to help search for my brother, Mr. Barrister. I understand Derrick disappeared on a hiking trip in your vicinity."

"That's right.'

"And he's been missing a day?"

"Two, actually."

"Two! Why on earth did you wait so long to get a search started?"

"I wanted to give him the chance to make it back on his own. He came back a day late once before, so I wasn't alarmed at first, not until I went out looking for him and came across his gear." He paused a moment. "I guess I shouldn't have waited, but I really hated to call in search-and-rescue until I knew for certain it was necessary. Those fellows are all volunteers. They have to leave their jobs and families."

"Volunteers? You mean it's not the police searching for him?"

"They're involved. But volunteers do most of the legwork. This is a remote area. It takes pilots volunteering to fly people in, Anchorage businesses donating foodstuffs. You have to appreciate how much people have come together on this."

Crysta had heard of search-and-rescue teams, and she admired the volunteers for their dedication. But when it came to Derrick, she wanted the very best trackers looking for him—professionals, if at all possible. Fear knotted her stomach. She yearned to hear Derrick's voice, to hear him laugh, to feel the warmth of his hand on hers.

"Are you saying the search for my brother is being left to amateurs?" Despite her attempt to be calm, Crysta couldn't keep the note of hysteria out of her voice.

When Sam Barrister spoke, his tone was silken and patient. "Search-and-rescue teams are well qualified. In addition to them, Blanchette Construction made arrangements to bring in a Huey helicopter with infrared devices that detect as much as a two-degree variation in temperature. Everything that can be done is being done. Bank on that."

"And has the helicopter detected anything?"

"Not yet, no. But they didn't start making sweeps until yesterday. There's endless territory to cover. All the high-tech equipment in the world can't perform miracles."

The helicopter sounded impressive, but beyond that, Crysta pictured a handful of unqualified men stumbling around in the woods calling Derrick's name. Her throat tightened.

"Do you have a spare cabin I could use?" Derrick was too important to let strangers handle everything. Her mother was right; Crysta should be there. "I'd pay, of course. I'd really like to be nearby, and I know my mom would feel better if a member of our family was up there."

He hesitated a moment. "How's your mom doing? Derrick told me about her heart problems, so I wasn't too happy when I heard the authorities up here had called her. I asked them not to, to try to get in touch with you, but I guess the fellow I talked to went off shift. I tried to get your number through information but couldn't. I figured they might have better luck. First thing I knew, your mom was calling me." He sighed. "I'm sorry about that. I wanted to get word to you so you could be there with her and cushion the blow when she heard the news."

"She's awfully upset, I'm afraid." Crysta fastened her gaze on Derrick's photograph. The concern she heard in Barrister's voice reinforced all the positive things Derrick had told her about him.

"It's an expensive trip, Crysta. I can waive my rates, but that won't help on your air fare or your float-plane flight inland."

His voice was deep and warm, filled with sympathy, yet Crysta detected an underlying tension. Something wasn't clicking here.

"I see."

There was another short silence. "No, I'm afraid you don't. Let's be straight with each other, okay? Your coming up isn't a good idea."

"Why on earth not?"

"What could you actually do to help? This is rugged country. A person who doesn't know his way around could easily become lost. As cruel as this may sound, you'll be more a hindrance than a help. It's pretty primitive up here, and right now every available person is out searching. There's no one to accompany you anywhere.''

"I see."

Actually, she didn't see, and she was infuriated with herself for making the same inane response twice. Why was the man trying to discourage her from coming? Crysta knew from Derrick's stories about Sam's lodge that all different types visited there: businessmen, actors, football players, families with children. The main lodge, though rustic, kept food laid out 'round the clock for any hungry guests who might trail in from the surrounding cabins. That wasn't what one would term primitive.

"I knew you'd understand," Barrister replied. "I'll keep you posted, okay? If Derrick's out there, we'll find him—you can count on it."

Bristling, Crysta said, "Derrick is my brother—my twin brother."

"And you love him. But loving him isn't enough in country like this. In fact, it could be a drawback. It's extremely difficult for family members to remain objective. You'll be better off if you stay home. And so will Derrick. Why don't you give me your number. I'll give you a call back tonight to let you know how the search is progressing and if we've found any signs of—"

The phone crackled loudly with static. Crysta pressed the receiver closer to her ear. "Mr. Barrister?"

She listened a moment, then clenched her teeth in frustration. Disconnected. She redialed the number and got a busy signal. Had he hung up on her? His phone might have gone on the blink again, but it seemed like mighty convenient timing.

Dropping the receiver into its cradle, she reviewed her conversation with the lodge owner, becoming more convinced by the moment that there was something he wasn't telling her. She had no idea what that might be, but she was convinced his reluctance to have her up there stemmed from something more than concern over her finances and her safety. What, though? That was the question. Was he hiding something?

Whatever his argument, Crysta knew she had no choice but to fly north. It wasn't just that her mother wanted her to go; Crysta loved her brother far too much to let his fate be decided by a bunch of weekend Rambos. No matter how she tried or how much she wanted to, she couldn't forget her dream.

With grim determination, she flipped the phone book back open. Within five minutes, she had reserved a flight to Anchorage. After that, she called Rosanne, asking her to take over at the shop until she returned, then quickly packed a bag and went to spend the night at her mother's. They both needed a little comforting.

Chapter Two

Sam rapped the phone receiver on the counter, then listened for a dial tone. Nothing. He gave it another rap, then heaved a frustrated sigh. With his luck, Derrick's sister would think he had hung up on her, and if she was anything like her brother, that would be all the impetus she needed to book the first possible flight to Anchorage. He glared at the phone, cursed under his breath and slammed the receiver into its cradle. There were days when nothing went right, and this was one of them.

He walked to the window, bracing his shoulder against the frame to stare through the steamed glass at a stand of cottonwoods. He considered sitting down for a moment but quickly discarded the idea. As if he had time to rest.

The lodge's main room, dining and sitting area combined, was filled with the delicious aroma of fried salmon cakes and Jangles's wonderful homemade yeast rolls. His stomach turned. He massaged the muscles in the nape of his neck, tipping his head back to ease the tension. The crackling of the fire usually soothed him, but not today.

What would he do if Crysta Meyers flew up here? Maybe he should have told her about the condition of Derrick's gear. The shredded backpack and scattered contents pointed to a bear attack, except for two minor things: no blood and no body.

That bothered Sam. Derrick was fast on his feet, but not that fast. He couldn't have outrun a grizzly for long, so there should have been at least some blood nearby. Not only that, but bears rarely attacked people in this vicinity unless provoked, and Derrick was too bear-smart to be that stupid. Sam couldn't, in good conscience, intimate to Derrick's relatives that Derrick had been the victim of a bear attack until there was more conclusive proof. Especially not when he had reason to suspect that Derrick had been murdered by men, not animals.

Heaving a sigh, Sam turned from the window and strode toward his office. He had to get started going through those papers in Derrick's briefcase. That alone would be a two-day chore. Maybe he was barking up the wrong tree, but he couldn't rid himself of the feeling there was far more to this than met the eye. If he didn't turn up anything, then a flight to Anchorage was in order.

Meanwhile, Sam could only hope Crysta Meyers took his advice and stayed at home in Los Angeles...where she would be safe.

ALASKA FROM THE AIR.

At any other time, Crysta might have thought this state beautiful, perhaps even mystical, but today her only reaction to it was dread. How could she hope to find Derrick out there? For too long now, the closest thing to a road she had seen was a moose trail. The tundra, dotted with small dark lakes, seemed to stretch into infinity, the snow-draped peaks of Mounts McKinley and Foraker standing sentinel, so immense their tops were wreathed in clouds.

As the tiny plane veered north, she stared down at a tannish-brown glacier river, the Big Susitna, according to her travel pamphlet. Along the river's banks, she saw several uprooted trees, bulldozed by nature when the ice had broken.

"The Yentna River's up ahead," the pilot, Todd Shriver, yelled, trying to make himself heard over the engine noise. "We'll follow her course right in to the lodge."

Crysta craned her neck to see. She had expected something more than spruce, cottonwoods and undergrowth.

"Aren't there other lodges out here besides Cottonwood Bend?"

"A few. You have to remember, though, that a real close neighbor in these parts is at least five miles away."

To Crysta, a wilderness area was a well-marked nature trail. Ordinarily, she might have enjoyed visiting a remote lodge. But knowing Sam Barrister wasn't going to be happy to see her made the isolation rather unnerving. To locate her brother, she needed to be here. What if Barrister refused to let her stay?

To take her mind off that unsettling possibility, Crysta tried to concentrate on the landscape. The shaking and shuddering of the Cessna made it impossible. The Cottonwood Bend brochure, which she had picked up at the Lake Hood Airport, had called the float-plane flight up the Yentna a once-in-a-lifetime adventure; it hadn't mentioned that it could well be her last.

She had only herself to blame. Rather than wait until tomorrow, she had bribed Shriver for passage on a supply run this afternoon, not realizing what she was bargaining for. Despite her mother's favorite aphorism, ignorance was not bliss. Her fellow passengers were numerous crates and two fifty-gallon drums of fuel for the lodge's generator. Behind those, she caught a glimpse of a partially open carton bearing an animal skull with macabre black holes where its eyes had once been. She couldn't shake the eerie feeling that it was staring at her. Doubtless Shriver often hauled hunters and their grim trophies to and fro from Anchorage, but she wished she hadn't encountered a victim on her first pontoon-plane flight. She was nervous enough as it was.

Crysta often made buying trips for her dress shop and considered herself a fairly seasoned traveler, but she flew in large jets. Being a passenger on this glorified tin can with no landing wheels was a new experience. The pilot, tall, blond and tanned to a leathery brown, looked as if he should be posing for a macho cigarette advertisement. And he lived up to the image.

In the two hours since meeting her, he had already tried to hit on her, flirting blatantly and inviting her out for a "night on the town." Crysta assumed "town" was Anchorage. No matter. She wasn't here for a fling. Even if she had been, Shriver wasn't her type. She supposed he was likable enough, but when it came to dating, Crysta preferred men of a more serious nature. The handsome bush pilot struck her as the type who probably had a girl in every port—or, in this case, behind every bush.

"Um, excuse me, Mr. Shriver, do you think it's wise to be smoking? The gas fumes are awfully strong back here."

"Not to worry, honey. I haul fuel all the time, and, as you can see, I haven't blown up yet."

Somehow Crysta didn't find that very reassuring. Reaching inside her blouse, she tugged her floral-print thermal undershirt away from her skin, hoping for a whisper of air. As her travel-tips pamphlet had warned, the temperatures here took dramatic swings, and, as advised, she had dressed in layers. Now the chill of the morning was rapidly giving way to steamy afternoon warmth, and she had already discarded her sweater vest and jacket.

The plane shuddered again, making her forget her discomfort. She clutched the edge of her black vinyl seat.

"Won't be much longer now," Shriver called back to her. "You anxious to start catching those big old king salmon?"

"I didn't come to fish. My brother is missing. Derrick Meyers. Maybe you know him?"

He threw her a surprised look. "You're Derrick's sister? You know, I thought you looked familiar. You were twins, weren't you?" A frown pleated his forehead. "Hey, I'm really sorry about Derrick. Enjoyed visiting with him. He knew this country, I'll tell you that. A helluva nice guy. Having him along always spiced up the trip. He was one of my favorite passengers."

"Was?"

"Like I said, he knew his way around out there. He should have been back by now unless he met with an accident or—"

"My brother isn't dead."

In response to that, Shriver shrugged and faced forward again.

Unwilling to let the matter drop, Crysta said, "If he had met with an accident, the searchers would have found his body."

"Not necessarily. You have to remember how many predators are out there."

A wave of revulsion washed over Crysta. She hadn't thought of that. Averting her face, she pretended sudden interest in the Yentna River below. Cottonwoods and an occasional spruce lined its banks. She found herself watching carefully for anything that looked familiar. A lone, wind-twisted spruce in particular. Or a splotch of red flannel.

"Look, ma'am, I didn't mean to upset you. I speak before I think sometimes. I liked Derrick. Why, I've even flown some of the searchers in, free of charge."

Crysta dug her nails into her palms. "I appreciate that. It's just hard, you know?" She studied the back of Shriver's head. "Tell me, have the police considered the possibility of foul play?"

"Foul play?" He nearly twisted his neck off to stare at her. "You serious? Who'd want to hurt Derrick?"

"I'm not certain." Crysta hesitated, then asked, "How well do you know Sam Barrister?"

"Well enough. If you're saying... Well, you can forget that. Sam may be the rough-and-rugged type, but violent? No way."

"How about his guests? Are there many regulars?"

"An easy dozen. Hey, look, if you want to learn more about that, I suggest you question Sam. He knows his guests better than I do. As for foul play, honey, I think you're way off the mark. It's one big happy family out here. You want mystery, go to the city."

Crysta forced herself to leave it at that. Could Shriver be right? Was Derrick dead, his remains devoured by animals? Perhaps that was why Sam Barrister had discouraged her from coming. Had he been trying to spare her? Crysta had been praying for a happy reunion with her brother, clinging to the belief that he would be found alive. Now grisly images flashed through her mind.

Fear made her hands start to shake. She couldn't start thinking like that. Not about Derrick. He was too much a part of her. If she lost him . . . Well, it didn't bear thinking about.

Squeezing her eyes closed, Crysta tried to block out everything—the gas fumes, the heat, the roar of the engines, the shuddering of the plane. None of that mattered. Derrick was all that counted—finding him by whatever means she had, even if it was self-destructive. As well it might be. Her failed marriage testified to that.

Derrick? She listened to that secret, inner part of herself, praying she would hear something, feel something. *Derrick, answer me. Oh, please, please, answer.* There was nothing. Just a horrible, dead silence.

"Check your safety belt," Shriver called over his shoulder. "We're about to land."

The plane began its descent. Pressing her cheek against her window, she spotted a bend in the river where a large log building perched on a rise, surrounded by rustic cabins. The lodge, she guessed. In a clearing nearby, she saw a group of tents, which she presumed were for the searchers. Miniature people were scurrying about on shore, some shading their eyes to see the plane, others waving.

The aircraft tipped crazily to one side, then the pontoons touched down. Crysta braced herself for a shuddering deceleration, but the landing felt more like gliding on glass. In the center of the river, joined to shore by a footbridge, was a small island, where several aluminum boats were moored. Todd Shriver cut the engines and coasted the plane toward the strip of land. She felt a jerk when the pontoons hit bottom.

"Safe and sound," Shriver called as he slid out of his seat. "When you get out, be careful. Not to say I'd mind fishing a pretty little gal like you out of the water, but that river's like ice."

A pretty little gal? Crysta nearly groaned. The pilot definitely needed to be metropolitanized. He wouldn't last a day among the women's activists in Los Angeles. Keeping her expression carefully blank, Crysta unfastened her seat belt and scrambled forward to the cabin door. Following Shriver's example, she stepped out onto a pontoon and leaped from there to semidry land. Had Derrick once stood in this very spot?

As she got her balance and turned to look shoreward, a stout man with a shock of grizzled red hair ran up, his arms laden with two large boxes. He didn't spare her a glance as he set the boxes down and struggled to assist Shriver in unloading a heavy barrel.

She scanned the tree-lined riverbanks, glad to finally be here. True, arriving was only a start, but Derrick was out there somewhere. He had to be. And she was determined to find him.

She heard Shriver and the redhead talking, their voices low. She strained to hear what they said, but the brisk breeze snatched their words away. She turned and spotted her luggage, tossed down on the soggy dirt alongside a gas drum and a galvanized tub filled with salmon, bloody water streaming down its sides. Caring less about her expensive suitcases and more about having clean, dry clothes to wear while searching for Derrick, she quickly pulled the suitcases to dry ground.

As Shriver removed the last crate of supplies from the Cessna and set it down by the others, he said, "Well, I wish you luck, hon. Hope you find him, hale and hearty."

As he headed back toward the plane, Crysta called, "Thanks for making room for me."

"No problem."

The redhead stowed his boxes inside the airplane, then turned to look at her. From the curiosity she read in his expression, Crysta guessed that Shriver had told him who she was. His unwavering regard made her uneasy. At a loss, she turned away.

The scenery seemed familiar, very much like the terrain in her dream. People fished the river in boats, but otherwise, there was nothing, just water and dense cottonwoods. Her one link to civilization, the plane, was about to leave.

"Um ... Mr. Shriver. Hold up a sec."

The pilot doubled back, blue eyes quizzical. "Problem?"

"No, not exactly. I was, um, just wondering. I may have some business to take care of in Anchorage. If I call you, can you pick me up that same day?"

"Depends."

"On what?"

"We fly VFR out here."

"What's that?"

"Visual Flight Rules. If I can't see, I don't go. Rain storms, low clouds."

"Oh." Anchorage suddenly seemed light-years away. She might want to visit Blanchette Construction's warehouse there if Derrick wasn't found soon. Just to see if the building in any way resembled the one in her dream. "And how often does inclement weather interfere?"

"That depends on Mother Nature. Like most females, she's pretty unpredictable. For the most part, though, I fly in at least once a day."

"Then I can catch a ride?"

"If there's room, you bet. I never turn down a pretty passenger." He gave her shoulder a consoling pat. "Hey, if there's anything I can do to help—fly you around so you can search from the air—anything, you let me know."

Ignoring the unwanted intimacy, Crysta asked, "How expensive would that be?"

"If it's worked in around my flight schedule, I'll only charge for the fuel."

"I may take you up on it."

"I hope you do."

The wind picked up, dragging wisps of her long hair across her eyes. Through the reddish-brown strands, she studied Todd Shriver's features. In the sunlight, she could see things she hadn't detected inside the plane: a smattering of freckles across his nose, a chin that wasn't quite squared enough to offset the sharp angle of his cheekbones. All in all, though, it was a nice face. A little too cookie-cutter handsome for her tastes, but nice.

Except for his eyes. Maybe it was their ice-blue color, but they seemed expressionless to her. Her aunt claimed the eyes were windows to the soul, and Crysta guessed that might be true in Shriver's case. With his lighthearted outlook on life, she doubted many serious thoughts crossed his mind. The lack thereof showed in his gaze. She thought of Derrick's expressive eyes, which reflected grief as well as joy. Her heart grew heavy at the comparison.

"Again, my thanks, Mr. Shriver, for everything." Her voice sounded a little shaky, but she couldn't help it.

Shriver clasped her shoulder, flashing her a smile. "Thank me when there's something to thank me for, hm? And forget what I said earlier. Positive thinking can work miracles." Dropping his hand, he swung around and strode toward the plane. "See ya, Riley. Don't clean the river out of fish!"

The redhead chuckled. "It'd take a better man than me. You have a safe flight."

"Always. Hey, buddy, keep an eye on the lady for me, would ya?" Shriver jumped onto the pontoon, his footing sure from long practice. Crysta fastened her gaze on his rubber boots. Military-green with yellow trim. Catching the door frame, Shriver swung one leg through, pausing to add, "If she needs anything, help her put a call through to me, okay?"

Riley nodded. "Sure, I can do that. If I'm here, anyway."

As Shriver disappeared inside the plane, Crysta glanced at Riley's feet. His boots were the same avocado green, trimmed with yellow.

The plane's engines roared to life. Loneliness knifed through Crysta as the Cessna pulled away from the island. Thus far, Shriver was the only person she knew in Alaska. Now that he was gone, she was on her own. Shoving her hands into her jeans pockets, she took a deep breath of astonishingly pure air and headed toward the footbridge. No sense in putting it off. She might as well confront Sam Barrister now.

The footbridge felt unsteady when she stepped onto it, and she found herself wishing for handrails.

"Hey, lady!" Riley yelled as he shouldered a box of supplies. "You forgot your gear."

Crysta had hoped the lodge would have an employee to carry guest luggage ashore. She sighed and started to retrace her steps. As she did, the bridge gave under additional weight.

Glancing over her shoulder, she saw a tall, dark-haired man striding toward her, his every step making the water-soaked structure bounce and sway. Preoccupied though she was with keeping her footing, she noticed three things about him. He was without question one of the biggest men she had ever seen. He was as attractive as he was tall. And he looked angry.

Chapter Three

Crysta turned to meet the man head-on. It was a narrow bridge, and the approaching stranger took up most of its width, not with fat but sheer bulk, every centimeter lean muscle. There was an air about him—the loose-jointed way he walked, the set of his broad shoulders, the gleam in his brown eyes—that made him seem at home in the rugged country around him. She sincerely hoped the unlucky person he was so furious with was somewhere behind her.

No such luck. He drew to a stop dead in front of her and said, "Crysta Meyers, no doubt."

"And you must be Sam Barrister."

He squinted against the sun, tiny lines creasing the corners of his eyes, his long lashes casting shadows on his cheeks. The wind lifted his hair, drawing it across his high forehead in unruly black waves.

Crysta shoved her hands deeper into her pockets. For some reason, she had never pictured Sam Barrister as so attractive or virile. A red sweatshirt molded itself to the impressive contours of his chest, its snug fit accentuating his narrow waist and flat belly. Faded denim skimmed the muscular length of his legs. A knife scabbard rode his hip. Like Riley and Shriver, he wore a pair of yellow-trimmed green rubber boots. Obviously her running shoes were inadequate for the terrain, but it couldn't be helped. She hadn't had time to go shopping before leaving home, and galoshes weren't among her usual accessories.

Crysta returned her gaze to his face. The sun touched his unshaven jaw, highlighting a sprinkle of silver whiskers among the black. Late thirties, early forties? She chose to ignore his anger and kept her voice carefully polite. "Is there any more news about my brother? How's the search going?"

"If I could have reached you last night, you would know the answer to that. I wish you had called back. After we were disconnected, I got the phone working again, but with your unlisted number, I couldn't get through to you."

"I stayed at Mom's. She's terribly upset, naturally."

Something flickered in his eyes. Concern? It was gone as quickly as it came. "Maybe you should have stayed there with her." He clipped the words short. "I told you your being here wasn't necessary."

"If it was your brother missing, where would you be?"

She had him there. His gaze shifted, as if he couldn't quite look her in the eye. "As much as I sympathize with your concerns, I don't have space for you." He nodded toward the group of tents. "All the cabins are full."

"If you have a spare sleeping bag, I'll manage. I tried to bring my own, but passengers are limited to two pieces of luggage on the pontoon flights. I had to leave it in a locker at the airport."

Silence hung between them. His gaze met hers again, hard and unyielding. Then he swiped at his cheek with the back of his hand, leaving a smudge of dirt along his jaw.

Crysta shot a glance at the cluster of tents. "I can always sleep under a tree."

His eyes warmed with a weary smile. "With the bears?"

"Bears?" Crysta echoed. She scanned the area again. It hadn't occurred to her that wild creatures might venture this close to the lodge. Still, if the volunteer searchers could sleep outdoors with nothing but canvas to protect them, she could make it through a few nights in the open. "Right now, my main concern is finding Derrick. If a spot under a tree is all you have available, then I'll settle for that."

He seemed amused by her reaction to the idea of bears, but she also detected a flicker of admiration in his expression at her willingness to brave it out. The smile in his eyes finally touched his mouth. "I think I can do a little better than that."

Crysta noticed that the warmth in his expression transformed his features. He was even more attractive when he smiled. "I appreciate your help; and I apologize in advance for any inconvenience I might cause. I didn't realize so many people would be here."

Tipping her head back to study him more closely, Crysta noted once again that he was not what she had expected. Derrick had described Sam, of course, but "big and rugged" didn't do him justice. He was at least six-five, maybe more, with a set of shoulders most of the weight lifters in Los Angeles would kill for. At five-ten, Crysta seldom met a man so tall and with enough breadth to make her feel petite.

His dark gaze searched hers. "I should be the one to apologize—for the surly greeting. I haven't slept more than a couple of hours at a stretch in days. I've been trying to run this place, organize the search parties, make sure the volunteers are fed, keep beds ready, and in between all that, I've been trying to search for Derrick myself. I'm afraid it puts a strain on congeniality."

Now that Crysta was looking for them, she could see the faint shadows of exhaustion beneath his eyes.

"A few minutes ago, one of my guests got a fishhook stuck through his finger," he added. "The ordeal of trying to get it out while he threatened me with a lawsuit destroyed what was left of my sense of humor." With a wry twist of his mouth, he admitted, "Not that I had much left to destroy."

A wave of guilt washed over her. Now she could see why Sam Barrister might not have wanted her here. She licked her lips. "I didn't realize so much responsibility for the search had been laid on you."

"It wasn't laid, I took it. Derrick's my best friend."

"I don't suppose an extra pair of hands might be useful? I worked one term during college as a short-order cook, so I might be a help in the kitchen."

"Somehow, I pictured you wanting to accompany the searchers."

"I want to go look for him. I won't deny it. But if I'll be more useful working here to free someone more experienced for the search, you won't hear me arguing. He's my brother. I have to help. Can't you understand that?"

"Of course I can. It's just that the thought of you getting lost out there scares the hell out of me. Derrick's being missing is bad enough." He placed his hands on his hips. "Let's get your luggage. It looks like you're stuck here, at least until tomorrow. We may as well make the best of it."

Crysta took one of the suitcases, and Barrister grabbed the other. He led the way back onto the footbridge. Crysta watched the rhythmic shift of his shoulder blades as she followed him. In all fairness, she really couldn't blame him for resenting her arrival. In the city, she could handle just about anything, but she was definitely out of her element here. He logically expected her to be more trouble than help. Crysta was determined to prove him wrong.

When he reached the end of the bridge, he leaped over a wash of mud to dry ground, then turned to hold out a hand for the suitcase she carried. Since she lacked his length of leg, Crysta didn't demur. Once unburdened, she gauged the distance and jumped.

As she drew abreast of him, he retained both suitcases but made little concession for her shorter stride. Crysta gave him a measuring glance, taking in his chiseled profile and clenched jaw. Deep within, she experienced a purely feminine response to him.

That surprised her. Normally she was attracted to a man more by his personality than by his looks. She laid her reaction off on nerves. Since learning of Derrick's disappearance, she hadn't been herself. Sam Barrister was the epitome of masculine strength; frightened and unsettled as she was, it was natural that she should feel drawn to him.

He headed toward the large log buildings set apart on a knoll. By the time Crysta made it up the incline, she felt as if she had run a footrace. He didn't slow until they reached the lodge entrance and then paused only to push the door wide with his shoulder.

He stepped back to let her enter first, juggling suitcases so she could slip by him. A blast of warmth hit her in the face, and she glanced at the stone hearth where the dying remains of a fire crackled, the feeble flames casting golden shimmers on the knotty-pine paneling. Around the hearth was an arrangement of sturdy wood furniture with orange-and-brown plaid cushions that lent the spacious sitting area a cozy feeling.

Had Derrick lounged there? She pictured him kicked back in a chair, leafing through one of the magazines about Alaska that were fanned across the coffee table. A heavy ache centered in her chest. What if Derrick never visited this lodge again?

At the far end of the room stood several planked tables, one laden with food, another occupied by three men whose low conversation and laughter blended with the crackling of the fire. Judging by the men's clothes, she didn't think they were searchers. Guests, more likely. Crysta scanned the walls, expecting to see hunting trophies. She was both relieved and puzzled not to find any.

"Mr. Barrister, when I asked you earlier how the search was going, you never answered me. Has any progress been made? Have they found any sign of Derrick, any clues as to what happened?"

Sam glanced at the three men in the dining area. "Let's discuss that when we have some privacy," he said in a low voice.

Her reluctant host stepped behind a cluttered check-in counter, then through a doorway. As she followed him, she spied a dog-eared calendar on the wall, a dingy picture of Mount McKinley at its top. Her attention was caught by some sloppy writing in the box for the fifteenth. *Phone due back—have check ready.* She paused. Today was the seventeenth of June. Derrick had called their mother, supposedly from the lodge, last week. How could he have if Sam Barrister's phone had been gone?

More determined than ever to press the man for some answers, Crysta stepped through the doorway into a small, untidy living room with another stone fireplace and more of the same rustic furniture. The back of the sofa was toward her. She spotted two very large white-socked feet propped on the wooden armrest at one end.

"My son," Sam whispered as he set her luggage down in a corner.

Crysta heard a low snore, a sputter and then a surprised grunt. In a husky, sleepy voice, the boy said, "Dad? I thought you were gone."

"Didn't leave yet. There's a guest you should meet, Tip. Derrick's sister, Crysta Meyers."

A dark head shot up over the back of the sofa, and Crysta found herself looking at one of the handsomest boys she had ever seen, a younger version of his father. His pale blue T-shirt struck a sharp contrast to his deep tan and liquid brown eyes. His sleep-tousled hair and nervous grin only added to his appeal. She guessed him to be about sixteen.

"Hi—hi. I'm p-pleased to m-m-mmeet y-you, Cr— Cr—" He dipped his head and swallowed, his face suddenly aflame. "Cr-Cry-sss—"

Crysta's heart went out to Tip as she watched him struggle to say her name.

Sam laid a hand on the boy's shoulder. "It's all right, son." Throwing Crysta a warning look, Sam added, "Tip gets a little tongue-tied when he first meets strangers."

"Tongue-tied, hm?" Anxious to put the boy at ease, Crysta moved forward and extended her hand, remembering that Derrick had mentioned Sam's son was handicapped. "Well, we'll be fast friends then. When I meet new people, I trip over my own feet."

Tip stared at her outstretched fingers. "Y-you d-do?"

"You should have seen me when I tried to be a waitress. I lasted two hours, and all my wages went to clean some poor lady's dress. I dumped a platter of spaghetti down her front."

"Y-you did?" Tip's eyes grew round.

"Yup. And the little meatballs went down inside her— Well, it was really a mess. I got canned before the dinner hour was over."

Tip's eyes grew even rounder. "Canned? Like a salmon?"

Sam's stern visage softened. "No, son. That's another way of saying she lost her job."

Tip finally grew bold enough to grasp Crysta's extended hand, his mouth spreading into a lopsided grin. "W-well, you don't have to w-worry around us. If you t-trip, we'll j-just help you up. R-right, Dad?"

Sam glanced at Crysta. "And you offered to help out in my kitchen? Help like that may put me out of business."

"Just don't serve spaghetti."

She thought she detected a hint of a smile at the corners of his mouth, but he squelched it before she could be certain. Then Tip distracted her by carrying through the handshake with such enthusiasm that he jolted her arm clear to the shoulder.

Before she thought, Crysta said, "Easy." Tip froze. When he tried to draw back his hand, though, she held on. Smiling at him, she modified the pumping action. "There, you see? The same way, just not quite as hard."

Tip glanced at his father as he released her hand. "I forgot. You d-do it soft with ladies."

"That's right." Sam glanced at Crysta. All trace of warmth had left his face.

Crysta squirmed. She certainly hadn't meant to offend. Would it have been better to endure a painful handshake with Tip, and then avoid letting him touch her again?

"I'm sorry, C-Crys— Crys—"

"Just call me Crys. Derrick used to when we were younger, and I kind of miss it."

"Crys." Tip appeared pleased when he had no difficulty with the shortened version. And, unlike his father, he didn't seem upset that she had corrected him about the way he shook hands. "I like n-nicknames. My r-real name's Sam, just like my dad's. Only when people c-called me, he answered, and when they called h-him, I did."

Crysta gave the boy another warm smile. "So you're called Tip?" She pretended to consider the name for a moment, then nodded. "I like it. It suits you, somehow."

Tip nodded. "It's b-because my dad won't let m-me work for f-free. He says I help p-people as good as the m-men he hires, so I sh-should get paid tips like they do. One guest said h-he had to pay me so m-many times, my m-middle name should be Tip."

"And the name stuck," Sam inserted.

"You wanna see my p-p-pictures, Crys?" Tip asked.

Actually, Crysta had a dozen questions for Tip's father: where Derrick had been heading the day he left the lodge, who had known his destination, where his gear had been found, whether any of it was still missing, what area the search was covering right now. She needed to procure a forestry map to help her keep track of the search. She also wanted to do some sleuthing as soon as the opportunity presented itself. But faced with the eagerness in Tip's expression, she held her tongue. Five more minutes would make little difference to Derrick, and she had a feeling they would mean the world to Tip.

"What kind of pictures?"

"Just p-pictures." Tip tugged his drooping socks up and sprang off the sofa, as lofty as his father when he straightened. "C-ome on. I have them in here."

He hurried to a door across the room and threw it open. Remembering his manners, he stepped back so she could precede him. In his excitement, he wasn't stuttering. "I do them without any help. Huh, Dad?"

"Tip, Crysta may want to freshen up. She's had a long trip, and she's worried about Derrick. Maybe you could show her later when—"

"No, really," Crysta cut in, "I'd like to see them."

When she stepped into the unfurnished bedroom, she felt as if she had entered an art gallery. Every inch of wall from floor to ceiling was taken up with oil paintings, mostly nature scenes but portraits, as well, one of Sam, another of Todd Shriver.

"Oh, Tip." That was all Crysta could say.

"Do you like them?"

"Like them?" Crysta took a step back to absorb the full impact of a lone wolf on a snow-swept knoll. The moonlight, the layered clouds against a slate sky—every last detail was perfect. She could almost hear the animal's forlorn howl. "I'm in awe."

Tip threw a questioning glance at his father. Sam flashed a weary smile. "That's a compliment, son."

"You're very talented, Tip. Have you given any shows yet?"

"Tip paints for pleasure," Sam inserted brusquely.

Crysta cleared her throat. Clearly, any talk of art shows was taboo. "When I can, I'd like to spend some time in here admiring each painting, Tip, and hearing the story behind it. Did you see the wolf in a book, or take a picture of him outside? The detail you've captured is breathtaking."

"Tip paints from memory." Sam's piercing brown eyes met hers. "With one glance, he sees more than most of us do after staring at something for an hour."

Tip rushed to the easel in the center of the room. "Come and see this one."

Crysta stepped around to view the canvas in progress. For an instant, when she spied the cinnamon-colored hair and hazel eyes, she thought it was an unfinished portrait of herself. Derrick. His facial features were still sketchy, not yet brought to life by Tip's brush. As her gaze lowered from Derrick's face to his shoulders, her heart began to slam.

"As you can see, Derrick's been on Tip's mind a lot," Sam said softly.

Crysta licked her lips. "That shirt. When did you see Derrick wearing it, Tip?"

"Wh-when he left that day. R-right before he got lost." Shadows crept into the boy's brown eyes. "I'm s-sorry. I didn't m-mean to make you sad."

For a moment, the room seemed to spin. In the portrait, Derrick was wearing a western-style, red flannel shirt with pearl snaps, just as he had in her dream.

Chapter Four

Twenty minutes later, Crysta still hadn't completely recovered from the head-on collision between her dream and reality. As she followed Sam Barrister behind the lodge for a tour of the buildings, she scarcely heard what he said. Derrick had been wearing a red shirt the day he disappeared. If that much of what she had dreamed was right, how much of the rest was? She couldn't forget the explosive noise that had ended her dream. Had her brother been shot?

"Are you listening to me?"

Crysta jerked herself back to the present and looked up at Sam's brooding features. "I guess I was woolgathering. What did you say?"

"I was telling you how to go about bathing in the sauna. It's more of a steam bath, actually. Luckily, it's pretty self-explanatory. All the toiletries you'll need are in the anteroom. And, as you can see, the fire is kept stoked most of the time. We all use the same steam room, and, for safety's sake, there's no lock. Turn the sign to read Occupied when you go in so you don't get company. Right around the corner, you'll find the necessary house. Again, there's only one for both sexes, so latch the door."

Still feeling separated from reality, Crysta noted a string of smoke trailing from the sauna building's chimney.

"Seeing that portrait really upset you, didn't it?"

She forced herself to focus, dismayed that he had cued in so easily on her feelings.

"I'm really sorry. Tip means well. He just doesn't think beyond the moment sometimes. You went so white, I thought you might faint."

"Tip's great. And the portrait is going to be wonderful. It was just—" She shifted her gaze, afraid he would see too much, read her too well. "I wasn't prepared, that's all."

He watched her closely. Too closely.

"Crysta..." His facial muscles tightened. "We both know I didn't bring you out here for a tour. Aside from the fact that you've got dozens of questions to ask me and would probably like to talk to the search coordinator, there's something I need to tell you before you hear it from someone else."

He looked so somber that she braced herself.

"It's about the condition of Derrick's gear when I found it. It looked like a—"

"Hey, Mr. Barrister?"

Sam turned at the call, focusing on a weary-looking man in soiled jeans and a safety-orange shirt. As the man strode toward them, Crysta noticed he carried a dark green garbage bag in one hand. Her stomach tightened.

Looking back at her, Sam said, "That's one of the searchers. Hold on a second, okay?"

Crysta nodded and watched Sam walk down the slight slope. The two men met about twenty feet away from her, but it was so peaceful here that she could hear everything they said.

"I wanted to report the news to you first thing. We finally found him—or what little was left of him. Several miles downstream. I'd guess it was at least five miles from where you found his gear. Bear, no doubt about it. Must be a renegade in the area."

The ground seemed to dip beneath Crysta's feet. Sam threw her a concerned look. "Jim, this lady is—"

"Still no body, I'm afraid," Jim rushed on, inclining his head at Crysta to acknowledge her presence. "But we found plenty of bear tracks and blood at the scene. He was either completely ingested or dragged away. We'll probably never know. In the surrounding brush, we found remnants of his shirt. At least we assume it's his.'' Jim stuck his hand into the garbage bag and pulled out a shredded piece of red flannel. A pearlescent snap shimmered in the sunlight. "The lab will run tests, of course, to check the blood type. I know there isn't much left of it, but could this be part of the red shirt you described?"

A cry tore from Crysta's throat. Sam spun and hurried back to her. "Crysta—"

"They're saying he's dead?" She couldn't drag her eyes from Derrick's shredded shirt. She would have recognized it anywhere. Had a bear's claws ripped it that way? "Derrick's dead?"

Sam gripped her arm, the pressure of his fingers firm enough to support her but strangely gentle. "Jim, this lady is Derrick's sister."

"Oh, hey, I'm sorry. I had no idea."

Crysta fastened pleading eyes on Sam's. "He can't be dead. I'd know it. I'd feel it. Don't you see? He can't be dead."

Sam said nothing, and his silence drove the horrible news home. Crysta threw a bewildered look at the retreating searcher, her thoughts a jumble.

"It can't have been a bear," she whispered. "I would have known. I know I would have."

"Crysta . . . Let's go up to the lodge, okay? I'll fix you some Irish coffee. Maybe you can lie down and rest."

The silken tone of his voice made Crysta realize how hysterical she must sound. She nodded, numbly following the lead of his hand. The searcher had sounded so positive. Surely they couldn't make a mistake like that. Bear tracks and blood. Maybe her dream had meant nothing, after all.

"They—they could be mistaken, couldn't they?" she asked, looking up at him.

"I—" He broke off and swallowed. "Jim Sales is one of the best trackers in the country. I've never known him to make a mistake. He wouldn't blame it on a bear unless he felt positive."

The walk back to the lodge passed in a blur for Crysta. At some point, Sam put his arm around her, and she dimly realized he was not only steering her but allowing her to lean into him. His strength became her only reality.

One foot in front of the other. She tried not to think. It hurt too much. A bear. Every time the horror of it skirted her mind, she shoved it away. Not Derrick. Please, God, let it be a mistake. Sam Barrister's lean strength and the warmth of his body gave Crysta something solid to hang on to. Derrick's friend. She didn't resist when he drew her closer to his side.

She had a vague impression of the lodge as Sam led her through it, of his private quarters, of being lowered to a sofa. She was seeing it all through a layer of cotton. Sam spoke to her, his voice low and gentle. Tip's voice rang out intermittently. Crysta felt separated from them, not registering reality because she couldn't bear it.

Time passed. How much, she didn't know. Her mind began to let the truth seep in, a fact at a time. Derrick was gone. Not just dead, but gone. No body. No funeral so she could say goodbye. Just gone, as though he had never existed. A bear. She couldn't envision the animal—nothing in her imagination was monstrous enough. Then Sam whispered, "I'm sorry," and it became a reality. People didn't say they were sorry in a shaky, rough voice like that unless something unspeakable had happened. "I'm sorry." She tried to focus on his face. His being sorry didn't make it hurt any less. How would she ever tell her mom?

Raised by proud, very private parents, Crysta seldom cried and never in front of people. She had broken her arm once in two places and hadn't shed a tear. At her dad's funeral, she had survived listening to the eulogy dry-eyed and with her head held high. But now her pride eluded her. The tears welled in her eyes, carried up from deep within her on the crest of a ragged moan she could not stifle. If only Sam and Tip would go away so she could be alone.

Instead, Sam tried to take her in his arms. Maybe he had been Derrick's friend, but to her, he was still a virtual stranger. In addition, he was extremely handsome, definitely not the type who could carry off a brotherly embrace. Though she knew Sam meant well, she felt self-conscious instead of comforted, and she pushed against his chest. He backed off instantly.

"I'm sad f-for you," Tip said softly.

Perhaps it was Tip's lack of pretense, that he didn't say he was sorry or pretend to understand how she felt, just a tremulous whisper that cut straight to her heart, but Crysta felt her self-control begin to slip further. Looking at him, at his stricken brown eyes swimming with tears, was a mistake. Her shoulders started to shake. "Oh, Tip. I don't want you to feel sad."

"Why? You're sad."

As if it were the most natural thing in the world, he sat next to her and drew her into his arms. His embrace was awkward, his hands clumsy as he stroked her hair, but Crysta buried her face in the crook of his shoulder. He was solid and warm, something real to hang on to while the horror of her brother's death sank in. Mauled to death by a bear. Crysta couldn't think of a more awful way to die. The images assaulted her mind, faster and faster, until a scream welled in her throat.

No. She wouldn't do this to herself or Tip. Curling her hands into fists, she forced the pictures away and focused instead on the boy who held her. She breathed in and out, concentrating on the rhythm. Don't think about how Derrick died.

Her tears slowly dwindled, drying to stiff trails on her cheeks. When at last she felt more like herself, she straightened. She gave Tip's hand a gentle squeeze. Words didn't seem enough, somehow.

"B-bears aren't bad," Tip whispered.

Until that moment, Crysta hadn't realized she had spoken her thoughts aloud. A denial sprang to her lips, but she swallowed it back. Tip was right. All bears weren't bad.

"D-Derrick liked the bears. They eat breakfast in our g-garbage heap every day, and he liked to watch them. We gave them all n-names. There's Grumpy and Snaggletooth. And Hog, because he won't share. Derrick'd be sad if you started hating them. He said the bears need f-friends to help protect them. Stupid people shoot them and make rugs out of their f-fur. I found a c-carcass yesterday.'' His eyes darkened with sadness. ''They killed it for its head and f-feet.''

Crysta stared at him, not quite registering the words.

''The t-teeth and c-claws can be sold f-for jewelry,'' Tip elaborated mournfully.

Crysta could barely control a shudder. ''I won't start hating the bears, Tip. I promise.''

As if he knew the shock had chilled her to the bone, Sam had built a fire, and soon the small living room was cozily warm. Though Crysta knew she should move away from Tip, she couldn't find the will. She had come here fired up with plans to find Derrick. And now there was nothing to find. She remembered how she had tried and failed to sense her brother's presence on the float-plane. Had that been a sign? Despite the fire, a cold numbness seeped into her mind and through her body.

''I'm going to go talk to the searchers,'' Sam said softly. ''I really don't think it's necessary for you to come. You can review the official reports later, when you feel more up to it.''

Crysta agreed with a nod. She couldn't handle hearing the gory details of Derrick's death, not yet. She sat straighter and finger-combed her tangled hair. Flashing both of them a quavery smile, she said, ''I'm sorry for losing it like that. You scarcely know me. It was just such a shock to hear that—'' She broke off, unable to put it into words.

Sam started to speak, but Tip beat him to it. ''We're fast f-friends. You s-said so.''

Puzzled for a moment, Crysta suddenly realized that to Tip her prediction that they would be fast friends meant they would become friends quickly. It followed that pretense between them was unnecessary. Patting the boy's hand, she said, ''I guess we are, aren't we?''

Tip beamed. ''I'm glad. You make me feel nice.''

The feeling was mutual. Tip was special, and Crysta knew she was richer in some inexplicable way for having met him. Not even her grief over losing Derrick could completely overshadow that.

THREE HOURS LATER, when Sam slipped back into his apartment, he saw Crysta had fallen asleep on the sofa. A blanket was tucked around her—Tip's doing, he guessed. Sam pulled the blackout shades on the windows so the light wouldn't disturb her rest. At this time of year, from midnight until around three in the morning, Cottonwood Bend experienced twilight, but darkness never descended. For someone unaccustomed to it, Alaska's midnight sun could make sleep difficult, and Crysta needed her rest. Tomorrow would be draining.

After drawing the last shade, Sam turned from the window. Shadows now obscured Crysta's features. He studied the outline of her face, a pale oval in the dimness. He felt an inexplicable urge to move closer. Something about her drew him, made him want to hold her, to—Sam cut the thought short, amazed at himself. He scarcely knew the woman. And he certainly was in no position to befriend her, not until this was over.

With only a few words, he could have eased her pain somewhat, but he hadn't. And he wouldn't now. She might insist on staying until he told her everything. It was better that she believe Derrick the victim of a bear attack so she would go home, where she would be out of harm's way.

Despite what the searchers believed, Sam didn't buy the theory that a bear had killed Derrick Meyers. He might have if it had appeared that Derrick had been killed near the site of his initial encounter with the animal. But Derrick's shredded gear had been found five miles from the scene of his death. The way it looked, the bear had taken exception to Derrick's presence in its territory, which wasn't unheard of, had torn up his gear and then chased him for five miles before killing him. No man could outrun a grizzly for five miles.

Sam knew the searchers felt satisfied with the evidence. After all, grizzlies sometimes did strange things. Sleeping campers had been known to disappear, bedding and all, never to be seen again. To the searchers, this was just another bizarre grizzly incident, and they were willing to call it a closed case as soon as the lab reports came back. They had no reason to suspect foul play.

But Sam did.

Straightening his shoulders, he went into the adjoining bedroom to check on Tip. When he was satisfied the boy was sound asleep, he slipped from the apartment and went to his office. From a cupboard along one wall, he withdrew a briefcase. Derrick's papers were inside. With luck, the name of his murderer would be there, as well.

DIZZINESS SWIRLED in Crysta's head. Light flashed before her eyes, and she felt as if she was falling. Mud. Cold and slick. It was everywhere. All over her arms, globbed on her hands. She was on a slope, an extremely steep slope, and sliding backward. Instinct took over, leaving her no time to wonder how she had gotten there. She looked down and saw white water surging around craggy boulders. If she lost her precarious hold, she'd plunge to her death. She clawed at the slimy earth. Pain. Like the mud, it seemed to surround her. White-hot pain so intense it took her breath away. She longed to rest but didn't dare. Panic filled her. She was slipping.

Crysta dug into the mud with her toes and fingers. She scrambled upward, blocking the agony from her mind. The roar of the water below filled her ears. So cold. So tired. She found a foothold and rested a moment, her lungs convulsing. A shudder racked her. Lifting her head, she gauged the distance she must scale to reach the top of the mud slide. It wasn't far, and desperation drove her. Arm over arm, one toehold at a time.

When she reached the top of the slope, Crysta rolled onto her back to rest. Turning her head, she spied a rickety log cabin nestled among some trees. It's chimney pipe rose above the roofline, one side badly bent. Smoke. They were still there. At the thought, her mind spun with questions. They? Fear clenched her guts. She couldn't waste time wondering who. Run, run, before they find you.

She struggled to her knees. Pain exploded in her shoulder and chest when she put weight on her left arm. She glanced down. Blood. Crimson ooze coming from a black hole over her heart. She gained her feet, still staring at the wound. The mud seemed to be staunching the blood flow. She took a step; knifelike pain shot through her right thigh. She gritted her teeth. There was a lake nearby, a deserted cabin. She'd be safe there.

WITH A GASP, Crysta woke. The sofa cushion pressed against her face, the weave of its fabric warm and slightly scratchy. Still gripped by terror, she lifted her lashes. A blur of brown and orange swam before her eyes. She jackknifed to a sitting position and grabbed her right thigh. Her head reeled. For a moment, she hovered between nightmare and reality, aware of her surroundings but still able to see the mud and blood. Frantic, she began brushing at her chest and arms.

"Are y-you okay?"

Tip's voice made her start. She stared at him, her hands frozen in midmovement. Then she threw wild looks around the room, taking in the plaid upholstery, the fire, her clean clothing and hands. Slowly the last traces of her nightmare disappeared.

"Y-you scr-screamed," Tip whispered. "Y-you said you were b-bleeding. Did you cut yours-s-s-self?"

"No." Crysta swallowed. "No, Tip. I guess I was having a bad dream."

He relaxed his stance. "Oh. I have b-bad ones sometimes. My dad'll let you s-sleep with him if you're still scared."

Heat crept up Crysta's neck. "I'll be fine out here." Her gaze shifted to Sam's closed bedroom door. "Thanks for checking on me, Tip. I'm sorry I woke you."

"I c-can tell you a story for a w-while. My dad's taught me some really good ones."

Never had Crysta known anyone as sweet as Tip. "That's thoughtful of you. Maybe another time? I'm awfully tired. I'll bet you are, too."

"Kind of." He looked reluctant to leave. "Good n-night."

She watched Tip disappear into his bedroom. After his door closed, she rested her elbows on her knees and dropped her head into her hands. What was happening to her? Even now, though she was wide awake, her right thigh still throbbed, and her shoulder felt stiff. Crazy, so crazy. Or was it?

A sudden flare of hope jerked Crysta's head up. She remembered the explosive noise that had ended her last dream, her certainty that it had come from a gun. The blood. The black hole in her flesh. A bullet wound? She leaped from the sofa, nearly falling before she disentangled herself from the blanket. Pressing her hands to her cheeks, she stared into the dying fire. Was she losing her mind? Or could Derrick still be alive?

Chapter Five

If there was a possibility that Derrick was still alive, Crysta had to do something. Finding her brother was the first priority, but she knew that only a fool would strike off searching for Derrick alone in so vast a wilderness. She needed help—from someone who knew the country. Who better than Sam Barrister, who was, according to Derrick, one of the best guides in Alaska?

When a soft tap on Sam's bedroom door failed to rouse him, Crysta ventured out to the front of the lodge, vaguely aware of a humming sound somewhere outside. A generator? Watery light came through the dining-room windows. Crysta glanced at her watch. Two o'clock. For a moment, she thought she had slept through the night and into the next afternoon. Then she recalled that Alaska didn't have darkness at this time of year, only twilight. The feeling of nighttime in Sam's apartment was due to blackout shades.

A glow of lamplight spilled from a partially open doorway to her left, and through the crack she glimpsed someone moving. She veered toward the door, raising her fist to knock. Then she hesitated. Through the opening, she saw Sam Barrister seated at a large desk, his dark head bent over a pile of papers, his forehead furrowed in a scowl.

Rapping softly on the door, she gave it a push and took in the cozy work area at a glance. A gorgeous painting of an elk hung behind Sam's desk. It was unmistakably Tip's handiwork. The pine walls shone in the aura cast by the reading lamp, and the rich aroma of coffee teased her nostrils. "Mr. Barrister?"

Sam Barrister flinched at the sound of her voice and jerked up his head, his piercing dark eyes arresting her as she started to step across the threshold.

"I, um, need to speak to you," Crysta said, feeling suddenly wary. Why was the lodge owner so jumpy? His behavior was completely at odds with the stories Derrick had told her about him. "Do you have a minute?"

"Sure." With a casualness belied by the tautness of his mouth, Sam shoved the papers he had been studying into a familiar-looking brown briefcase and snapped it closed. He lifted it from his desk and stowed it in a drawer. "Come on in."

He shoved back his chair and stood up, giving the bottom of his red sweatshirt a tug in an attempt to cover his smudged undershirt. Crysta closed the door behind herself, then immediately wished she hadn't, her hand tightening on the cool knob.

She tensed as Barrister stepped out from behind the desk. In the small room, he seemed even larger than he had before, his long, well-muscled legs skimmed with worn-soft denim, massive shoulders emphasized by the undersized sweatshirt. He was the only man Crysta had ever met who made her feel small. Given the circumstances, she could have done without that.

"Coffee?" he offered, voice strained. "Just made fresh."

Crysta's gaze slid to his desk. It was impeccably neat, the wood surface agleam with wax, which clued her that Barrister's untidy apartment and unkempt appearance were probably uncharacteristic of him. She longed to walk over and open the side drawer to look more closely at the briefcase he had hidden from view. "Yes, please. Hot coffee sounds wonderful."

He strode to a battered white serving cart near the window where an automatic coffeemaker was giving its final sputter. Crysta noted that the coffee utensils were in tidy order, too, a curious contrast to their unshaven, weary-looking owner.

He took two mugs from a wooden wall rack and sloshed coffee into each. Derrick aside, Crysta was accustomed to men in suits and polished dress shoes, nails manicured, the pads of their hands as soft as hers. Sam Barrister was anything but soft.

"Don't you ever sleep?" she asked.

"Cream? Sugar?" He glanced over his shoulder at her.

"A lump of sugar, thanks."

"In answer to your question, yes, I do sleep. But these last few days, I've been too busy to do it much."

As he spoke, he moved toward her, extending one of the steaming mugs. She crooked a finger through the handle of the cup and murmured still another thank-you, feeling self-conscious and uncertain of what to say next. Gesturing toward a spare chair in front of his desk, he relieved the silence. "Have a seat."

As she lowered herself onto the leather cushion, he perched a hip on the desk, one leg straight to support his weight, the other slightly bent. There was an air of the woodsman about him, even indoors. Crysta decided his dark, rugged looks probably gave most women butterflies.

Not that she herself didn't find him attractive—amazingly so, considering that he had made no effort to look his best. Once again she noted the dark circles of exhaustion under his eyes and the telltale specks of silver peppering his unshaven jaw. His age was stamped in tiny lines upon his countenance, those bracketing his mouth deeper than those at the corners of his eyes, both giving testimony that he had laughed at life and wept over it. She got the impression he didn't realize how handsome he was or else didn't count it important. She liked that in him.

She couldn't help wondering what was so pressing that he had passed up a chance to shower and sleep to come in here and work. She shifted her attention back to the top of his desk and the papers lying on the blotter. The direction of her gaze seemed to make him uneasy.

"What was it you wanted to talk to me about?"

Crysta took a sip of coffee, then lifted her gaze to meet his. "Where are my brother's personal effects?"

"I'm sorry. I thought I told you. They were found along a trail . . . destroyed by the bear."

"Derrick carried his briefcase when he went hiking?"

One of Sam Barrister's eyelids twitched, but otherwise his expression remained poker straight. "I didn't realize Derrick even carried a briefcase."

"In his line of work, Derrick had contacts to make even during his off-hours. He was worse about carrying his briefcase than most women are about their purses."

Shrugging one shoulder, Barrister frowned. "Maybe Cottonwood Bend was the exception. He did come here to get away from it all, you know. And with mobile phone rates as costly as they are, he seldom contacted people from here. Maybe he left his briefcase behind in the hotel safe at Anchorage."

The skin across Crysta's cheekbones felt as if it were smeared with drying egg white. Tight-lipped, she studied this man whom Derrick had called friend. She felt certain he had just lied to her about Derrick's never bringing his paper work to the lodge.

"Speaking of your mobile phone, Derrick called my mom from here last week, yet I noticed a note on your calendar that leads me to think your phone was being repaired. How did Derrick place a call from here when there wasn't a phone?"

Sam shot a glance toward the doorway. "Since mine was on the fritz last week, Riley O'Keefe let me borrow his."

"Riley O'Keefe?"

"He's a regular here at the lodge—the stocky redhead you saw on the island when you arrived?"

She recalled the man. "How well does he know my brother?"

"Fairly well. Riley works for Blanchette Construction."

"In what capacity?"

Barrister hesitated. "He's a warehouse supervisor."

"Are there other Blanchette people who come here regularly?"

Barrister searched her gaze, his jaw muscle flickering. "Several. Steve Henderson comes the most—the tall, brown-haired kid? Maybe you didn't notice him. Riley brings him along fairly often, probably to take Steve's mind off things at home.''

''He has problems?''

Sam's eyes clouded. ''A sick son. Leukemia. He's just a little tyke. It's hard on Steve. I don't think the financial squeeze he's under has helped any.''

Acutely aware of the compassion revealed in Sam's eyes, Crysta remembered her original reason for coming here. Surely a man who cared so deeply about another man's sick child could be trusted. Emotion clogging her throat, she blurted, ''I don't believe my brother was killed by a bear.''

His eyes went deadpan. ''What do you think killed him, then?''

Careful, Crysta. ''I—I don't think he's dead.''

Sam grew unnaturally still, watching her in that unnerving way he had that made her feel he could read far more from her expression than she wished.

''Let me rephrase that,'' she whispered. ''I *know* he isn't dead.''

He gave a nervous cough. ''How can you possibly know he's not dead?''

Wrapping her fingers around the warm mug, Crysta bent her head, staring at the coarse weave of her denim jeans, fighting back the urge to tell him about her dreams. Her credibility was on the line; she mustn't forget that.

''I just know, that's all. I want to resume the search. It's imperative. We have to find Derrick before it's too late.''

There followed another taut silence. Then she heard the click of porcelain on wood. With no warning, he leaned forward and grasped her shoulder, making her start. ''Crysta, I know how difficult it must be for you to accept Derrick's death, especially the way he died. It's natural to go through a time of denial, even rage. Is there anything I can do to help you?''

Crysta kept her head bent. The heavy warmth of his hand and the concern she heard in his voice tapped emotions she had been fighting to ignore. Weakness. The need to be consoled. This was the same man who allowed his frightened teenage son to sleep with him, the same man who told bed-time stories to chase away nightmares. Isolated as she was from the rest of the world, Sam was the only person she could turn to. Derrick was out there somewhere. She wanted, needed, to believe in Sam Barrister, to know that he cared. "You can help me find my brother."

The request rested heavily between them. Slowly, Crysta lifted her head.

"What makes you think he's alive, that there's—" He relinquished his grip on her shoulder and shoved strong-looking fingers through his dark hair, avoiding eye contact with her while he uttered the distasteful words that followed. "What makes you think there's anything left of him to find, Crysta? You heard what the searcher said."

When he looked back at her, Crysta's turmoil increased. Sam Barrister seemed like a nice man, and she instinctively liked him. Was she responding to his good looks? To Tip's revelations about him? Or did she feel she knew him better than she actually did because of the many stories Derrick had told her about him? She knew foul play factored into Derrick's disappearance and she should trust no one at this lodge, but she needed help.

"I just know he's alive," she whispered, her voice ragged.

"You just know?"

He seemed to consider that. With the incredulous tone of his question still hanging in the air, Crysta was forced to ask herself how much or how little she could trust her own instincts. Looking at it from Sam's point of view, she had to admit that her convictions sounded absurd. Yet they stemmed from a lifetime of experiences, and she couldn't discount them, not when Derrick's life might hang in the balance. She didn't care if she looked the fool.

He finally broke the silence. "If you have one iota of proof, I'll organize a search. But, please, understand I can't do it without a darned good reason. Those men have jobs to return to in the morning, families to support."

"I'd feel it if he were dead. We're twins. Twins are—more attuned to one another than other siblings."

That was as close as Crysta dared get to the truth about her relationship with Derrick. And it wouldn't be enough. If she read Barrister right, he was a facts-and-figures man, the pragmatic sort who discounted anything he couldn't see, hear or touch.

Feeling defeated but defiant, she set her mug of coffee on Sam's desk and pushed to her feet, feeling very like a disobedient child called onto the carpet. He studied her, his expression unreadable, his jaw set in a stubborn line.

"If you won't help me look for him, then I'll hire a guide."

The corners of his mouth tightened. "The guides up here are booked for months in advance. Finding a reputable one on such short notice would be nigh unto impossible."

Crysta's flare of hope died with his words. She knew by the look in his eyes that he was telling the truth; she'd never be able to find a guide in time to help her brother. She stood there staring at him, her hands knotted into fists. Never had she felt so impotent. "Then I'll look for him myself. You'll at least steer me in the right direction, won't you?"

He raised his hands and shook his head. "No. Another lost person is the last thing I need. We're talking a bear attack, Crysta! Raw power, enough to take your head off with one swipe of a paw. You're not going out there alone. I won't allow it."

Her frustration mounting, Crysta cried, "You won't allow it? Excuse me, but I happen to be over twenty-one. You have no authority over me."

"Oh, yes, I do. This is my lodge. You're here as my guest. You get yourself killed, and I'm liable."

"I'll sign a disclaimer."

"You'll stay within sight of the lodge, that's what you'll do. In court, a disclaimer wouldn't be worth the paper it's written on. I know the dangers out there, you don't. It would be criminal to let you take the risk. Like it or not, I'm responsible for you as long as you're here. And my livelihood depends upon my reputation."

"You let Derrick take off hiking."

"Derrick was an experienced woodsman. You aren't. If I let something happen to you, it'll be a clear-cut case of negligence."

"Please . . ." she whispered. "It's my brother out there."

Sam met her gaze, his own stony. He had the look of a man who longed to say yes but couldn't. Sensing that he was teetering on the edge, she stood her ground, hoping he'd relent.

When the silent waiting became unbearable, she spun and left the office, trembling with frustration and fear for her brother. She felt utterly helpless, and she hated that. In her everyday world, she prided herself on being a take-control type, someone who could think quickly on her feet.

Once outside the office, she pressed a hand over her eyes, so confused by her conflicting emotions and thoughts that she couldn't make sense of anything. She wanted to trust Sam Barrister, yet common sense told her she shouldn't. Derrick's friend or his enemy, that was the question, and Crysta had no answer.

Her neck stiff with tension, she stared at the closed office door. Had that been Derrick's briefcase on Sam's desk? There was only one way to find out.

SAM STUDIED the closed office door, his ears tuned for the sound of Crysta Meyers's footsteps so he could determine what direction she took. Outdoors. He heard the front door hinges squeak as she let herself out.

"I'd feel it if he were dead." Sam knew better than to take that statement lightly. Whether or not the Meyers twins were actually able to communicate telepathically wasn't an issue Sam cared to wrestle with at the moment. The important thing was that both twins believed it. Sam knew, through his long association with Derrick, that if Crysta had a feeling about her brother, she'd act on it as if it were fact.

Weary and discouraged, Sam tipped back his head and studied the shiplap planks in the ceiling. Crysta Meyers posed more problems than he had ever anticipated. She could be in danger if she stayed here, and Sam didn't know from what quarter the danger might come, which made it impossible to protect her. Yet how could he convince her to leave?

Being curt and unfriendly hadn't worked, and telling her the truth was out. If he revealed to her that he thought Derrick had been murdered, that he believed Derrick had stumbled across some sort of criminal activity being perpetrated by Blanchette Construction employees, she'd be determined to stay until she brought her brother's killers to justice.

Taking a slow sip of coffee, Sam cast a worried glance toward his desk drawer, wondering if Crysta had recognized Derrick's briefcase. If she had, she'd press the point until he told her the truth. He couldn't let it come to that. He wanted her safely out of here. He owed Derrick that much.

An ache centered itself behind Sam's eyes. He groaned and set aside his coffee mug to knead the back of his neck. Self-recriminations did no good, but Sam couldn't stop himself. If only he had listened more closely to Derrick when his friend had mentioned his suspicions.

I don't want to make any wild speculations at this point or finger innocent people, so I won't elaborate right now, but something fishy is going on up here in Alaska, Sam. I'm not sure what, not yet. But I'll find out, mark my words. When I do, I'll hang the creeps.

Sam, preoccupied with a discrepancy he had found in his books, had been tense the evening Derrick had come to him and had listened with only half an ear. Now the conversation haunted him.

All Sam could do was follow a paper trail in hopes of discovering what had made Derrick suspicious. Some kind of proof, that was what he wanted, something he could present to the authorities. If he approached the law empty-handed, no one would heed anything he said. *"Something fishy."* Sam had to find out what. And he had to find out quickly, before Crysta Meyers started asking the wrong people unsettling questions—people who would do anything to avoid answering.

THERE WAS more than one way to skin a cat.

Raised as she had been by an aphorism-prone mother, Crysta had a wealth of adages stored in her memory for every situation she encountered, and she didn't have it in her to give up easily. Going to Sam Barrister had proved a dead end, but that didn't mean she was going to stand back while the search for her brother was terminated. If Sam wouldn't or couldn't help her, she'd go above his head, directly to the search coordinator himself.

Panic nibbled at the edges of Crysta's mind. The clock was continually ticking, the seconds mounting into minutes, the minutes into hours. Time was being wasted, time that could mean the difference between life and death for Derrick.

As she walked down the slope, she scanned the circle of pup tents among the cottonwoods, hoping someone in the search team would be awake. She wasn't disappointed. Outside one tent, a man sat on a stump, a clipboard angled across his knees, one hand clasping a pen, the other holding down the paper he was writing on so the wind coming in off the river wouldn't ruffle it. She approached him slowly, trying to compose herself and rehearse what she was about to say.

"Excuse me, sir? I'm Crysta Meyers, Derrick Meyers's sister. Is the search coordinator up and about anywhere?"

The man paused in his writing and glanced up. Crysta immediately recognized him as Jim, the man who had approached Sam on the slope and broken the bad news. "You're looking at him."

Crysta couldn't believe her good luck. "Could I ask you some questions?"

His gray eyes skimmed her rumpled clothing and softened with sympathy. "I'm real sorry about your brother, ma'am. If answering questions will help you through this, I'll field any you have until our plane picks us up." He indicated a stump next to his own. "Take a load off."

Crysta perched, pressing her hands between her knees. Gazing at the nearby fire, which had burned down to coals, she recalled camping trips she had taken with Derrick, sitting on a stump or rock, her cheeks warmed by the fire, singing along while he strummed his ukulele and made up silly ditties. Pain washed through her, and her sense of loss was so acute, she ached with it. In the recent past she had wished that she could distance herself from Derrick and have a normal life. Now she would give anything to hear his voice whispering inside her head, to feel connected to him again.

"Without a—a body, how can you be positive my brother is dead? Couldn't you continue looking for him for a couple more days?"

Jim shoved his pen behind his ear and gazed off into the cottonwoods. Crysta focused on the grizzled tufts of brown hair that curled down over his upturned shirt collar. He needed a haircut and a shave. She wondered if he missed his family, if he understood her grief. She decided he must. He wouldn't be here, volunteering, if he were an uncaring man.

"It isn't easy to lose someone this way," he said softly. "I know that. But you have to accept it. We found parts of his shirt, shredded and soaked with blood. There were bear tracks and signs of struggle all around the scene."

Straightening her spine, Crysta asked, "Did you search for any evidence of foul play?"

"Foul play?" The look he gave made her feel the question was ridiculous. "No. Why would we look for something when there was no indication we should?"

Because I heard a gunshot. Crysta nibbled her lip. "Did you notice any human footprints?"

"Naturally there were some. Your brother's."

"Any others?"

He was beginning to look irritated. "We didn't make any plaster molds and compare the shoe marks, if that's what you mean. There were signs of a violent struggle, slide marks in the mud, bear track, blood, broken branches on the surrounding bushes, dislodged rock and your brother's shredded shirt."

Not to be deterred, Crysta pressed on. "Isn't bear track common up here?"

"Of course it's common."

"Was the bear track indicative of an attack?"

A flush crept up the man's neck. "Everything was indicative of an attack."

"Were the bear tracks just ordinary tracks? You mentioned slide marks. Were any of those marks made by the attacking bear? Or were they all made by boots?"

The muscles in his face tightened. "Ma'am, it was a clearcut case of a renegade bear attack. There's no reason, absolutely none, to think otherwise. The authorities are satisfied with our findings. Why can't you be?"

"You found blood, but how do you know it's my brother's?"

"Whose would you guess it to be, the bear's?" He pinioned her with a steady stare, then sighed. "I'm sorry. That was uncalled for. Tests will be run, ma'am. If it isn't your brother's type or if it's animal blood, we'll resume the search."

"By then it will be too late!"

"We'll get preliminary reports back this afternoon."

"And if there's any question that it's his blood, you'll come back and begin another search?"

"It's a promise."

Crysta blinked and glanced away. Out at the island, she saw the redhead, Riley O'Keefe, disembarking from a boat. She wondered if he had been night fishing. Her brother was missing. How could people go on as if nothing had happened? "I don't think my brother's dead. We're twins, and because of that, we're closer than most siblings. I'd know. You understand?"

The search coordinator gave her a pitying look. "It's hard to accept, I know it is."

"No, you don't under—"

Crysta broke off, struggling to stop the violent shaking that had attacked her limbs. It was such a horrible feeling to pour out her heart to people and not be able to reach them. If only telepathic phenomena didn't make people so wary! But Crysta had learned long ago that she must guard her words. Saying the wrong thing could alienate this man even more than he already was. She felt badly about grilling him, but she had so many questions and so few answers.

"Do you ever get a gut feeling? Deep down, you just know something, and you can't really explain how?"

He continued to study her, clearly at a loss.

Crysta leaned toward him, as though drawing closer would somehow convince him when words alone failed. "I know my brother isn't dead. He's out there somewhere, and every wasted second decreases his chances of survival. Please don't call off the search. Please."

"Ma'am, the evidence is overwhelming. I can't keep these fellows here. Our organization would never sanction more expenditures to cover their wages, not on the strength of a gut feeling. I'm sorry."

"Their wages?"

"Like it or not, it's a consideration."

An image of Derrick's face flashed through Crysta's mind. Her brother, whom she loved so dearly, and he was being written off because of expenses. Heartbreak prodding her, Crysta shot up from the stump and whirled on the coordinator. "So the bottom line is money, is that it? How can you place a price on a man's life? You can't just give up and leave him out there!"

Her voice had risen to a wail. When she realized how she sounded, she swallowed and swiped her sleeve across her mouth, acutely aware that the surrounding tents probably sheltered sleeping searchers who needed and deserved their rest. She gazed upriver, fighting for control, watching Riley O'Keefe bounce along the footbridge toward shore. From the surreptitious glances he shot her direction, she guessed that he had heard her outburst and probably thought she was hysterical. Not that he was far off the mark. Derrick needed her, and her ignorance of the area held her trapped here, unable to make a move on her own.

The sound of a snapping twig made Crysta glance around. A thin, brown-haired man in jeans and a powder-blue sweatshirt strode through the trees. For an instant she wondered if he had been eavesdropping on her conversation with the search coordinator, then discounted the suspicion as ridiculous. She couldn't distrust everyone she saw.

Crysta swallowed again and took a bracing breath, returning her attention to the coordinator. "I—I'm sorry for raising my voice. I should be thanking you for all you've done."

"Don't be sorry, ma'am. As hard as it is for you to believe, I understand how you feel, truly I do. I wish I could continue the search, but I can't. Not without cause. If you'd like, you can call headquarters and see if they'll authorize our staying. Or the police in Anchorage. All I need is a go-ahead."

A sense of futility swept over Crysta. Nothing she could say or do would change things, not even if she blurted out the entire story and gave them a blow-by-blow account of previous instances when she had experienced telepathic communication with her brother. Who would believe her? Except for her parents, Derrick and her aunt Eva, who had ever believed her? Not her ex-husband, certainly, not the family doctor, not her analyst. Why expect more from a bunch of strangers?

"I don't suppose you'd be interested in hiring yourself out as a guide?"

He gave her a regretful smile. "Like everyone else, I have a job I have to get back to. My boss excuses me for official searches, but when those end, he expects me back."

Crysta swallowed. "Could you recommend a guide to me then?"

"An easy dozen, but none will be available. Their time is usually booked up well in advance, sometimes as much as a year."

"Where exactly did the bear attack occur?" she asked softly, hoping he would be more informative than Sam had been.

His gaze sharpened. "You're not thinking about going out there, are you?"

What did he expect her to do? Nothing? Crysta knew she was a lousy liar, so she chose silence as an answer.

"No way." He jerked his pen from behind his ear, suddenly all business, his body language clearly stating that, as far as he was concerned, their conversation was over. "I'm really sorry about your brother, ma'am. If you have any more questions, you know where I am."

"I have a right to know all the pertinent facts."

"If you wanna get yourself killed, you'll do it without my help."

"You're withholding information from next of kin."

He leveled a stubborn glare at her. Then, eyes revealing nothing, he pointed downstream. "The scene of the attack was thataway."

The sarcasm made Crysta want to shake him. "How far?"

He seemed to consider the question. "Several miles."

"Several meaning three, four, five? How many would you guess?"

"More than two, less than ten. I didn't log the exact location."

"Was it along the river, at the mouth of an inlet, along a slough?"

He frowned, feigning bewilderment. "I think it was along the river, but then again, it could have been a slough. It was definitely along the Yentna somewhere, and it'd be hard to miss if you came across it. We flagged the area."

Blazing with anger and fighting off tears, Crysta turned away before she lost her temper. It certainly wouldn't help Derrick if she alienated everyone who might be able to find him. As she walked up the slope back to the lodge, she weighed her options, trying to decide what she should do next. It didn't look as if she was going to convince anyone else to resume the search for her brother. She needed a map of the area.

Weariness blurred her thoughts, and the maze of disjointed ideas in her head made her wonder if she wasn't losing her ability to be rational. Overwhelming evidence indicated that Derrick was dead, the victim of a bear attack. Was she insane to believe otherwise?

A gust of wind caught Crysta's hair, whipping it across her face. She stared through the reddish-brown strands, wondering if she would ever again see her brother's hair gleaming in sunshine, ever again hear him call her name.

As a greenhorn in rugged country, she would be taking a perilous step if she ventured far from the lodge alone. She must think things through, plan her strategy. If her dreams were accurate, there was a whole lot more than bears out there to worry about. She would need all her wits about her, that was a certainty. Maybe a hot bath would clear her head.

She slipped quietly into Sam's apartment and gathered fresh clothing from her suitcases, then slipped quietly out again, relieved that she hadn't encountered Sam. As she approached the sauna building, the hair on her nape prickled. Hesitating, she glanced uneasily around. When she spied no one, she shrugged off the sensation, blaming it on exhaustion and raw nerves.

Proceeding up the steps to the building, she flipped the sign over to Occupied, as Sam had told her to do, and opened the heavy outer door to the anteroom. After hanging her fresh clothing on the provided hooks, Crysta selected a few chunks of wood from the supply along one wall, then opened the stove door and refueled the fire. Grabbing soap, shampoo and a towel off the stack, she stepped through the interior doorway into the steam room, pulling the massive door closed behind her.

Amazed at how effectively Sam's rustic sauna system worked, Crysta deep-breathed the steam. The structure had soaked up the mist until the foot-thick walls were swollen and airtight. Now she could appreciate Sam's reasons for not putting latches on the doors. The air was so hot and thick that someone less fit could easily stay in here too long and get woozy.

Crysta felt as though a hundred years had rolled away. On one side of the room was a recessed area in the planked floor, bedded with rock that was somehow heated by the wood stove. A huge galvanized tub sat on the rock, the simmering water within sending up a continual mist of steam. Nearby was another tub, filled with cool water. The opposite wall supported handmade steam benches. The slatted floor provided drainage.

She had always imagined coming to the lodge with Derrick, to have him be the one to show her around.

Remembering only sketches of Sam Barrister's instructions, Crysta was on her own in figuring out the bathing procedure. Feeling uneasy because there was no latch on the door to guarantee privacy, Crysta undressed, then sloshed water over the rocks so she could enjoy the calming effects of the steam. She filled the large bucket by the tub of hot water, added cold water to get the temperature right, and dumped the contents over herself. Definitely not the Ritz, but she guessed that was the appeal of Cottonwood Bend. People came here to escape the strictures of their citified lives.

After a brisk shampoo and scrubdown, she returned to the anteroom and dressed, forgoing makeup and giving her hair only a few cursory swipes with a brush.

En route back to the lodge, Crysta spotted a flash of red down by the river. Riley O'Keefe. Remembering that Sam had said the Irishman worked for Blanchette, Crysta decided to talk to him, just to see if she might glean some new information. Stowing her damp clothing by the lodge entrance, she struck off toward the river, shivering as a cool breeze whipped up off the water to cut through her denim shirt and jeans. For the first time since coming to Alaska, she wished she had on her thermal undershirt.

Riley O'Keefe, who had been cleaning fish, smiled when she approached. Scooping a wad of chewing tobacco from inside his cheek, he shook his hand clean and spat. "Sorry to be caught with a chaw, but I wasn't expectin' company this time of morning. Nice to know I'm not the only night owl up and around."

Appalled that anyone would stick a fish-bloodied finger in his mouth, Crysta hid a shudder and said, "It doesn't seem like night to me." She shot a glance at the sky. "It's kind of like twilight, isn't it?"

"Yeah, but this time of year, it's the only nighttime you'll get. Makes for a great growing season, but newcomers often have trouble sleeping. It'll catch up with you, though, and when it does, you'll crash and sleep like the dead.''

The dead. Everything reminded her of Derrick and her race against time. Crysta raked her fingers through her wet hair, forcing herself to smile. "I understand you know my brother.''

"I knew him.''

Crysta flinched at his use of the past tense. "You work for Blanchette, Sam tells me.''

"That's right.'' Opening a Coleman cooler that sat beside him, Riley fished out a dripping can of beer. "Want one? Might help you sleep, and I've got plenty more where this came from. I'm heading into Anchorage later. Shriver's making the loop today, so I can put in a few hours at work, pick up another rack of beer, then pull a U-turn and do more fishing. The life of Riley.'' He chuckled at his joke, then arched an eyebrow. "Wet your whistle with me?''

Crysta couldn't help wondering how Riley O'Keefe could afford frequent trips to the lodge and all the beer he wanted to drink on a warehouse supervisor's wages. Maybe she was in the wrong line of work. "I'm not much of a beer drinker unless the weather's extremely hot. Thanks for offering.''

He pulled the can tab. Tipping back his head, he guzzled, his larynx bobbing. For a moment, she thought he meant to drain the can. Giving a satisfied burp and an apologetic smile, he wiped his chin with his shirt sleeve.

"I guess you're the type who comes prepared,'' Crysta said lightly.

"How's that?''

"Well, you have a stock of brew.'' She inclined her head at the cooler. "And I understand you even travel with your own phone. You lent it to Sam last week, didn't you?''

"The mobile phone?'' He nodded. "Yeah, I brought mine up. His was gone for repairs. In a remote place like this, a phone is a must. Never know when an emergency might come up.''

Crysta's throat tightened as she glanced downstream. "Yes, my brother's disappearance proves that.''

Riley finished off his beer, tossed the can into a sack beside him, and promptly reached into the cooler for another. Nearby, Crysta saw a pile of discarded beer cans in the brush, and she was surprised that Riley's hadn't joined them. His regard for the environment made her reverse her first unfavourable impression of him. Just because a man had poor chewing-tobacco habits didn't mean he wasn't a nice person.

"I'm real sorry about Derrick, by the way. Started to tell you so when you landed, but I wasn't sure what to say."

The sympathy in his expression made a lump rise in Crysta's throat, and her eyes started to burn. To maintain control over her emotions, she gazed at the beer cans in the nearby brush. Alaska wouldn't remain beautiful and untouched very long if people threw litter all over the place. She wondered why Sam didn't lay some ground rules for his guests. Perhaps he had, and some simply chose to ignore them.

"I guess there isn't much anyone can say," Crysta finally replied, dragging her gaze back to Riley. After a moment, she asked, "You wouldn't happen to know exactly where my brother's clothing was found, would you?"

O'Keefe gave her a knowing look. "Why don't you ask the search coordinator?"

"I did, but he was rather vague."

His voice gentle with concern, he asked, "You aren't thinking about going down there, are you?"

"I might. That's my decision."

"True. Unfortunately, I don't know the exact location. Just that it was downriver somewhere."

Frustration seethed within Crysta, warming her skin. She had a hunch O'Keefe knew more than he was telling. "If you do know, I'd appreciate your telling me. I realize the risks."

He gave her a pleading look. "Don't put me on the spot. It's not my business, you know? I'm just a guest here. If I get on Sam's bad side, my weekend retreat is shot all to hell, and I like coming here."

Crysta could see pressing him for more information would be fruitless. She understood everyone's concern and appreciated their reasons for trying to protect her, but it was frustrating, nonetheless. She decided to explore another subject. "I gather you come here a lot?"

"Every chance I get."

"Must be nice. Most people can't afford the rates or the air fare in."

"All the pilots give me a break on my air fare, and Sam gives me a discount."

"It still must be expensive. Especially if you bring your friend often. What's his name?"

"Steve Henderson. He's not the only guy from work I bring, but I do bring him the most. It's all what your priorities are, I guess. Me, I'm single, don't have kids. I figure I may as well enjoy myself. And if a few weekends away help Steve to cope, it seems little enough for me to do, paying his way up. Nice kid, Steve. Closest thing to a son I'll ever have."

"It's good of you to care. Nowadays, too many people don't." Crysta focused on O'Keefe's wristwatch, wondering if it was a genuine Rolex or an inexpensive look-alike. "I gather you and Sam must know each other well."

He nodded. "Sam's good people."

"You like him, then?"

"Everybody likes Sam."

"I know my brother did."

Riley O'Keefe took another swallow of beer, sighing with satisfaction as he drew the can from his mouth. "Yeah, they got along real well. Most of the time, anyway."

Crysta's skin prickled. "Most of the time?"

O'Keefe shrugged. "Nobody gets along a hundred percent."

"I wasn't aware they ever disagreed."

"Wasn't any big deal."

Crysta took a moment to phrase her next question, not wishing to sound too eager. "When were they on the outs?"

He squinted and leaned over to retie the laces on his boot. Another green boot with a band of yellow at the top. "Derrick had been coming up a lot lately, more than usual. You know how it goes. Too much of a good thing. Don't misunderstand—they were good friends. Hell, Sam's been half out of his mind since Derrick came up missing. They just didn't see eye-to-eye sometimes, that's all.''

That was news to Crysta. "I guess we all feel cross at times." She caught the inside of her cheek between her teeth, worrying the soft flesh, her gaze fixed on O'Keefe's ruddy face. "They weren't quarreling last week, were they? Right before Derrick disappeared?''

He glanced up, his eyes sharpening. "What if they were?''

Crysta shoved her hands into the pockets of her jeans. "Just curious. That could account for Sam's reaction to Derrick's disappearance. He might feel a little guilty, which always makes losing someone hurt all the more.''

He seemed to relax. "It was no big deal. Something silly, I think. Sam was a little hot when Derrick left, but he would have been over it by the time your brother got back.''

"So you haven't any idea what they were upset about?''

"Even if I did, it wouldn't be my business to repeat it.''

She gave a shrug, feigning an unconcern she was far from feeling, questions burning within her. Pressing O'Keefe for answers right now might be unwise. He could relate her curiosity to Sam, forewarning the lodge owner that she knew he had quarreled with Derrick. Crysta preferred to spring that knowledge on Sam when he didn't know it was coming and when it might be to her advantage.

She studied the trees, filled with resentment toward Sam, pretending she had run out of things to say. "Well, I guess I should at least try to sleep. It was nice talking to you, Mr. O'Keefe.''

"Same here. And, once again, I'm really sorry about your brother. He was a favorite around here, a real nature enthusiast and a helluva nice man to work under. I'll miss him, in more ways than one.''

Crysta bit back a rebuttal. Derrick wasn't dead. She just knew he wasn't. Not yet.

Chapter Six

A delicious smell wafted to Crysta as she approached the lodge. Curious about who would be up cooking at this hour, she followed her nose, circling the building until she came upon a plump Indian woman busily placing trays of salmon on racks in a makeshift smokehouse. Though Crysta had little interest in salmon-smoking techniques, she was keenly interested in learning all she could about Derrick's last visit here. If this woman worked at the lodge, she might have answers to some of Crysta's questions.

"Hello," Crysta called softly.

Stooped over a burdensome tray, the woman turned slightly at the waist and fixed her black eyes on Crysta, her square face expressionless. Making no attempt to be friendly, she grunted and returned her attention to her work. She was bedecked in jewelry, her arms striped with colorful bangles, her neck with gaudy strands of beads and ivory pendants, her earlobes weighted with dangling ovals of scrimshaw. Even her black braid was interwoven with handmade jewelry.

"I'm Derrick Meyers's sister."

"I know who you are," the woman replied, her voice toneless.

"You have me at a disadvantage."

The woman ignored that.

"If you know who I am, then you must know my brother."

She graced Crysta with another glance. "I knew him."

Crysta's heart caught, and she glanced uneasily at the ground, struck speechless by the woman's ill-concealed animosity. What reason could the Indian cook have for disliking her?

"He would not want you here."

The words were spoken so softly that Crysta almost thought she had imagined them. She looked up, confused and shaken. "Why do you say that?"

"Because it is true. The Tlingit Indians speak only truth. You walk in the shadow of the great black bird, Crysta Meyers. Death is your companion. Go home. Back to the living. There is nothing for you here but sorrow—great sorrow."

So she was a Tlingit. Crysta knew very little about the Alaskan tribes, but it seemed to her she had once read that the Tlingit hailed from the southeast section of the state. If so, this woman was a long way from where most of her people lived. "Wh—what do you mean?"

"What I said. Go home." The woman returned her black gaze to the salmon racks. "Go now, before it is too late."

With that, she closed the smokehouse door and walked toward the lodge, an emptied tray swinging in one hand, her colorful gathered skirt swirling around her plump calves, her braid bouncing along her spine. Crysta longed to pursue her and demand that she elaborate.

She longed to but didn't. The people at Cottonwood Bend were not what they seemed. Sam Barrister had quarreled with her brother right before he disappeared. Now this Indian woman spouted veiled threats. Crysta had a bad feeling, a very bad feeling.

She circled the lodge and retrieved her bundle of clothing. As she drew up at the front entrance, Sam Barrister was coming through the doorway. He was looking back over his shoulder and speaking to someone, so he didn't see her. Though Crysta tried, she couldn't sidestep him quickly enough to avoid a collision. Stunned, teeth snapping together on impact, she dropped her clothes, staggered and would have fallen if not for Sam's quick reaction.

Seizing her shoulders, he righted her. "Are you okay? I should have been watching where I was going."

"I—" Crysta closed her eyes, then opened them, still disoriented. "I'm fine, just a little rattled."

Focusing on the lodge owner's dark face, Crysta could have sworn his concern was genuine. His grip on her shoulders tightened, hinting at the leashed strength in his hands. She looked past his arm into the dimly lit lodge. "It seems to be my day for unsettling encounters. I just had a skirmish with a Tlingit."

"A Tlingit?" One of his eyebrows shot up. "Jangles?"

"Is that her name? She was so busy trying to scare me, she didn't introduce herself."

Sam's mouth quirked. Releasing her, he bent to pick up her clothes. "Don't mind Jangles. Her heart's in the right place. She's just a little abrupt at times."

He called that abrupt? "She threatened me."

"Jangles?" He looked amused by the thought. "That doesn't sound like her. Threatened how?"

"She told me to go home, back to the living, before it was too late. Something about walking in shadows."

Sam pressed the bundle of clothing into her arms, his expression turning wry. There was something different about him, but she couldn't pinpoint what. She only knew he was even more attractive than she had first thought, which was unsettling, and she missed the comforting warmth of his hands on her shoulders, which was doubly so.

"Probably her superstitious nature coming out," he offered. "Some of the natives are frightened by death or any dealings with it. Maybe she's afraid because you've come here searching for Derrick."

"Are Tlingits particularly superstitious?"

"Most Indian cultures are rife with superstitions."

Crysta had to admire the neat way he had avoided giving her a direct answer. Somehow, she felt sure Sam knew as much about Tlingits as he did about Alaska. She wondered if he would be equally evasive when she cornered him about his quarrel with Derrick.

Shoving the door open wider, he stepped aside to allow her through. "You're sure you're okay?"

Crysta's mind raced, trying to sort the questions she wanted to ask him. All she could manage was a weak "I'm fine."

Since she couldn't just leave him standing in such an awkward position, bracing the door open, she ducked under his arm, amazed, even in her agitation, that he was so tall. So large a man would have no difficulty overpowering someone Derrick's size. It was an unsettling thought, but one she couldn't banish once it slipped into her mind.

Sam inclined his head, then continued on through the doorway before Crysta could voice any of the questions she had hoped to ask him. When the door swung closed behind him, she stood staring at the wood. Only then did she realize what was different about Sam Barrister. He had showered, changed clothes and shaved. The brown plaid shirt he wore was far more flattering than the grungy sweatshirt he'd sported earlier.

After stowing her soiled clothing in Sam's apartment, Crysta returned to the front of the lodge. On the check-in counter, she spied a rack of maps, some of them the forestry type that plotted the surrounding wilderness. Helping herself to one, she sat at one of the long dining tables, smoothing the large map open on the planks. Within seconds she was absorbed in the spidery network of lines, trying to decipher the small print and pinpoint where along the river Derrick might have been when she had dreamed of men chasing him.

"I DON'T BELIEVE Derrick is dead. I know he isn't." The words ate at Sam. After sharing a few pleasantries with Riley O'Keefe, Sam stared downstream, his thoughts fragmented. What if Crysta was right and Derrick was out there someplace, alive and in need of help, while he wasted precious time going through a briefcase for clues?

In his mind, Sam relived every detail of his initial search for Derrick, which had culminated with his finding Derrick's shredded backpack and scattered camping gear. Had he overlooked something, some telltale clue?

Torn, Sam cast a furtive glance at the lodge, then sauntered toward the trees. One thing was for sure, he didn't want Crysta to realize he'd given credence to anything she said. If she found a single chink in his armor, she'd work at it until he confessed everything. And then she'd be in on this until the bloody end.

The word *bloody* stuck in Sam's thought grooves like a scratchy needle on a phonograph record. He circled the lodge, then struck off through the trees, hoping the indirect route would prevent anyone from noticing his departure. It was quite a trek to the spot where Derrick's gear had been found, a good twelve miles, but Sam knew he could pace it off, do a more thorough search of the area and return before anyone became unduly alarmed by his absence. Sometimes, though not often, his long legs were an asset.

A MOVEMENT CAUGHT Crysta's attention, and she glanced up from the map. Through the window, she saw Sam Barrister skulking through the cottonwoods and casting furtive looks over his shoulder, as though he didn't want to be seen. With the mystery of her brother's disappearance foremost in her thoughts, Crysta deduced that the lodge owner's secretive excursion involved Derrick. She didn't take time to think beyond that.

Shooting up from the bench, she raced outside, determined to follow Barrister without his knowing it. She could only hope Riley O'Keefe, who still sat on the riverbank, had drunk so many beers that he wouldn't notice her as she slunk around the sauna and darted into the woods.

Before long Crysta was cursing Sam Barrister for his lengthy stride. Not an easy man to tail. She was forced into a trot half the time, just to keep him in sight. Along the riverbank, the brush was thick and tall. While it provided her with necessary cover, it presented a problem when it came to following someone.

Sam disappeared from view. Crysta strained to catch a glimpse of him through the tangled undergrowth, then increased her pace, cringing at the noise she was making. At a run, it wasn't easy to be quiet, and she had no ready explanation if he should turn around and discover her.

Three miles later, Crysta's side ached from exertion. She stopped a moment to catch her breath, scarcely able to believe Barrister or any other man could cover ground so quickly at a walk. Peering through the trees, she once again tried to spot his brown plaid shirt. He was nowhere in sight. Momentary panic set in. Not only did she hate to lose him, but she wasn't too thrilled about being out here alone.

A crackling noise made Crysta whirl to look behind her. Footsteps? Frustrated by the low rushing sound of the river, she strained to hear, eyes scanning the woods for movement, heart racing, her senses bombarded by unfamiliar smells and sights. Poised for flight, she felt the muscles in her legs quiver. Suddenly, all the conversations of that morning came back to taunt her. What if everyone else was right, and she was wrong? What if her brother was indeed dead?

One word bounced off the walls of her mind. *Bears.* Still, if there was anything as big as a grizzly out there, surely she would see it. Or hear it. A renegade bear wasn't likely to be furtive before it launched an attack. A picture of Derrick's shredded shirt flashed in her head, and her stomach lurched. She listened a few more seconds, flinching when leaves, caught by the wind, rustled overhead. Nothing. Whatever she had heard, it was gone now. She hoped.

A more cautious person probably wouldn't be out here. It was a fault of hers, acting before she weighed the consequences. She drew little comfort from her proximity to the river, by which she could retrace her footsteps. After all, bears ate fish, didn't they?

Bears or no, Crysta knew she was out of her element and should follow the river back to the lodge. But she didn't want to. What she wanted was to dog Barrister's heels and see where he was going. Was she going to let thoughts of a four-legged man-eater scare her off?

Determined, she slogged through a narrow slough, wetting her jeans to the knee. Common sense told her that since

Barrister had followed the river this far, he wasn't likely to alter his course. If she discovered that he had, she could turn back.

She ran across a stretch of marshy grass and back into the brush, darting right and left through the maze of dappled cottonwood trunks and undergrowth. Straining for a glimpse of the lodge owner up ahead, Crysta was taken totally off guard when a dark shape hurtled out at her from the thick brush.

A bear? Fright flashed through her, but there was no time to react. One instant she was on her feet, and the next she felt as if a brick wall had mowed her down. She spied a blur of brown plaid. Then coarse wool grazed her cheek. Sam Barrister. When she tried to move, she found herself vised in a tangle of muscular arms and legs. The instinctive scream that had welled in her chest came out as a grunt when he rolled, flattening her body with his, slamming her face into the dirt.

It quickly occurred to Crysta that Sam Barrister must think he had tackled a man. She was proved correct an instant later when he clamped a palm over her breast and froze. The contact made Crysta's nerves leap.

"Son of a— What in the—?" He jerked his hand away. "Don't you know better than to sneak up on someone like that? It's a good way to get yourself hurt."

With her face buried in dirt and moldy leaves, Crysta couldn't have replied if she wanted to. It was all she could do to gather her wits and regain her shattered composure. Her skin still tingled from the touch of his hand, and the unwelcome, purely feminine reaction at such an inopportune moment made her unreasonably angry, with him and herself.

Twisting her face to one side, she spat out dirt and other things she didn't want to identify. Then she ran her tongue over her throbbing front teeth, none too sure they were all intact.

He muttered something that sounded suspiciously like a curse, then rolled, came up on one knee and extracted his arm from around her. "I could hear you but couldn't see you. If I'd known it was you, I—" He let out a ragged sigh. "I'm sorry. I just reacted."

Crysta pushed up on her elbows, shoulder throbbing, scraped cheek afire. He reached to help her, seeming uncertain where to touch. By the flush rising up his muscular neck, she guessed that he was as unsettled as she by the physical awareness that had flared between them.

"I'm really sorry. I didn't mean to—Is anything broken?"

"I'm fine." Squelching her anger, which she knew was due more to embarrassment than outrage, Crysta gave her sleeve a tug and brushed debris from her hair, taking advantage of the brief silence to mend her shattered dignity. Testing her shoulder, she said, "You pack quite a wallop."

"It never occurred to me it might be you, and with everything that's been going on, I decided to act first and ask questions later."

Crysta focused on only part of what he said. As she flicked the leaves and dirt off her favorite denim shirt, she countered, "Exactly what *has* been going on?"

The flush on his neck deepened. He flexed his shoulders, bracing one arm on his upraised knee. The breeze ruffled his dark hair across his forehead, and Crysta had a sudden urge to smooth it with her fingertips. She stifled the wayward impulse, determined to ignore the attraction she felt to him. For some reason beyond her comprehension, she was drawn to this man in a way that defied all her attempts to squelch it.

Frustration mounting, Crysta fired another shot. "You've been keeping things from me. I know you have."

His eyes met hers, teeming with indefinable emotion, but he said nothing.

"You quarreled with Derrick right before he left. Do you deny that?"

"No."

"What did you argue about?"

His jaw tensed. "That isn't any of your concern."

His response so infuriated Crysta that she shot to her feet. How could she allow herself to be attracted to this man? He clearly wasn't being up front with her, and his reasons for that remained to be seen. She could only assume the worst.

"Not my concern? My brother is missing! Anything involving him is my concern! Don't play games with me, Mr. Barrister. I don't appreciate it."

"Sam."

"I hardly think we should be on a first-name basis. I want answers."

"I'm your brother's best friend, have been for nearly ten years. Doesn't that count for something? How can you possibly think I had anything to do with what happened to him?"

"If that bothers you, then level with me!"

For a moment, Crysta thought he might do just that. The shutters lifted from his dark eyes, and she saw pain reflected there. In that instant, she would have sworn he loved her brother, possibly as much as she did. With Derrick's life at stake, though, she couldn't afford to go on intuition. She also wasn't sure, judging from the tangle of her emotions when she was near this man, that she could trust her instincts.

"How about your leveling with me?" he retorted. "What makes you so sure Derrick's alive? Why did you come to Alaska when I asked you not to? Why are you acting as though some*one* hurt your brother when you've been told repeatedly that he was the victim of a bear attack? And why on earth did you follow me out here?"

Crysta clenched her teeth to keep from answering those questions. A part of her wanted to tell him everything. She also reasoned that she was out here alone with him. With his size as an advantage, he needn't engage in a war of words for long. On the other hand, he had to realize that two disappearances in less than a week were bound to raise eyebrows.

Reassured by that thought, she said, "If you're so certain my brother was killed by a crazed bear, Mr. Barrister, then why aren't you carrying a gun?"

She could see the question caught him unprepared. Her determination bolstered, she rapped out another question. "Where were you going?"

"For a walk."

Crysta knew that no one would take such precautions to avoid being seen simply to go for a walk. She braced her hands on her hips. "I know whatever it was you intended to do somehow involved my brother, and I want to know what it was."

He gave her a look far too innocent to be genuine. "You must read too many mysteries. I came for a walk, that's all."

"I *never* read mysteries." Two could play this game. Crysta shrugged. "I saw you coming out here and decided to join you. Nothing mysterious about that, either, is there?"

His expression registered *touché* as clearly as if he had spoken. Pushing to his feet, he regarded her steadily. Then, with a half grin, he reached to pluck a leaf out of her hair, his hand lingering longer than was necessary, his thumb grazing her temple. "You not only *look* like Derrick, you act like him."

Crysta had the uncomfortable feeling that he was trying to distract her, and she was loath to admit that the tactic might work. The notion and all it implied frightened her in some indefinable way she didn't have the energy to deal with right now. "Why do I get the feeling that isn't a compliment?"

His grin broadened. "Possibly because you know Derrick as well as I do. When they came up with the word *bullheaded*, it was with him in mind."

Drawing on the store of maxims her mother used so frequently, Crysta quipped, "Birds of a feather flock together. According to Derrick, you two were very close." She paused, gauging the seconds so her next words would catch him off guard. "Is that why you quarreled, because Derrick's bullheaded?"

His face tightened. "Like I said, that's not your concern."

"If my inferences bother you, why keep secrets? Your having a quarrel with Derrick looks bad. Even you have to admit that. If it was over nothing important, why hide it?"

He arched an eyebrow. "Excuse me, but do I in any way resemble a bear, Crysta? A quarrel wouldn't look bad if you would take things at face value."

"Face value isn't good enough, not when my brother's life rides on it. I want answers, and I'm not getting them, not from you or anyone else. You've no right to keep secrets from me."

His eyes gave her no quarter. "And you've no right to accuse me of things without proof."

"But I do have every right to see where my brother's gear was found, where this *alleged* bear attack occurred. Yet you refuse to tell me where either of those places is. And you've seen to it that no one else will tell me, either. I resent being treated as if I were a child."

"A child? This is Alaska, not the Los Angeles zoo. A renegade grizzly could spot you in his territory from a mile away and go into attack mode. Grizzlies don't cotton to interlopers at the best of times. Hikers learn to respect their habits and go out of their way to accommodate them. But a crazed bear? We're talking totally unpredictable."

"Then why don't you escort me downriver? I'd be safe with you, and I could satisfy my curiosity."

"You *wouldn't* be safe with me, that's just it. Do you see a large red S emblazoned on my shirt?" The sound of a snapping twig caught his attention. He glanced over his shoulder, looking uneasy. Crysta wondered if his behavior was a ploy calculated to frighten her. She scanned the woods behind him. When he looked back at her, she met his gaze. "I couldn't protect myself from a grizzly, let alone you," he finished.

"Come on, Sam. Derrick's told me what an expert guide you are. You're as at home out here as in your living room. You don't let grizzlies or any other bears stop you from hiking."

"Under ordinary circumstances, no. It's safe enough, if you know what you're doing. But these aren't ordinary circumstances, and that's no ordinary bear out there. And, contrary to what you seem to think, I'm a very ordinary guy. Besides, I told you flat out before you came that I didn't have time to escort you downriver.''

"Yet you have time for a walk?" Shaking with anger, she gestured upstream toward the lodge. "Shall we head back? Or do you want to *stroll* a little farther?"

Sam bit back a frustrated groan. She had pluck, he'd give her that. But there was such a thing as being too fearless for one's own good. If he was correct and Derrick had fallen victim to foul play, the last thing Sam needed was a daring and stubborn sleuthing partner. He wanted Crysta on the first flight out, safely away from here before she followed the wrong man into the woods or pressed the wrong person for answers. So much for re-examining the spot where he had found Derrick's gear.

"We may as well head back," he growled.

She glanced around. "How much farther is it?"

So exhausted that he was operating on automatic pilot, Sam said, "It's about—" and then caught himself. She had almost nailed him. "You don't give up, do you?"

"Would you?"

Her hazel eyes lifted, filled with such pain and fear that Sam yearned to comfort her. The answer to her question was no, if it was his brother missing, he would never give up, but he couldn't admit that. Nor could he acknowledge, even to himself, that her expression tugged at his heart.

Over the last ten years Sam had formed a vague picture of Crysta from Derrick's stories about her, but even so, she'd been little more than a name to him. Now the reality of her was hitting him like a well-placed blow to his solar plexus. She was a living, breathing, feeling person, grappling with grief and terror. And he was helpless to do anything about it. The fact that she appealed to him more than any other woman ever had made the situation he found himself in even more difficult.

ONCE BACK AT THE LODGE, Sam dropped Crysta off at the door and went down to the river, presumably to oversee his paying guests but in actuality to think and wait for a more opportune moment to sneak away. Until he was certain Crysta wouldn't follow him, he didn't dare go downstream again.

A feeling of helplessness dogged Sam everywhere he went. Derrick. He couldn't get his friend off his mind. *"Something fishy."* What had Derrick meant by that? And whom had he suspected? Sam was totally in the dark. Surely Derrick had come across an illegal activity of some kind within his company. But what? *"Something fishy up here in Alaska,"* he had said. *"I'll hang the creeps."* Derrick had suspected something serious, definitely. Something so serious that the perpetrators had killed him to protect their anonymity.

Or had they? *"I don't believe my brother is dead. I know he isn't."* Sam sat on the riverbank, arms braced on his knees, shoulders slumped with weariness. There was only one consolation in all of this. If Derrick was indeed alive, he was an expert woodsman and could survive in the Alaska interior for quite some time. Unless, of course, he was badly hurt. In that case, he probably wouldn't have lasted this long.

MORE DETERMINED NOW than ever to search for her brother on her own, Crysta returned to her map the moment she got back to the lodge. She was deeply engrossed when Tip's voice snagged her attention. She glanced up to spy him walking across the dining hall, hair rumpled from sleep, his cheek lined from where it had pressed against his pillow.

"H-hi, Crys. Wh-what are you d-doing?"

His shy smile made it impossible for Crysta to say she was busy. She patted the table across from her. "I'm looking this map over. Have a seat."

"Am I b-bugging you?"

Crysta forced a smile. "Certainly not. Whoever said such a thing to you?"

"Lots of people." He swung a jeans-clad leg over the opposite bench and sat astraddle the wood, one elbow propped on the table's edge. "I don't bug my dad, but he loves me."

Crysta was pleased to note that the boy's stuttering had stopped, a sign that her warm welcome had put him at ease.

"Well, I *like* you. Does that count?"

His cheek dimpled as he smiled, giving Crysta an idea of what Sam might look like if his expression wasn't so stern all the time. Cocking his head, Tip regarded the map. Jabbing a finger at a spot upriver from their location at the lodge, he said, "I walk to that place a lot."

"Do you?"

It occurred to Crysta that Tip might know the area well enough to give her some direction. But before she could pursue that train of thought, he jerked her offtrack.

"D-do you really think my p-pictures are good enough to sell?"

The return of his stammer told Crysta just how important to him her reply was. Recalling Sam's disapproval of this subject, she hesitated, but she couldn't bring herself to lie. "I not only think they would sell, but for premium prices. I believe you could become famous if you showed your work."

Beaming with pleasure, Tip shot up off the bench. "I'm going to go paint."

Crysta gazed after him, momentarily distracted from her worries about her brother. Tip clearly wanted to display his paintings, yet Sam wouldn't allow it. Crysta couldn't imagine why. Surely Sam could see that his son wanted and needed to excel in something, that he yearned to be accepted by others as an equal. It was cruel to keep him secluded here, exposed only to the guests. In addition, many people who patronized an establishment seemed to feel it acceptable to snipe at those who worked there. As a designer and dress shop owner, Crysta had been on the receiving end of such behavior. Someone like Tip couldn't understand that the jabs made at him weren't personal.

With a weary sigh, Crysta eyed a nearby window. As much as she might like to champion Tip and to make Sam understand his son's needs, she didn't have time right now to play family counselor. Pushing to her feet, she sidled over to the glass and peered out at the river to see if Sam had tried sneaking off again. Sunlight glanced under the eaves, making her squint. It should be dark outside at this predawn hour, yet it wasn't. Was Derrick out there somewhere, gazing at that same river? Hurt, possibly, and growing weaker? The thought made Crysta ache, and the need to be doing something hit her with such force that she stiffened.

She saw Sam Barrister in one of the boats out on the river, helping a guest wield a large fishing net. As she watched him work, it occurred to her that as long as he was thus occupied, she had a perfect opportunity to snoop.

A tingle crept up the nape of her neck as she turned from the window to contemplate the closed office door. Was it locked? Her heart picked up speed. Invading someone else's privacy wasn't something she felt comfortable doing, and yet, how could she not? She wouldn't rest until she examined the familiar-looking sienna briefcase she had seen on Sam's desk. Was it Derrick's, as she suspected, or a look-alike?

The few feet to the office seemed like a mile as she moved across the rustic planked floor. Checking over her shoulder, Crysta made sure no one was watching before she tried the doorknob. It turned easily. Afraid of being discovered, she pushed quickly into the room and eased the door closed behind her, leaning her back against the wood. Her heartbeat resounded in her ears while she stood there, half expecting someone to burst in after her.

To her dismay, she felt no lock button when she glided her fingers over the cool surface of the doorknob. Someone might walk in and catch her there. She sped to the desk. The more quickly she checked the briefcase and got out of there, the better. A good plan, except for one thing: she felt like a common thief. When she reached to open the drawer, her hand hovered over the handle, fingers trembling.

Her love for Derrick strengthened her resolve. This was no time to be a faintheart. Taking a deep breath, she jerked the drawer open. Disappointment coursed through her when all she saw was a thick, leather-bound book, the same shade of brown as Derrick's briefcase. Was this what she had seen on Sam's desk?

No, she distinctly recalled Sam shoving papers back into a folder, closing the briefcase and pressing the latches. She had been tired, yes, but not so exhausted that she had started imagining things.

Was this a plant, then? Had Sam hoped she would come here, see the brown book and believe her eyes had tricked her? The thought unsettled her. If such was the case, she was dealing with a very crafty fellow. Removing the book from the drawer, Crysta flipped it open.

The heavy pages parted about a third of the way through. Crysta stared at a lock of dark hair affixed to the paper with clear tape. To the right of the hair was a notation, written in bold, masculine longhand, *Eighteen months*. On another page was a tiny tooth, stained a peculiar lavender shade, with the footnote, *Tip's first tooth, lost at six years when learning to blow bubbles with grape bubble gum.*

Feeling an irresistible need to learn all she could about Sam Barrister, Crysta leafed through several more pages. Snapshots of Tip. Crayoned artwork done by a child's clumsy hand. An arrowhead. Dried flowers. All annotated in that manly script. Crysta's mouth inched into a reluctant smile. A scrapbook, filled with a father's treasured memories.

She could almost see Tip, as a much younger child, eyes bright with excitement, scurrying into the lodge with surprises for his dad. It said a great deal in Sam's behalf that he had not only saved everything but had so painstakingly recorded the memories. One of Tip's crayon drawings depicted a stick-figure man holding a child on his lap, a storybook opened on his knee. Knowing Tip's penchant for detail, Crysta guessed Sam must have read to his son frequently. Was a man without feeling capable of loving so deeply? Crysta didn't think so.

Shoving the scrapbook back into the drawer, she checked all the other desk compartments, then went to the cupboards along one wall. Door after door revealed nothing but lodge-related paper work—daily sheets, receipts and past years' tax documents. Dust burned in her nostrils as she shifted stack after stack of papers.

Then Crysta opened a middle cupboard. The edge of a brown briefcase peeked out at her from beneath a pile of yellowed folders. She recognized the case by the deep, Z-shaped gouge at one corner, put there by Saksi, her mother's Pekingese, during one of his puppyhood teething frenzies. Derrick had teased Ellen for weeks about the damage.

With quivering hands, Crysta pulled the case off the shelf, all sense of guilt vanishing. Sam Barrister had lied to her. Not only had he lied, but he had tried to throw her off by planting a sentimental scrapbook in the drawer where he had known she would look first.

Was he a loving father, as he clearly hoped she would believe, or a killer?

Shaken by the implications of her discovery, Crysta carried the briefcase to Sam's desk, emboldened by her sense of outrage. Now if Sam caught her in here, he would have as much explaining to do as she did. As she popped open the brass latches and lifted the lid of her brother's briefcase, another thought ricocheted through her mind. Sam wouldn't have hidden this unless there was something inside he didn't want her to see. But what?

Crysta spent the better part of a half hour trying to find an answer to that question. The documents in Derrick's file folders were simple and unmysterious, records of Blanchette business transactions, inspections sheets, purchase orders, job assignments, return credits, jotted notes. Nothing Sam Barrister should have been afraid for her to see.

So why had he hidden the briefcase? Maybe there had been something in one of the folders, something incriminating, and before Sam could remove it, she had burst unexpectedly into his office. Put on the spot, he had been forced to say he hadn't seen the briefcase, and once he had lied, he had no alternative but to keep the case hidden, even after the incriminating evidence had been removed.

The slamming of a door outside the office brought Crysta's head up. Heavy footsteps crossed the dining hall. Heart pounding, she closed the briefcase and returned it to the cupboard where Sam had hidden it, expecting him to walk in on her at any moment. All her bravado evaporated.

If Sam was involved in her brother's disappearance—and it certainly looked as if he might be—it wasn't likely that raised eyebrows would stop him from getting rid of her if he thought she was on to him.

When the footsteps faded away, she felt limp with relief.

Since she hadn't been discovered, Crysta saw little point in abandoning stealth now. The less Sam knew of her activities, the more chance she would have to watch him. She crept to the door, tensing at the smallest noise. After a final glance at the room to be certain she hadn't left anything out of place, she slipped out of the office and wandered over to the sitting area, pretending interest in one of the magazines.

Her skin prickled. The picture on the front cover of the magazine was of a beheaded walrus. Crysta had never seen anything so gory. An inset in the upper righthand corner of the cover showed a lonely stretch of Alaska beach littered with similarly mutilated corpses. The headline read: Walrus Killings Continue. Repulsed, she let the magazine drop from her fingers back onto the table.

Had anyone seen her sneak from Sam's office? She didn't want to appear suspicious by glancing over her shoulder, so she brazened it out, half expecting a heavy hand to clamp over her shoulder.

When no one confronted her, Crysta allowed herself to relax a little. Then it occurred to her that Sam might wonder what she'd been up to during his absence. After their run-in downriver, he'd never believe she'd been lounging around reading, no matter how convincing her act.

She should look busy, but doing what? The clatter of pans from the kitchen reminded her that she had promised to help out in any way she could. There was nothing like killing two birds with one stone, and she had a feeling that Jangles, the cook, would be a font of information, if only she could be persuaded to talk.

Striding toward the rear of the lodge, Crysta pushed open the swinging door to the huge, antiquated kitchen. Jangles spared her only a glance before returning her attention to the batter she was stirring inside a gigantic metal mixing bowl.

"I was hoping you might let me help," Crysta offered in her friendliest voice. "I promised Sam I'd carry my own weight while I was here. Could you use a hand? I understand you've been overworked since the searchers arrived."

"I've survived worse," the Tlingit woman replied. "And I only have one more meal to get through before they all fly out."

"Still, the work load has been heavier than usual, and you must be running behind. Maybe I can help you catch up. I'm pretty good in a kitchen." In actuality, Crysta's forte was designing fashions for the problem figure, not preparing the calories that created it. Playing it safe, just in case she might be asked to cook something unfamiliar, Crysta added, "I can fetch and carry, wash dishes, scrub floors. Just name it."

Jangles's dark eyes gleamed with unspoken challenge. "You can clean those fish behind you."

Heart sinking, Crysta rolled up her sleeves and approached the double utility basins along one wall. One tub was chock-full of salmon, all of them staring at her with round little eyes that made her skin crawl. The fish she had encountered up to now had already been beheaded, cleaned and arranged attractively on beds of ice at the neighborhood market.

"I thought the guys cleaned their own fish down at the river," she ventured weakly.

"Some do, others don't. My pay is the same no matter what the work, so I do not complain."

Planting her hands on her hips, Crysta stared into the tub and wondered how one went about cleaning a salmon. It wasn't something the average Los Angeles woman learned. Behind her, Jangles bustled about the kitchen, opening oven doors and banging pans. Ellen Meyers's voice piped into Crysta's mind. *"Use that head of yours for something besides a hat rack, Crysta."* Cleaning a fish couldn't be that difficult. Nauseating, perhaps, but not difficult.

Picking up the knife that rested on the edge of the sink, Crysta advanced on a dead fish, her gorge rising as she began the nasty task. If it hadn't been for her brother's plight, she might have begged off. But getting on Jangles's good side was crucial.

One fish later, Crysta was mentally calculating ways Derrick could make this up to her. Dinner at Navaho's, one of the glitziest restaurants in her neighborhood, would be nice. By the time she finished the second fish, she was thinking more along the lines of a Caribbean cruise, all expenses paid. It was a cheering thought, imagining Derrick, alive and well, trying to make good to her on a debt. And he would definitely owe her when this was over.

"When you get finished, it would be nice if there was some meat left to eat," Jangles said matter-of-factly.

The sound of the other woman's voice so close to her elbow made Crysta jump. She turned and raised an eyebrow. "Can you give me some pointers?"

Jangles's mouth quirked, but she didn't smile. Taking the knife from Crysta's hand, she picked up another fish and, with a few deft strokes of the blade, gutted and scaled it. "It is simple," she said as she tossed the cleaned salmon into the other sink. "When you finish, rinse them all, and then we will fillet them and cut up the steaks."

Crysta eyed the next fish, none too eager to resume her chore, but determined. She read Jangles as being a woman who had little use for wimps. Not that Crysta did, either. It was just that in her environment, it wasn't considered wimpy to do one's fishing over a meat counter.

A soft knock at the outside door brought Crysta's head up. It would be just her luck that the caller was a guest bringing more fish. Sighing, she returned to her task. Jangles threw a wary glance over her shoulder as she went to answer the knock. Then, the instant she cracked the door, the Indian woman stiffened.

"What is it?" she asked in a sharp voice. "I told you not to come here."

A masculine voice replied in a language Crysta couldn't understand. Jangles abandoned her use of English and responded in kind. Then, after throwing a worried look at Crysta, she opened the door wide enough to slip outside.

Crysta rose on her toes and angled her body across the utility sink, trying to see out the window. She glimpsed Jangles and a stoutly built Indian man hurrying away from the lodge. Before Crysta could get a clear look at the man's face, the two entered the trees. There, beyond earshot, they stopped. It looked to Crysta as though they were arguing. Heatedly. Jangles kept casting glances over her shoulder, as if she feared she might be seen.

Perplexed, Crysta rinsed her hands and turned to regard the various pots Jangles had left unattended on the stove. She turned down the flame under a huge skillet of frying potatoes, then gave them a cursory stir with the oversize spatula. What could the man have said that was so important that Jangles had dropped everything to talk to him?

Crysta wandered back to the sink and looked out the window to see Jangles scurrying back to the lodge. When the Tlingit woman reentered the kitchen, she looked breathless and agitated. Crysta busied herself cleaning another fish.

"I turned down the flame under the potatoes."

"Ah. Thank you."

Crysta hoped Jangles might explain who the man was, but she didn't. "A friend of yours?"

The Indian woman threw Crysta a stony look and didn't answer. Crysta wondered if perhaps the man was Jangles's lover. Maybe Sam had rules against his employees socializing during the work week, and the woman feared that Crysta would tell on her. It was difficult to imagine the plump little Indian woman caught up in a torrid affair, but what other explanation was there? If the man had come to the lodge for a legitimate reason, Jangles wouldn't have reacted the way she had.

Crysta grabbed another salmon and went to work on it, trying not to think about the cold, scaly skin against her palm. In between fish, she threw longing glances out the window at the dense cottonwoods, wishing she had the know-how to strike off on her own to search for her brother. If only Derrick had become lost in intercity Los Angeles, where she maneuvered like a pro, then she wouldn't be wasting precious time, elbow-deep in raw salmon.

It was little comfort knowing that she had come in here not to waste time but to pry information from Jangles. Though Crysta made several attempts at conversation, the Indian woman remained distant. When the fish were all cleaned, Crysta stood beside the Tlingit at a large work center in the middle of the room, watching to see how she filleted the pink meat. When Crysta felt she had the technique down pat, she began filleting herself.

After several minutes had passed with no conversation, Crysta could bear the silence no longer. "Have I done something to make you dislike me?"

Jangles continued slicing salmon steaks without pause. "I like you fine. I think you should leave, that is all. Derrick would want you to."

Crysta considered her next words carefully. "Why do you feel I should leave, that my brother wouldn't want me here?"

Jangles at last stopped working to pin Crysta with her black gaze. "Because you are in danger here."

"Other people are here. Are you telling them to leave?"

"They are different," the woman rasped. "You are walking in shadows, courting death."

"That's nonsense."

"Is it? I speak seldom. My silence makes many forget that I have ears. Leave, Crysta Meyers, before it is too late. You cannot help your brother now."

"What have you heard?" Crysta pressed. "Oh, please, Jangles, tell me. My brother isn't dead. I know he isn't. I need your help."

"And I am giving it. *Leave.*"

"You believe someone harmed my brother, don't you? You don't think it was a bear that got him. Have you told anyone? Mr. Barrister, the search coordinator, anyone? You must, Jangles, you *must.* They're abandoning the search for him. He could be alive out there!"

"I know nothing," the woman said. "Bits and pieces that make no sense. There is nothing I can do, nothing you can do. You take great risks staying here, asking questions and following Sam. Desperate people can be dangerous. Leave before it is too late.''

Desperate people? ''Convince me.'' Crysta met the woman's gaze. ''Stop talking about birds and shadows. Tell me something concrete.''

Jangles averted her face. No matter how Crysta tried to prompt her, she refused to say anything more. They finished filleting the salmon in taut silence, Crysta so frustrated she wanted to cry. Jangles's vague references to having overheard something suspicious was the closest thing to a clue Crysta had unearthed. How could she give up and leave the kitchen when she knew Jangles had information that might save her brother's life?

Chapter Seven

In the end, Crysta felt she had no choice but to stay to help Jangles prepare breakfast. *"Desperate people can be dangerous."* The woman's words replayed ceaselessly in Crysta's mind. She tried not to reveal her disappointment when the Tlingit woman refused to say any more about Derrick's disappearance.

When the meal was cooked, Crysta remained true to her word about making herself useful and busied herself carrying food to the dining room, arms aching from the heavily laden serving trays as she maneuvered her way through the doorway and down the aisles between tables. Hotcakes, salmon and beef steaks, cottage fries, eggs, toast, biscuits, sweet rolls. Cholesterol heaven. She couldn't believe the variety or the amounts of food Jangles had provided.

Guests and soon-to-be-departing searchers trailed in to eat as the items were placed in the warming pans along one wall and on the tables. Crysta tried not to get angry about the aborted search for her brother. Her mother having often reminded her that one could attract more flies with honey than vinegar, Crysta forced herself to smile at each man who offered her his condolences.

The rich food smells made her feel a little nauseated, probably a result of not having eaten in so long. Now that she came to think of it, she couldn't recall her last meal.

When she had finished helping Jangles, Crysta filled herself a plate and sat at an unoccupied table, determined to eat at least a few bites. As she chewed a piece of steak, she felt someone staring at her. Glancing up, she met the gaze of a lanky, brown-haired man with worried blue eyes. She recognized him as the same young man she had seen in the woods earlier when she was conversing with the search co-ordinator.

The intent, anxious way he watched Crysta unnerved her. The meat in her mouth turned to sawdust. With an effort, she managed to swallow. Averting her gaze, she studied the remaining food on her plate, her determination to eat vanishing.

"You have to get something under your belt," a deep voice chided her. "You can't run on willpower and caffeine for long. Trust me, I know."

The sound of Sam's voice made Crysta leap. As he sat down across from her with his plate piled high, she prayed he wouldn't read the guilt on her face. Had he gone to his office yet? Would anything out of place clue him to her visit there? "It's hard to eat when I feel I should be doing something." She met his gaze. "Time is slipping by, and so far, I've accomplished nothing."

"You've only been here—" He glanced at his watch. "It's only been about twelve hours, tops."

"It seems like days." One table down, a fisherman hooted with laughter. Distracted by the sounds of merriment, Crysta glanced in that direction, then back at Sam. "It's my brother out there. I keep telling you that, but it doesn't seem to sink in."

After a lengthy pause, he replied, "Oh, it sank in, believe me. It's just that there's nothing you can do. I tried to tell you that over the phone before you wasted air fare coming here."

Visions of Derrick swept through Crysta's mind, and she felt angry tears welling in her eyes. "I disagree. I think there's plenty I can do, and I intend to."

Crysta knew that was an overstatement. She had failed to convince Jim Sales to continue the official search. There were no guides available. At the moment, her only option seemed to be searching for Derrick on her own. She knew that doing so would be dangerous and that only a fool would try it. She was no fool. But she was desperate. Desperate enough to risk her life if she had to.

"Why don't you start by trusting me?"

Trust him? If Crysta hadn't been so upset, she might have hooted with laughter herself. She had to hand it to him; the husky concern in his voice sounded so real, he deserved an Oscar. She wished he truly did care. Never had she needed a friend more.

The scalding tears in her eyes spilled over onto her cheeks. She made an angry swipe at them, outraged with herself for losing control again in front of him. He wasn't what he seemed. The proof of that lay hidden in a cupboard in his office. For an instant, she considered telling him that Jangles might know something, just to see his reaction, but caution ruled that out. She mustn't betray Jangles to anyone—least of all to him.

"You expect me to trust you?" she countered. "Why won't you trust *me?* You could start by answering my questions. No one here will so much as point me in the right direction so I can look for Derrick."

The dark depths of his eyes eddied, the swirl of emotion revealed there too fleeting to identify. His jaw tightened. "I don't think you're equipped to look for him on your own. Do you?"

Crysta knew she wasn't, but she couldn't bring herself to admit it to him. It struck her as ironic that a brief pontoon flight had plucked her out of a world in which she felt capable of handling almost anything and had deposited her in a place so foreign to her that she was rendered all but helpless.

"You're very frightened for your brother," Sam went on in a soothing, reasonable tone. "Fright can lead anyone to make unwise decisions."

"If so, then the consequences of those decisions would be my own fault."

"And mine for allowing you to make them. You're in unfamiliar country and under a great deal of stress. You're also exhausted. You can't be thinking clearly right now."

"Do you always take responsibility for other adults?"

The corner of his mouth lifted in a halfhearted smile. "Only when the circumstances dictate. Besides, you're not just anyone—you're my best friend's sister."

"Yes, and your best friend is lost out there, possibly dying. How will you live with it if you don't do something to save him?"

He studied her for a long moment. "Don't judge me on appearances, Crysta. Derrick trusted me. Why won't you?"

"Because you—" Crysta bit back the words. She had nearly mentioned the briefcase. An ache of exhaustion spread across her shoulders.

He sighed and shoved his plate to one side. "Crysta, why don't you fly back to Anchorage with the volunteers? Why torture yourself like this? Let me handle the search for Derrick."

"What search?" she cried, a little more loudly than she intended. The dining room went suddenly quiet, but she was beyond caring who might hear her. "Show me one person who's been out there looking for him today!"

"What if I were to promise I'd go on looking? Would you consider leaving then?"

Once again thinking of the briefcase, Crysta could scarcely credit how worried about her he looked. His duplicity made her long to reach across the table and slap him. A dozen accusations crawled up her throat. She voiced none of them. "If you're going to search for Derrick, there's not a single good reason I can't accompany you."

"No, there are more like a dozen—the first, a killer bear. I'll have my hands full just keeping my own hide safe."

Passing a hand over her eyes, Crysta glanced down the table. The man with the worried blue eyes was still staring at her. "Who *is* that man? He keeps staring at me."

Sam followed her gaze. "Steve Henderson. He's probably not staring so much as spacing out. He's the fellow with the sick son."

Crysta's heart caught. No wonder there was such a worried expression in his eyes. She felt a sense of kinship with him.

"I'm surprised he's not at home, spending every spare moment with his son," she whispered.

"He says the doctor advises that family members continue with their regular activities. If not, the kid will sense how desperately ill he is and may not respond as well to treatment. He doesn't enjoy himself here, as you can see. Half the time, he just sits, gazing at nothing. When I try to imagine how he must feel..." The muscles in Sam's face tightened. "Sometimes I feel guilty because I'm so glad it isn't Tip."

Crysta curled her hands around her coffee mug, wishing she could do something to help Steve Henderson, knowing she couldn't. Just as no one seemed able to help her. "Is there any hope?"

"Maybe a bone marrow transplant. They're waiting for a match, and then he'll be flown down to Seattle for the procedure. If they can afford the initial fees, that is."

"Won't it be horribly expensive?"

"More than a hoister driver like Steve can afford. His insurance had a ceiling amount per illness, and that's been exhausted. From what Riley O'Keefe tells me, Steve's in debt already." Sam poked at a clump of scrambled eggs with his fork, looking none too hungry. "We took a collection last month for a television and VCR for Scotty's bedroom, so he can watch movies when he's too ill to leave his bed. But that's only a scratch on the surface. He wants a Nintendo. He wants to visit Disneyland. They'd like to buy him some tutoring videos so he won't fall behind in school. The costs are endless."

Pictures of Steve Henderson and his wife hovering at their dying child's bedside filled Crysta's mind. The pain they must feel. A knot lodged in her throat. She didn't even know Steve Henderson and his little boy, Scotty. It was insane to feel so perilously close to weeping.

"Crysta..." Sam's voice trailed off, and he reached to grasp her wrist, his fingers curling around her flesh like heated bands of steel. "You're exhausted. Why don't you lie down for a while. My bed has fresh linen on it. If I get a chance to rest, I can bunk in Tip's room."

Gazing at his handsome face, Crysta decided he was the epitome of the romantic hero: tall, dark, powerfully built, and irresistibly attractive—the proverbial bridge over troubled water, the sort a woman could fancy herself leaning on. But what lurked beneath the facade Sam Barrister presented to the world? Was he as mysterious on the inside as he was on the outside? It occurred to her that if she accepted his offer, she might be using the bed of her brother's murderer. The thought made her skin crawl.

"I couldn't take time for sleep." Crysta blinked and straightened. "After I help Jangles clean up, I want to study one of those forestry maps again."

"Why? So you can go out and get lost? Do you think Derrick would want that?"

Crysta wanted to say that Derrick had called to her, pleading for help, but that wasn't within Sam's scope of reality. Her dreams were her curse, never to be shared with anyone, unless she wanted her sanity questioned. "I'm going out to look for him. I don't suppose you have any spare pairs of rubber boots?"

He gestured toward a wall cupboard with his chin. "They're mostly men's sizes. I don't know if any of them will fit you."

Crysta made a mental note to check the boots later. "Before I go, I need to study the area, so I have my bearings." She turned her mug within the circle of her palms, forcing Sam to release his grip on her wrist. Recalling her last dream and the ramshackle structure she had seen in it, Crysta licked her lips and let her gaze trail past Sam's shoulder. "Are there any cabins downstream from here?"

"No. Why?" His voice sharpened, compelling her to look at him.

"In case I need shelter," she lied. "There must be a cabin out there someplace."

"Abandoned cabins pepper the interior, but there are none nearby along the river. At least if there is, I haven't come across it. We aren't exactly in a metropolis out here." He raised one dark eyebrow. Clean-shaven, his strong jaw line complemented his striking features even more than before, perfectly offsetting his prominent nose and angular bone structure.

There was something about Sam Barrister, possibly the sheer size of him, that undermined her usual self-assurance. Under other circumstances, she would have deferred to his judgment. He knew this country; everything about him testified to that. It would be foolish to disregard his warnings. Yet she had no choice.

"Is there anything I can say to dissuade you?" he asked softly.

Instead of answering his question, she replied, "I'll take every precaution."

"If you lose your bearings, can you read a compass?"

"I'm not expert at it, but it can't be that hard. Besides, there's always the sun to guide me."

He laid his fork down on the edge of his plate. "You're forgetting we don't get the same sunrises and sunsets here that you're accustomed to seeing."

"I'll figure it out."

"You'll get lost, that's what you'll do."

"That's my risk to take."

"And my livelihood you're gambling with."

"I said I would sign a disclaimer."

He leaned forward, his eyes glittering. "I'll have it engraved on your headstone, shall I? Do me one favor. At least get some rest before you go out there. Otherwise, you'll collapse five miles from the lodge."

With that as a parting shot, he left the table, looking far angrier than Crysta felt he had any right to be. What did he care if she got herself killed? She didn't buy that his primary concern was his reputation. It was a free country; he couldn't be held responsible for every ding-a-ling city slicker who ignored his advice and insisted on taking risks.

It wasn't until after he was gone that Crysta realized he hadn't touched his meal. She eyed her own with mounting distaste. Only her realization that she needed nourishment prompted her to once again pick up her fork.

AFTER CRYSTA HELPED Jangles clean up the kitchen, she checked the boot cupboard to see if any of the spare rubber boots came close to her size. All where far too wide and would rub blisters. Disappointed, she abandoned the closet and followed her earlier plan of action, retrieving the map she had been studying from its rack on the check-in stand. Spreading it open on the table, she traced a finger along the spidery network of lines, trying to make sense of them. When she noticed the mileage scale in the bottom right corner, her heart sank. An inch represented fifty miles? Crysta sat back, taking in the map with renewed dread. She hadn't realized until now just how large an area she was trying to familiarize herself with.

Panic fluttered in her stomach. Sam was right; she had no business attempting a search on her own. She hadn't the vaguest idea how to find her way around out there. To her, one tree looked exactly like another.

A picture of a wind-twisted spruce flashed in Crysta's mind, rekindling her determination. The tree of her dream had been growing along the bank of a waterway. She need only find it to know she was hunting for Derrick in the right area. The problem was that there were probably numerous rivers in this region, not to mention hundreds if not thousands of small sloughs. Which waterway had Derrick been following?

So weary that she ached, Crysta slumped over the map, staring blindly. As she contemplated the enormity of the task she was undertaking, a frisson of fright coursed through her. She'd be risking her life out there, and if she got lost, as Sam predicted, her death might not be swift. Regardless, she had to search for her brother. If she didn't, she'd spend the remainder of her life hating herself.

Black spots danced before Crysta's eyes. With a defeated sigh, she passed a hand over her forehead. Sam was right on another count: she had to grab a little sleep. If she didn't, she'd be dead on her feet before she had walked a mile. Her sleeve cuff brushed against her nose, and the strong smell of salmon hit her. Grimacing, Crysta drew back and glared at the stained denim. She needed another bath, thanks to Jangles's tub of fish.

Wrinkling her nose, Crysta pushed to her feet and refolded the map, tucking it under her arm. There wasn't time for another bath, not until she found her brother. After a couple of hours' sleep, absolutely no more than that, she had a search to begin. God willing, it would lead her to Derrick.

SAM BARRISTER'S BEDROOM was a reflection of the man himself, the colors earthy and quiet. Remembering her ex-husband's penchant for chrome and glass, Crysta decided she much preferred Sam's plain and simple approach. This was a place where one could stretch out and not worry about leaving fingerprints.

His furniture was large and sturdy, the finish, like its owner, handsomely weathered and marred. The rumpled quilt on his bed, a wedding ring pattern, was handstitched yet somehow masculine, the clean cases on his king-size pillows as crisp and white as Alaskan snow. The leather boots sitting neatly by the bedstead were stained mud-brown. Above the headboard hung a painting of the northern lights captured so beautifully in oils that Crysta stood mesmerized for a moment. Was it any wonder Sam loved Alaska?

Crysta pictured him living a hundred years ago, a big, rugged man carving out an existence in the wilderness, his gaze always fixed on the horizon. Perhaps that was why he lived in Alaska, where the wave of civilization had not yet struck.

She picked up the book on his nightstand. Scanning the title and blurb, she ascertained that it was about wolves and the human threat to their survival, the sort of material she might have found in Derrick's library. Clearly, Sam and her brother had a great deal in common.

Everything led back to Derrick.

Sighing, Crysta returned the book to its resting place, feeling lost and frightened. She knew why. There were no whispers inside her head. Was Derrick still alive? If so, why

the ominous silence? Maybe he was deep in a dreamless
sleep. Or unconscious. Please, God, let him be alive.

As she turned from the bed, Crysta realized this was the
perfect opportunity to search Sam's room. Not that he
would have offered to let her sleep here if he had hidden
anything from Derrick's briefcase in the drawers. Still...

Methodically and thoroughly, she searched everywhere,
even going so far as to run her arm under the mattress. She
found nothing. Heavy of heart, she drew the blackout
shade, plunging the room into darkness. *Hold on, Derrick.
I'm coming. I won't let you down.* As she peeled off her
clothes, Crysta thought of Sam in this room, tugging his
shirt off over his head, sitting on the bed to doff his boots.
The picture made her feel self-conscious, as if he were here
with her, watching. The masculine scent in the room, his
scent, added to that illusion, a pleasant blend of flannel and
denim, fresh air and after-shave, laced with faint traces of
musk. Cool air washed over her skin, making her shiver.

She hoped Sam remembered offering her the use of his
room and didn't barge in on her. Drawing on her flannel
nightgown, she wriggled her toes against the braided rug and
stretched her aching arms. A wind-up clock on the headboard drew her attention, its loud ticking reminding her of
just how quickly each second passed. Time had become her
enemy. And Derrick's. With numb fingers, she set the alarm
so she wouldn't oversleep.

Flipping back the corner of the quilt, Crysta slid into bed,
pleased to feel that the crisp linen was stretched tight. From
the rumpled condition of the quilt, she had half expected
wrinkled sheets, one of her pet peeves. Punching the pillow, she arranged it just so under her head and angled a
forearm across her forehead, so exhausted that she felt
wired. Determined, she closed her eyes.

The sickening stench of dead fish crawled up her nostrils. Crysta frowned and drew her forearm away from her
face, wondering how the smell could possibly still be clinging to her. She had washed her hands and wrists thoroughly, and now her soiled shirt lay in a heap by her
suitcase.

Rolling onto her side, Crysta drew up her knees, snuggling her cheek against the pillow, bent on ignoring the odor. She had more important things to worry about than personal hygiene. Warmth stole over her, and her muscles slowly relaxed. The hypnotic ticking of the clock began to soothe her. She closed her eyes, twisting her hips slightly so one leg was angled forward.

Something cold pressed against her knee—something cold and wet. Crysta stopped breathing and lay motionless, her skin prickling. There was something in the bed. For an instant, the years rolled away and she felt like a child again, afraid of the dark and tormented by Derrick's stories of bloody hands reaching under the covers to grab her.

It took all Crysta's strength of will to extend her hand toward the wet lump. Her fingertips encountered something cold and slightly rough. She slithered away, pushing up on her elbow. Throwing back the quilt, she stared through the shadowy gloom at a long, dark shape against the white backdrop of sheet. What on earth?

Reaching behind her, Crysta grasped the shade and gave it a jerk, sending it into a rattling ascent on its roller. Sunlight spilled into the room.

"Oh, my God!"

Crysta sprang from the bed, eyes agape, frantically rubbing her hand clean on her nightgown. A huge king salmon lay in the center of the mattress, its gill gaffed with a wicked-looking hook, its guts spilling forth from the jagged rip in its underbelly. Crysta glanced down to see that her gown was smeared with gore. She recoiled a step, stomach heaving.

"Oh, my God . . ."

SAM'S OFFICE DOOR flew open with such force that the doorknob cracked against the wall. He glanced up, amazed to see Crysta standing in the doorway, a white bundle clutched in her arms, her slender, jeans-clad legs spread wide as if she were trying to keep her balance on rocky seas, her auburn hair in a glorious tangle around her fury-whitened face, her hazel eyes afire. For a moment, he was so taken aback that he forgot he had Derrick's briefcase out on his desk, in plain view.

"I want to talk to you, Mr. Barrister!"

It was more a hiss than a request. And then she advanced on him like a general coming to do battle. There was no time to gather Derrick's papers. Sam snatched the briefcase off his desk and shoved it into a drawer, uncertain what had set her off but hoping, all the same, that she was so mad she hadn't noticed her brother's briefcase.

As insurance, Sam decided diversionary tactics were called for and opted for counterattack. "Good, I've been wanting to talk to you, too. Now's as good a time as any. I was speaking to Tip a little while ago. You've been filling his head with nonsense about his paintings making a big splash in the art world." Sam shuffled papers, trying to hide those belonging to Derrick beneath some of his own. Then he shoved back in his chair, striving to look irritated rather than unsettled. "I want nothing more said to him on the subject. Is that clear?"

Crysta swept around his desk. Anger became her, heightening her color, adding a sparkle to her already beautiful eyes. With a cry of indignation, she tossed the white bundle at him, keeping one of her fists knotted in the linen. The sheet unrolled, and something heavy plopped into Sam's lap. When he saw what it was, he nearly shot from his chair. As accustomed as he was to salmon, he'd never had one dumped in his lap, gaff, guts and all.

"What in the hell?"

"I took you up on your offer to use your bed. Somehow, I found the other occupant offensive, to say the least!"

Sam looked up to find a slender finger wagging before his nose. No one could ever say Crysta Meyers was easily intimidated. She leaned toward him, and Sam had no doubt she was angry enough to punch him if he chose to stand up.

"Your son and his wasted talent is your business. I won't say another word about his paintings. By the same token—" her finger drew closer "—my brother is *my* business, and your sick little prank won't change that."

"This was in my bed?" Sam inched his head back as her finger advanced . "Crysta, I didn't—"

"Get this straight, Mr. Barrister, once and for all. I'm not leaving here until my brother is found. It'll take more than bears and fish guts to scare me off. Is *that* clear?"

It was crystal clear. Sam hadn't been confronted like this in years, not by a man, let alone a woman he towered over. "I didn't put this in the bed, Crysta. How could you think—"

She grabbed a fistful of the papers on his desk and waved them before his face. "How could I think you'd do something so despicable? What are these, Mr. Barrister? Papers from my brother's briefcase, which, according to you, didn't exist! I was in here earlier and found them myself. I've listened to enough of your lies!"

Sam stared at the papers crumpled in her fingers. The game was up. Like it or not, he had to tell her everything. Her presence was making someone uncomfortable. The fish in her bed was proof of that. If he didn't level with her, she might blunder her way right into a deathtrap. "Please don't rumple those," he said quietly. "They may prove helpful in discovering what happened to Derrick."

"Really?" She slapped the documents down. "You mean to admit, at long last, that a bear didn't make him his main course for dinner? Congratulations, Sam! The truth for once. Please, don't stop while you're on a roll."

"We need to talk. But not here." Gingerly, Sam lifted the stinking salmon from his thighs and rewrapped it in the sheet. "Let's go to my apartment where we won't run the risk of being overheard."

Dumping the linen-wrapped fish into the waste basket, he glanced up just in time to see the wary expression that crossed her face. Now that her anger was flagging, she was clearly having second thoughts about coming here. For all she knew, he might be planning to get her off alone so he could shut her up—permanently.

That thought strengthened Sam's resolve to tell her everything. Crysta wasn't the sort to avoid confrontations. She was more the type to say what was on her mind, the devil take tomorrow. It was a quality Sam admired and tried to cultivate in himself. But if Crysta confronted the wrong person, her straightforwardness might land her in a situation she couldn't get out of.

She retreated a step when he met her gaze, looking none too thrilled at the prospect of accompanying him to a more private setting. He didn't suppose he blamed her for not trusting him. He was doing an awfully quick about-face and, from her viewpoint, without any reason.

"Crysta, the dining room is within yelling distance of my living quarters."

She took another step back, giving her head a toss to get the hair out of her eyes. "If I was able to yell."

Sam stood. Though she was tall for a woman, Crysta's head barely cleared his shoulder. And after their tussle in the woods, both of them knew he had the advantage physically. Sam decided to challenge her pride. "Running scared, Crysta? Maybe you're not as much like Derrick as I thought."

Her chin shot up, and her eyes flared. "Lead the way."

Sam did, painfully aware that she wasn't about to turn her back on him.

A LOG SHIFTED in the grate, sending up a spray of sparks. Crysta, who had settled herself onto the sofa and was waiting for Sam to speak, stared at the fireplace, hands clasped in her lap, spine rigid, trying, unsuccessfully, to appear relaxed. Sam sat in the recliner, arms braced on his knees, shoulders forward, feet planted wide, looking ready to jump up at any second. After their wrestling match in the woods that morning, she had no delusions. Sam was big, strong and fast. If he should leap at her, she didn't stand a chance of escaping him.

"I don't know where to start," he said.

The sudden sound of his voice in the brittle silence made Crysta jerk. He cast her a knowing glance.

"Why not start with the quarrel between you and Derrick?"

His mouth tightened. "That's peripheral to the entire situation."

"So you say."

His eyes narrowed. "If you must know, it was about Tip. Like you, your brother has an irritating habit of interfering, and I told him so. We had words. End of subject."

"Not the end of your friendship?"

"Our friendship was as strong as ever. It wasn't the first time we've gotten into it over Tip, and pray God it won't be the last. Friends can agree to disagree, Crysta."

Crysta took a moment to digest this new tidbit of information. "Am I right in assuming that the argument was over Tip's artistic talent? It's the only thing I've come anywhere close to interfering in."

"With a bang," he amplified, shooting her another look, this one bordering on a glare. "You have Tip all but ready to pack his bags and head for the big city."

"He asked me a question. I told him the truth. Should I have lied?"

"The truth as *you* see it. He's my son. I know better than anyone else what he's been through, and I know what's waiting for him out there. I've seen how people—" He broke off, his mouth twisting with disgust. Raking a hand through his hair, he sighed. "Like I said, my argument with your brother has nothing to do with Derrick or what happened to him, so let's drop it."

Crysta inclined her head, acquiescing. He was telling the truth about the quarrel. The fire in his eyes told her that. But if he was innocent, why had he hidden Derrick's briefcase? Why had he tried to sneak off downstream?

"I see your point," she said softly. "The argument about Tip was none of my business, and I can see why you felt it unnecessary to tell me about it. I'm sorry I kept pressing you."

He ran his fingertips along his jaw, making a faint rasping sound on the growth of beard that had cropped up since his last shave. "Yeah, well . . . I should have just told you what it was all about. I'm sorry I didn't, but the truth is, it isn't easy even to think about it. We, um . . ." He turned to stare out the window, his voice going suddenly husky. "I let him leave without telling him goodbye. I was ticked, he was ticked. If he is dead, it was a hell of a way to end a ten-year friendship."

Crysta returned her gaze to the fire, resisting the urge to comfort him. His pain was evident in his voice, but was it real? From the corner of her eye, she studied him, alert to his every move.

"Why did you lie about having Derrick's briefcase? Why did you try to discourage me from coming here?" Crysta fixed him with a relentless gaze. "Why did you try to slip away from me? I want to trust you, Sam, but you haven't given me a single reason to."

He smiled slightly. "No, I haven't, have I? Can we take that one question at a time, beginning with the second one? I didn't want you coming here because I was afraid it might be dangerous."

"Dangerous? As in bears?"

His eyes met hers. "I was more worried about two-legged killers, Crysta." Briefly, he told her about the night Derrick had visited the office. "He had come across something at Blanchette that looked fishy—his word, not mine."

"Something fishy." Intent, Crysta scooted forward to the edge of the cushion. "Did he say what? And how do you know it was something at Blanchette and not somewhere else?"

"He wouldn't elaborate. You know Derrick and his ethics. Until he had some solid evidence, he didn't want to make any accusations. As for it being in Blanchette, that's an assumption on my part. 'Something fishy going on up here in Alaska' was what he said. I took that to mean it was something he'd run across that wasn't occurring at the construction sites in the lower forty-eight. That's why I'm going through his briefcase, looking for clues. So far, I've found nothing."

The nape of Crysta's neck prickled. She couldn't help recalling her dream, the report of a gun echoing in her ears. "So you think Derrick came across something illegal within Blanchette and that the perpetrators tried to silence him?"

"Exactly."

"And earlier, when you sneaked off downstream. Why didn't you want me to know?"

"I didn't want you involved." He pinched the bridge of his nose between thumb and forefinger, sighing. "When you seemed so certain that Derrick wasn't dead, I got to wondering if maybe the searchers had missed something. I figured you'd never leave if you knew what I suspected, so I kept up the pretense about the bear."

"Is my knowing such a bad thing?"

"It will be if you start pressing the wrong people for answers. You could end up a bear statistic, like your brother."

"That goes for you, as well. I'm a big girl, Sam."

"And Derrick's sister. I wanted to put you on the first flight out, safely away from here. He would expect that of me."

Some of the tension eased out of Crysta's shoulders. She wasn't entirely convinced he was telling her the truth, but at least this story made a lot more sense than the bear attack theory.

"Flying me out to safety isn't in the cards, I'm afraid. Until Derrick's found, I'm here to stay."

His mouth twisted in a smile. "Well, if you're bent on staying, Derrick would want me to keep an eye on you."

Crysta rolled her eyes. "Let me set you straight, Sam. Derrick is the twin who usually needs caretaking."

"Humor me."

Pushing up from the sofa, she walked to the fire, hugging herself and rubbing her arms. "I want to be involved in everything. I won't be set on a shelf. If that's your idea of looking after me, it won't work."

"I was planning to go downstream while you were asleep."

"Then I'm going with you."

"It's a long walk. And you're already tired. You might slow me down. I don't think—"

"I'm not that tired," she insisted, though she was.

He stared past her at the fire for a moment. "All right. At least if you're with me, I'll know you're safe and not following me or searching on your own."

Crysta had expected more of an argument. She hesitated, studying him. If he was deceiving her, it would be much easier for him to harm her once they left the lodge.

Chapter Eight

As a precaution, Crysta made it a point to let Jangles, Riley O'Keefe and two other guests know that she was leaving the lodge to go for a walk with Sam. As they struck off along the river, Sam flashed her a knowing grin.

"Are you sure you wouldn't like to invite someone else to come along?" he asked. "There's safety in numbers."

Crysta felt heat rising up her neck, from embarrassment or anger, she couldn't be sure. On the one hand, if Sam was on the level, it was inexcusable to let him know she didn't trust him. Just the same, she preferred to play it safe, and if that offended him, there was very little she could do about it.

Her second trip downriver seemed far less strenuous than her first, due, she was sure, to the slower pace Sam set. The fact that he altered his stride to match hers was reassuring. Surely it wasn't second nature to a killer to be so considerate.

When they reached the slough, he searched for the narrowest place, leaped across, then turned to give her a hand. The distance she had to jump was intimidating. Even as tall as she was, she couldn't compete with a man of Sam's stature. She hesitated to take his hand, reluctant to give the impression she needed coddling. She had waded through the slough only hours ago, though, and knew how chilly the water was. It would be foolish to risk getting soaked again.

"Coming?" he asked.

The trace of impatience in his tone prompted her to take his hand. His warm grip was disconcertingly strong. She was in big trouble if he had brought her out here to get rid of her.

Gauging the distance, Crysta tightened her fingers around his and leaped. When she landed, right foot first, her running shoe slipped in the mud. Sam braced himself to catch her. When he did, he lost his footing, as well. Crysta thought they were both in for a mud bath, but at the last second Sam scrambled and found purchase on the slick bank, catching her around the waist with a steely arm.

Crysta's breath caught. With her back arched, her thighs were pressed intimately against his, and her breasts were flattened against the broad ladder of his rib cage. They both froze.

Sam's dark eyes fixed on hers. Unbidden, a frisson of electricity shot through her. Until this instant, she had been so suspicious of Sam and so worried about her brother that she had fought her attraction to him. Now all her reasons for doing so seemed to have disappeared. As Sam bent his dark head toward hers, Crysta remained perfectly still, wanting his kiss in a way she couldn't fully comprehend. For a fleeting moment, just as his warm, silken lips touched hers, she wondered what it was about him that so disarmed her. Then sheer sensation wiped rational thought from her mind.

His kiss began in the predictable way, a hesitant exploration, but in less than a heartbeat the shyness vanished, replaced by a raw, primal hunger that Crysta sensed in him and felt within herself. Forgetting all else, she let the strong circle of his arms pull her closer and allowed her body to mold itself against him.

As suddenly as it had begun, the kiss ended. With a dazed and unmistakably incredulous expression in his dark eyes, Sam gently set her away from him and proceeded along the riverbank as though nothing had happened. But Crysta sensed his discomfiture in the long strides he was suddenly taking. She guessed that he had been taken as off guard as she.

At any other time, the situation might have been amusing, given the fact that for years Derrick had tried fruit-

lessly to get Crysta and Sam together. This wasn't another
time, though, and Crysta had far too much on her mind to
deal with overactive hormones, hers or Sam's. Clearly, Sam
felt the same.

She lengthened her stride to catch up. Within minutes she
was panting with exertion, the sounds issuing from her
throat short and shallow. Sam cast her a surprised glance
and slowed his pace.

Relieved to have the tension between them eased, Crysta
fell in beside him again. But her nerve endings were sensi-
tized now to his nearness, and her gaze kept shifting sideways to rest on the coarse blue denim stretched tight over the
corded muscle of his legs.

She had no business thinking of Sam as anything but a
means to her end, which was finding Derrick. What was
wrong with her? She couldn't be certain Sam was even
trustworthy. She sneaked a look at his profile. Sunlight
glinted in his hair where it fell in tousled waves across his
forehead.

Crysta laid her feelings off on the desperateness of her
situation. Though she might manage to search for Derrick
on her own, the odds of her success were slim. Sam Barrister's assistance was her only hope. Her emotions were a
powder keg, and he was merely the spark to set them off.

The seconds became measured by the steady thud of their
feet on the earth, her sneakers tapping out a soft counter-
point to the heavy impact of Sam's boots. Crysta became
lost in the rhythm, her thoughts focused on Derrick as her
legs churned to keep up with the man beside her.

They had to cross two more sloughs, each wider than the
last, which gave Crysta her first glimpses of the tranquil
marshlands and meadows that lay beyond the camouflage
of trees along the river. She had no idea how much time
passed. A great deal, judging by the ache in her thighs. She
began to get the disconcerting feeling that she and Sam were
the first people ever to have come here. On occasion,
though, she spotted footprints that dispelled that notion,
probably left there by the men who had searched for Derrick.

How far had she and Sam walked? Five or six miles? The only sounds that drifted to her ears were those of the water, the rustling leaves, the wind. She could see why her brother loved it here.

"So what do you think?"

She glanced up. "About what?"

"About that fish in the bed. Who do you think put it there?"

Wondering why it had taken him miles of walking to address that issue, she replied, "My first inclination was to blame you."

He snorted. "Put a stinking fish in my own bed? Besides, give me credit for *some* brains. It would take more than a few fish guts to send a woman like you running."

It was an offhand compliment, but a compliment just the same. She didn't know why it mattered to her what he thought, but, strangely enough, it did. "Who do you think did it?"

"The dining room was full of people. Any number could have heard me offer you the use of my room. My question is, was it someone's sick idea of a joke, simply because you're an attractive single woman here alone, or was it an attempt to frighten you into leaving?"

"I lean toward the latter. When I thought you'd done it, my first assumption was that you were trying to scare me off. Let's face it, fish guts aren't very funny."

Sam stepped around a bush. "I agree. Now that that's settled, the question is who?"

"I haven't been here long enough to make enemies. Jangles, possibly. I don't think she cares for me."

Sam shook his head. "Jangles likes you fine. She's just bent on getting you out of harm's way."

Crysta tensed, then plunged ahead, praying she wasn't subjecting Jangles to danger. "She knows something. She won't say what, but she doesn't believe Derrick was eaten by a bear any more than I do."

"I sensed that, too."

"And you haven't questioned her?"

"I tried." He shot her a troubled frown. "Jangles is one of the last of a dying breed, clinging, in many ways, to the old customs, fiercely proud of her Tlingit heritage, even though she's the only one in this immediate area. She loves Alaska, its natives and its wildlife, with a passion. And she prizes the strength often found in silence. If she takes it into her head not to talk, for whatever reason, she won't. Trying to force her is—" He lifted one shoulder in a shrug. "One thing I know—she'd never put a gaffed fish in your bed. Sneaking around behind a person's back isn't her way."

Crysta remembered the animosity that had gleamed in the woman's dark eyes. "I realize she's a friend of yours, but—"

"That's not the only reason I'm so convinced it wasn't her. Don't forget, whatever else Jangles may be, she's Indian. Heritage is extremely important to her. Even today, many Tlingit homes feature lineage crests."

"Lineage crests?"

"Totem poles," he explained, a smile touching his mouth.

Crysta found herself recalling the touch of those firm, silken lips on hers, how mesmerizing they had seemed.

"Courage and honesty are very much a part of that heritage," he continued. "I'm not saying she's above doing something mean, but if she does, she'll do it right to your face. To sneak would be cowardly."

He seemed so convinced that Crysta decided to concede the point. "Do you realize she has a gentleman caller? A Tlingit?"

Sam gave her a sharp look. "A caller?"

"A boyfriend, I assume. He came to the kitchen door this morning. She seemed upset and told him he wasn't supposed to come to the lodge. Then she went out into the woods and appeared to be arguing with him."

Sam's forehead creased in a thoughtful frown. "You're sure he was Tlingit? Not to say there couldn't be others in the vicinity, but if there are, I've never met them."

"He spoke in another language, and Jangles replied in kind. If they weren't talking in Tlingit, then what?"

As if he was considering that, Sam gazed ahead of them for a moment. "It's possible she knows more than one of the native languages. Or maybe the guy *was* Tlingit."

"Have you any idea why she would want to keep his visit secret from you?"

"No." He turned worried eyes on her. "She knows her friends would be more than welcome at the lodge."

A tingle crept up Crysta's spine. She had gotten the impression that Jangles hadn't wanted anyone to see the man. If Sam had laid down no rules restricting employees from having callers at the lodge while they were on his time, why had she hustled the man off into the trees?

"Is it possible she's up to something she doesn't want you to know about?"

"If she is, I'm sure it's nothing for me to worry about. The bottom line is, I trust her. Completely."

Crysta could see from Sam's firm expression that pursuing the Jangles angle would be fruitless. She wasn't quite so trusting, however. She made a mental note to keep an eye on the Tlingit woman.

"So, if not Jangles, then who?"

"Someone staying at the lodge—that much is a given. If I'm right that Derrick was referring to Blanchette when he talked about finding something fishy, then we have to assume the culprit is someone who works for the company."

"Any suspicions?"

Sam hesitated. "I don't like accusing people without proof."

"Let's forget the innocent-until-proven-guilty thing and toss ideas around. We aren't going to do irreparable damage to anyone's reputation if it's just between you and me. That was Derrick's mistake, remember? If he had pointed the finger at someone, we'd have an idea now of who to go after. As it is, we're shooting in the dark."

Sam gave a fleeting smile. "We? You sound as if you might be starting to trust me."

She jumped over a marshy spot, then dragged the soles of her shoes clean on the grass. With more certainty than she felt, she said, "You think I'd be out here with you if I had any doubts?"

"Unfortunately for my peace of mind, yes. You take too many risks, Crysta, without weighing the consequences. Like following me today. Then searching my office. And then confronting me about the fish. Did you even once stop to think what might happen if I caught you or turned on you?"

"I considered it."

"Did you? Somehow I doubt it. Understand something, okay? This isn't Los Angeles. The cops can't drive up to your door within five minutes of your call. You're a female, and you're alone. The modern woman's mind-set could get you into big trouble up here."

"I've taken self-defense training. I can handle myself."

He braked to a sudden stop, squinting against the sun at her. The impact of his gaze brought her to a halt. Looking up at him, she found her training in self-defense small comfort.

"We're about seven miles from the lodge," he reminded her. "I outweigh you by at least a hundred pounds. You don't have a weapon of any kind as an equalizer. You can't outrun me. I'd say that could spell trouble—in capital letters. What's your solution? A karate chop to my neck? What if I brought you here to shut you up? Have you thought of that?"

Crysta had indeed thought of that. "I told several people I was taking a walk with you. It'd cast you in a pretty bad light if something happened to me out here," she retorted. "As for my self-defense training, my instructor taught me to aim much lower than the neck."

Her pulse leaped at the grim twist of Sam's mouth, but before she could react, he struck off walking again.

"And what if I did away with you and made it look like an accident? Don't trust anyone—that's all I'm asking. Not *anyone*, is that clear? You're right—we are shooting in the dark. My first instinct is to suspect Riley O'Keefe, but since I'm not positive Derrick was referring to something fishy at Blanchette, I can't act on that. Besides, Riley flew back into

Anchorage with Shriver shortly after breakfast, so it isn't likely he would have had time to sneak something into my bedroom."

He heaved a weary sigh and ran his hand over his hair. "I suppose Derrick could have come upon something here at Cottonwood Bend," he went on. "It's a possibility we can't ignore, anyway. There are two other lodges within five miles. Planes galore fly in 'round the clock. People and cargo of every conceivable kind come and go."

Crysta scrambled after him. When he entered a line of trees and stopped to wait for her, she slowed her pace. He settled a thoughtful gaze on her, his lips softening.

"I didn't mean to sound condescending a minute ago. It's just that—" He grasped her arm to help her over a fallen cottonwood. "You weren't sure of me when you agreed to come out here. You can't deny that. It was foolish to take such a chance. It scares the hell out of me to think you might do it again, next time with the wrong person."

Crysta opened her mouth to retort, but before she spoke, she remembered how vulnerable he had made her feel a minute ago. As much as it rankled, he had a point. It was lucky for her that he hadn't brought her out here to kill her. Against an ordinary mugger, her self-defense training and the element of surprise might stand her in good stead, but the odds were considerably poorer here, with no one to intervene if she cried for help.

"I realize Derrick's your only concern right now," he added patiently, "but as much as you hate to think it, he may be dead. If he is, sacrificing yourself won't help him."

"I'll do whatever I have to."

He tightened his hand on her arm. "Crysta, if he's alive, he can survive out here for an indefinite period of time."

"Not if he's hurt!"

"A small cut on the head can bleed a great deal. The blood the searchers found isn't necessarily an indication that Derrick was badly wounded. He's bear-smart. If an enraged grizzly was on his heels, he might have taken off his shirt and tossed it down as a distraction. Sometimes an animal will go after anything with its prey's scent on it. That could explain the shirt's being shredded by a bear's claws."

A picture from her second dream flashed in her mind—of the puncture wound over Derrick's heart. "You don't believe that. You don't even believe a bear was involved. You think it was a man." She gestured at his empty hands. "If you thought for one minute a killer bear was out here, you'd be carrying a gun."

He pinched the bridge of his nose and heaved a weary sigh. After a long moment, he dropped his hand. "I can't make sense of any of it," he said in a husky voice. "There's only one thing I'm certain of at this point. I don't want something to happen to you."

The sincerity in his expression made Crysta forget whatever it was she had intended to say. For an instant she experienced an almost overpowering need to feel his arms around her again, to pour out her frustrations and fears, to believe he could somehow make everything all right.

She knew it was a childish wish. But, like Sam, she was so weary of trying to make sense of it all that she could scarcely think straight. A respected tracker was convinced Derrick had been slain by a bear. Yet Derrick had said things that gave Sam reason to believe her brother had been the victim of foul play. Who was right? Had the men who harmed Derrick staged a bear attack to throw the searchers off track? Crysta didn't know. And if all that wasn't enough, she had her dreams to consider. Were they telepathic visions, sent to her by Derrick? Or was she losing her mind?

At the moment, Crysta was none too sure of her sanity. Nothing seemed clear to her except that she felt inexplicably drawn to Sam Barrister. Yet common sense warned her that she still couldn't be entirely certain she should trust him.

As if he sensed how close she was to tears, he took her arm and drew her into a walk beside him. They emerged from the dappled shade into bright sunlight. Crysta blinked, momentarily blinded. When her vision cleared, her footsteps dragged to a stop.

"What's wrong?" Sam whispered.

Crysta stared ahead. "This is the place where it happened."

Sam glanced around them. "It's a little farther, I think. I found Derrick's destroyed gear farther ahead."

"No," she said with certainty, her attention fixed on a wind-twisted spruce on the riverbank several feet ahead of them. "No, Sam, this is the place."

Sam began scanning the ground, his expression dubious. Crysta stood frozen, her head swimming with images. This was the spot along the river that she had dreamed of, where the three men had caught up to her.

"You're right," Sam said softly, pointing at something to her left.

Feeling strangely numb, Crysta turned to follow his gaze. A flutter of orange caught her eye. She focused. Someone had driven a flagged stake into the ground to mark the spot. Sam moved cautiously forward, head bent to search the area.

"This is it. That's amazing—that you knew, I mean."

Still with that same feeling of separateness engulfing her, Crysta followed him, her gaze fixed on the ground. The toe of her running shoe touched a black splotch. She stopped to study it, then recognized it as dried blood. Derrick's blood, according to the search coordinator. Her knees went weak.

"It's just like Jim said, plenty of bear track, lots of blood." Sam touched the broken branch of a bush, his expression grim. "God, they're right. I've been off all along. It *was* a bear attack."

His voice, thick and husky with emotion, raked down Crysta's spine like chalk skidding over blackboard. Nausea rolled up her throat. Closing her eyes for an instant, she whispered "No," the sound almost inaudible.

Sam glanced up. "What do you mean, no?" He pointed at the many bear tracks. "The proof's staring us in the face."

Crysta's feeling of unreality wouldn't dissipate. She turned to stare at the twisted spruce. There couldn't be another tree exactly like it. Derrick had been here. Men had been chasing him. She wasn't losing her mind. She didn't care what evidence there was to the contrary. The bear attack had been faked; she knew it as surely as she did her own name.

"It wasn't a bear that got him," Crysta amplified.

Like a sleepwalker, she strode toward the water, envisioning herself lying there, dazed from a blow to the head. In her dream, she had been trying to reach safety someplace up ahead and the twisted spruce had been to her right. Crysta turned, putting the tree to her right, and found herself looking back the way she and Sam had just come. Derrick had been trying to reach Cottonwood Bend . . . and his friend, Sam Barrister.

More images from her dream assailed her as she drew closer to the water. A flash of silver arcing over her shoulder to plop into the water. Derrick's buckle. She had bent to pick it up and had put it in her left breast pocket.

Sudden excitement shot through Crysta, making her forget, momentarily, that there were some things best left unsaid. She bent at the waist to scan the earth. "Was Derrick's silver-dollar belt buckle found in the pocket of his red flannel shirt?"

"The shirt he was wearing when—?" Sam broke off. "No, I don't think so. Jim would have mentioned it."

"Then it must be here somewhere. When they picked him up after shooting him, it must have fallen from his pocket." Crysta waded into the water, peering through the murky ripples. "Help me, Sam. It's here, it has to be."

"What are you talking about? What buckle? And what shooting? You aren't making sense."

"I'm making perfect sense. Help me look. In my dream, I put the buckle in my pocket. Then someone hit me. I fell, stunned. When I turned over, they were talking about getting rid of him. Not *her,* Sam, *him!* I heard a gunshot right before the dream ended and—" she pressed a hand over her heart, lifting her face to stare at him "—I woke up with a terrible pain in my chest. Don't you see?" She waded from the water onto shore, not caring that her feet were soaked. "I knew this place because I had seen it before, in my dream! It wasn't me I was dreaming about, but Derrick!

They shot him. And then they tried to make it look as if a bear got him.''

In a rush, she went on to describe the dream in more detail. So intent was she on recounting everything exactly the way she had seen it that she scarcely noticed the wariness crossing Sam's face, growing more pronounced by the moment.

''And all you saw of the men were their legs and boots?'' He arched an eyebrow and glanced at his feet. ''Green boots with yellow bands at the tops? Crysta, everyone up here wears them. I'm sorry, but that's not particularly conclusive.''

''You have to believe me, Sam. Derrick's life depends on it.'' Her breath caught, and she swallowed. ''Derrick and I, we aren't like other brothers and sisters. Though we're not identical twins, somehow there's a special link between us.''

''A link?'' He avoided meeting her gaze.

''We—'' She caught her lip between her teeth and paused, feeling as if she were about to leap off a cliff. Sam was going to think she was crazy, she just knew it. ''Our minds are linked, telepathically linked.''

''Interesting theory.''

''It isn't a theory, dammit!''

Her curse brought his gaze careening back to her. After studying her a moment, he said, ''You're serious.''

''Of course I am. Do you think I'd joke at a time like this? Derrick can send me thought messages, kind of like...'' she made a futile motion with her hands. ''Sort of like radio waves. Only sometimes I get pictures, too. In turn, I can contact him.'' Crysta knew how insane she sounded, but she couldn't stop herself. Sam had to be convinced. ''It's happened. I swear it.''

In a rush, she told him about several instances from childhood when Derrick had been ill or hurt and she had been simultaneously stricken. ''I was miles away from him, Sam. Every single time. There was no way I could have known.''

"So why are we out here searching and playing guessing games?" A challenging glint crept into his eyes. "Why don't you just *call* him and find out where he is?"

The sarcasm in his voice was veiled, but there. Crysta swallowed down anger. And pain. "I can't. He isn't answering me. But he called to me for help, Sam. Forty-eight hours before the police contacted my mother. That's how I recognized this place. I'd seen it before! In my dream."

He cast a dubious glance around.

Crysta moved toward him. "I didn't tell you before because I was afraid you'd think I was crazy. But more importantly, I was afraid to let on how much I knew! If you were involved, Sam, my link to Derrick would be dangerous to you."

"So why are you telling me now?"

"Because now I know you had nothing to do with it." She gestured toward the spruce. "In the dream, I was running, trying to reach safety up ahead. That tree was on my right. I was running toward Cottonwood Bend, Sam! Don't you see? I wasn't dreaming about myself, but about Derrick. You were the safety he was running toward! His friend. He knew you'd help him."

In her desperation, she grabbed Sam's shirt. As quickly as she could, she recounted her second dream, in detail.

"You have to believe me! He isn't dead. It wasn't a bear."

Sam grasped her shoulders. The frantic appeal in her eyes caught at his heart. Derrick had told Sam about the "link" between him and his sister, but until now, Sam hadn't truly understood how deeply they both believed in it. Or how much it might mean to Crysta that he believe in it, as well. By nature, Sam was a doubting Thomas. He found it extremely difficult to believe in anything he couldn't see or touch or feel. But, for Crysta's sake, he was willing to try.

Giving her a slight shake, he said, "Crysta, I believe you. Just calm down. I believe you."

It was the first time in Crysta's life anyone had said that—other than family, of course, who had seen the proof—and she was momentarily taken aback.

Get 4 Books FREE

SEE BACK OF CARD FOR DETAILS

FREE MYSTERY GIFT

We will be happy to send you a
free bonus gift along with your
free books! To request it,
please check here and mail this
reply card promptly!

Thank you!

Canada Post
Postes Canada
125

DETACH ALONG DOTTED LINE AND MAIL TODAY! – DETACH ALONG DOTTED LINE AND MAIL TODAY! – DETACH ALONG DOTTED LINE AND MAIL TODAY!

"You believe me?" Her amazement came through in her voice. "Does this mean you'll bring the searchers back?"

Sam tightened his grip on her shoulders. "I think you dreamed the dreams, exactly as you described them, and that you believe with all your heart that they were messages from Derrick."

Her heart sank. "You believe I'm telling the truth, as I see it, in other words."

"I'm *trying*, Crysta. You can't blame me for having reservations."

Frustration welled within her. She jerked away and turned her back on him to stare blindly at the water. People had been skeptical all her life. Just once, why couldn't someone believe her? "I should have known not to say anything. You'd think, after all these years, that I'd learn. But, oh, no, I never do."

"Crysta..."

She waved a hand. "No, no! It's all right. I'm used to it. At least I should be." She gave a bitter laugh. "Have you any idea how many friends I've lost over this? I can even list my marriage as a casualty. You get a thick hide after a while."

"If only you had some proof," he said quietly. "There's a great deal at stake here."

She whirled around. "Like your reputation? Your credibility? Other than that, what have you got to lose?"

"Not me so much. I have to think of the searchers. I can't keep them from their jobs without some tangible proof to go on."

"I *can* prove it!" she cried. "The buckle, Sam! If it wasn't in his shirt, it has to be here someplace."

She began another frantic search. For several seconds Sam stood back, looking nonplussed, but then he began helping her comb the area. Ten minutes later, Crysta admitted defeat.

"Well it isn't here." She lifted her hands and shrugged. It was all she could do not to cry. Derrick had counted on her to come through for him, and she was failing, miserably. "I guess as far as tangible proof goes, we're back to square one and the bear theory."

Sam, who stood a few feet away, clamped a hand around the base of his neck, tilting his head back, clearly exhausted.

"In my second dream, I saw a wound over Derrick's heart." A cool breeze came in off the river, funneling around them. She wrapped her arms around herself, shivering. "In the first dream, he picked up the buckle and slipped it into his left breast pocket. What if the bullet went through the buckle, Sam? It may have been damaged. If those men found it, they wouldn't have dared leave it. It would have been evidence of foul play."

"You're grasping at straws, aren't you?"

"Maybe, but right now, I'll grasp at anything!"

"Crysta..." Sam walked slowly toward her. Taking her by the shoulders again, he said, "Honey, I know how upset you are and that the dreams seemed real to you. But isn't it possible that they were products of wishful thinking? That you love Derrick too much to accept the unthinkable—that he's dead and you'll never see him again? There's no sign here of two-legged attackers. Other than the more recent footprints of the searchers, there's nothing to indicate Derrick encountered anything other than a bear. I looked, believe me."

"Two things," she said, placing a hand on his chest to keep a distance between them. "One being that I had the first dream forty-eight hours before I was notified of Derrick's disappearance, which rules out wishful thinking. The second is, don't call me honey. It's condescending and infuriating. You wouldn't consider using an endearment like that if you were having this conversation with a man, would you?"

"I suppose not." His eyes filled with irritation when she pulled away from him. Folding his arms across his chest, he fell into step beside her as she headed back upstream. "Where are you going?"

"Back to the lodge. We've seen what we came to see. I'm going to study the map to familiarize myself with this area while I have Jangles pack me some food. Then I'm coming back here.''

"To do what?''

"To look for my brother.''

"Where?''

"Everywhere. I'll comb every inch of the area.''

Sam sighed.

Crysta rounded on him. "Look, I understand that you don't believe me. That's your choice, and I really can't blame you. That doesn't mean I'm giving up.'' She struck off walking again. "I know what I know. I can't prove it, but there it is. I'm coming back, and nobody, including you, is going to stop me.''

"Even though you just saw the evidence of a bear attack with your own eyes?'' he countered.

Crysta raised her chin. "Evidence can be faked.''

"It might be a little difficult to get the bear to cooperate,'' he came back.

A sudden thought hit her. "Not if it was dead.'' Her gaze flew to his. "The bear carcass, Sam—the one Tip said he found, minus its head and paws. What if Derrick's attackers used the teeth and claws to tear up his clothing? Bear track is common everywhere, right? They wouldn't have had to fake that. If they were extremely careful about the other evidence they left, not even a forensics lab could tell by examining the clothing. Naturally, the searchers would be fooled.''

His eyes narrowed in thought. "It's possible, I suppose. It'd be a mighty clever trick, using a dead bear, but if it was done right, even an expert might be misled by the hair and saliva traces left on the clothing.''

"So you admit it's possible.''

"Possible, yes.''

"But unlikely,'' she added hollowly. With a little shrug, she accepted that and picked up her pace. "For me, a possibility is enough.''

"What if I was to say I'm willing to go on your instincts?''

The question made her falter. "What do you mean?''

"That I'll forgo proof and logic, just this once. I can't have the searchers resume their hunt, but that doesn't mean I can't continue the search."

"I'm not one to look a gift horse in the mouth, but why?"

"Let's just say, for now, that I concede there may be such a thing as mental telepathy and that it might manifest itself between twins. There *was* a bear carcass found, a fresh kill, at just the right time. I care a lot about Derrick, and as long as there's a possibility he's alive, I'd be a fool to ignore what you're telling me."

"Oh, Sam, I could kiss you!"

"Kiss a man who calls you demeaning names like honey?"

She ignored the dig. "So you'll come back here with me?"

"I didn't say that."

"Sam, in my dream, Derrick was badly wounded! We have to make finding him our first priority!"

He shook his head. "If the wound was that serious, time has already run out. If not, then Derrick will manage to hang on until we reach him. A frenzied search isn't the answer. We have nothing to base it on." He held up a staying hand. "I know you saw a cabin in your dream. That's great, but it doesn't help. There are a lot of abandoned cabins in the interior. We might waste days searching and not find it."

"It's a sure bet we won't find it in Derrick's briefcase."

"We may get a lead there. You dreamed about a warehouse. If your dreams are messages from Derrick, that's proof my suspicions about Blanchette are accurate. If we can find out what Derrick found, we may be able to identify his attackers."

"Marvelous. Without Derrick to testify, we'd have culprits, but no evidence against them. What good would that do?"

"The 'culprits' can tell us where Derrick is, or at least point us in the right direction."

"Why would they be so accommodating? They'd be incriminating themselves."

"If we find them, Crysta, I think I can persuade them to cooperate," he replied in a silken voice.

She glanced down to see that his hands were knotted into fists. As frightening as it was to envision Sam losing his temper and using those fists on someone, it was also strangely reassuring. For the first time since coming to Alaska, she felt as if she had a friend in all this, someone who would stand by her and help her find her brother.

As they walked along, she noticed that Sam paused frequently, as if to listen, and scanned the surrounding area.

"What are you looking for?" she whispered.

His mouth settled in a grim line. "Grizzly sign. Territorial markings. Like it or not, we can't disregard what we saw back there. Where there's smoke, there's usually fire, and I'm not willing to risk our lives gambling that all that bear sign was planted."

The hair on Crysta's neck prickled. "If there *is* a renegade bear out here, what'll we do? You haven't got a gun."

"More fool I. I should have known Jim wouldn't have been so convinced of a bear attack without plenty of reason."

"Can grizzlies climb trees?"

He grimaced. "They usually just knock them down." He settled somber dark eyes on hers. "If we run across a bear, drop to the ground, pull yourself into the fetal position, tuck your head under your arms and play dead. If it mauls you, try not to move or cry out. If you're lucky, after a while, it'll grow bored and leave you alone."

"And if I'm not lucky?"

Sam's response to that was to scan the woods again. The worried look on his face was answer enough for Crysta.

Chapter Nine

During the return trip to the lodge, Crysta's legs grew quivery with exhaustion. The slightest projection in her path caught the toe of her sneaker, making her stumble.

With no warning, Sam touched her elbow and nodded toward a grassy sweep of high ground. "I need to take five."

He sat down and she stumbled after him, drooping to the ground like an overcooked strand of spaghetti. Despite the breeze coming off the water, her face felt hot, her forehead filmed with sweat. Sam stretched out on his back, head on his folded arms. With far less grace, she flopped over on her stomach.

She knew he had stopped not for himself, but for her. His legs were accustomed to long treks; hers were not. She drew a shaky breath, running her parched tongue over dry lips, longing for a drink. The river water looked too muddy for consumption.

As if he had read her mind, Sam removed a small flask from his belt and offered it to her. "Care to wet your whistle?"

Crysta uncapped the canteen and took a drink. After wiping the mouth of the container, she handed it back to him and watched as he took a long swallow and sighed with satisfaction.

"You okay?" he asked as he clipped the canteen back onto his belt. "This is quite a trek for someone not used to it."

After she had tried so hard to keep up with him, the husky concern in his voice pricked her pride. "I'm fine. How about you?"

The comeback was ridiculous. He would have to be blind not to see how trembly her muscles were. However, just because her body had given out on her didn't mean she should lose her sense of humor. "If you don't think you can make it the rest of the way, I'll let you lean on me," she offered.

She heard a choked laugh. "I appreciate that."

Abandoning pretense, she rolled onto her side and tipped her head back to study his profile. Against the backdrop of thick grass and swaying cottonwood, he struck a contrast to the wildness, yet seemed strangely a part of it. "Are we walking uphill?" she asked.

"The incline is pretty slight."

"Tell my legs that." ·

His firm lips inched into a wry grin. "I'm sorry. I should have stopped sooner. I had my mind on other things."

Crysta wished her own thoughts could transcend the physical. The last mile or so, even her obsessive musings about Derrick had dimmed, edged out by muscle fatigue and the struggle to keep walking. "What other things?"

"Derrick's papers. I've gone through at least half of them, possibly more. My instincts tell me there's something there, something I'm missing." He closed his eyes. "There *has* to be something. It's our only chance."

Crysta made a fist in the grass, giving the tender shoots a twist. The bittersweet smell drifted to her nostrils, making her think of the times in high school when she had tussled with Derrick on their front lawn while he practiced his wrestling moves. The memories brought a lump to her throat. She needed to share the pain and seek reassurance.

Since their talk at the site of the alleged bear attack, Crysta felt more at ease with Sam. She had revealed a side of herself she seldom shared with anyone, and he hadn't mocked her.

"Sam, tell me honestly, do you think Derrick's dead?"

He turned his head to look at her. "I did. Now that you've told me about your dreams, I'm not so sure." As if he sensed how desperately she needed a friend's assurances just now, his eyes softened, delving deeply into hers. "If he's contacting you, he can't be dead, can he?"

"That's just it. Since I had that dream last night, he hasn't." A shiver coursed through her, cold as death. "There's just silence now—an awful silence. For as long as I can remember, I've always *felt* him. I can't explain. I suppose you think I'm insane. It's part of me I don't often share. People—even those I thought were good friends— tend to shun me if I talk about it." Her mouth trembled as she tried to form the next words. "I can't feel anything, Sam. It's as if Derrick's gone."

"I don't think you're insane." His voice turned gravelly, but it soothed her in some indefinable way. "And even if I did, what difference would it make? Those people you thought were friends? You're you, Crysta. Your feelings, your relationship with Derrick, the telepathy thing—that's all uniquely you. Anyone who shuns you for being yourself isn't worth your time."

"I'm frightened," she whispered.

"I know you are."

Such a simple answer, yet somehow, it was exactly what she had needed him to say. No judgments, no analytical preaching, no cruel gibes. She hadn't expected him to understand, and perhaps he didn't. Maybe no one could. But that wasn't important. What counted was that Sam accepted her as she was.

She had been longing for a friend. Now she realized she had one. Tears sprang to her eyes. "Thank you for that."

It might have been a silly thing to say, given his response, but he seemed to understand. He shifted onto his side and placed a hand on her cheek, his fingertips feathering lightly over her ear and the tendrils of hair at her temple. As recently as this morning, Crysta probably would have pulled away. But now the familiarity seemed right. She supposed circumstances might be fostering emotions between them that they might not feel at another time—Derrick's best friend and his sister, drawn together by fear and grief—but it didn't seem like that.

His hand was large, warm, heavy. Even though she knew he only meant to comfort her, his touch made her skin tingle. She let her eyelashes drift closed, absorbing the solidness of him. He said nothing. When she thought about that, she realized there was very little else he could say. His touch was enough. It helped to know that he cared, even though he couldn't comprehend.

"Maybe he's unconscious," she whispered raggedly.

"Maybe," he agreed. "Or too exhausted to communicate. You're weary, too. That has to have some bearing."

She was glad for his seeming acceptance, but she still had to face the reality that the channel of communication between her and Derrick had gone dead. She might need to assimilate, deal with and accept what that might mean.

"I love him more than a sister usually loves a brother. I guess it's not true of all twins, but with us, there's a closeness, a sense of oneness." She opened her eyes. "Even when we fought, as brothers and sisters always will, the bond was there between us."

"I know. Derrick and I go back a long way. I could tell you two had something special, just by the way he spoke of you."

"I need to call my mother, update her. I'm not sure what I should say." Her throat closed around the words, making them sound tinny. "If he's dead, how will I—"

Sam moved his arm slightly, his thumb grazing her lips to silence her. "Crysta, if he *is* dead, your mom will deal with it. You'll both survive and go on living, just like everyone else who's lost someone dear. Until you know for sure, though, you have to concentrate on finding him. Not on what people might think. Not on what you should tell your mom."

She took a deep, steadying breath. "You're right. I know you are. I'm sorry."

"Don't be." He withdrew his hand from her cheek and sat up, looping his arms around his knees. The wind ruffled his dark hair. "You're handling this better than most people would. If the roles were reversed, Derrick would be over the edge."

Crysta pushed to a sitting position, keeping an arm braced behind her. "Yes, Derrick was—" She broke off, shattered that she was referring to her brother in the past tense. "He *isn't* so strong sometimes. Especially not since his breakup with Eileen. Emotionally, he's been walking a tightrope, and sometimes he—he loses his footing." Brushing hair from her eyes, she stared hard at the river, still fighting tears. "He changed after she left. Then there was the car wreck.... Without Eileen, the only comfort he seemed able to find was at the bottom of a bottle." She glanced sideways at Sam. "You knew him then, didn't you?"

"Yes. I visited him at the hospital, in fact. Drinking and driving. I couldn't believe it when I found out."

"I'm surprised we didn't run into each other. I practically lived outside the intensive care unit."

"If I remember correctly, you had gone to pick up your husband at the airport that afternoon. We probably just missed each other. I didn't get to visit Derrick for long. I was lucky even to get in, not being a relative, but they made an exception because I'd come so far."

Unpleasant memories assailed Crysta. Now that Sam mentioned it, she recalled that afternoon vividly—the grudging trip she'd made to the airport to pick up Dick, their ensuing argument over Derrick, Dick's ultimatum. She had been forced to make a choice that afternoon, a choice no woman should ever have to make.

The memories still hurt, not because of any undying love for Dick—bitterness had killed that long ago—but because a marriage that should have been strong had crumbled. Crysta knew Dick had tried his best, and so had she. The problem was that no marriage could survive the intrusion of a third party, and Derrick had intruded constantly.

Facing those memories now was too much for Crysta. She shoved unsteadily to her feet. "I'm rested enough to go on."

Sam rose beside her, his eyes hooded. Crysta wondered if he already knew why her marriage to Dick had failed. Had Derrick told him? Unsettled by the thought, she struck off walking.

Sam fell in beside her, setting his stride to match hers. The silence between them, at first uncomfortable, slowly mellowed. Then, without warning, Sam grabbed her hand fiercely. Crysta spun to a stop to find Sam looking over his shoulder. Tension radiated from him. His gaze, alert and suspicious, scanned the woods. Then, so slowly the movement was almost imperceptible, he stepped between her and the brush.

"Wha—what is it?" she whispered. Envisioning a hungry grizzly, she clutched the back of his shirt and instinctively moved closer to him. "Did you hear something?"

He motioned for her to be quiet. Crysta stared into the trees, afraid on the one hand, yet not nearly as frightened as she might have been had he not been there. After a moment, he relaxed and resumed walking, keeping his hold on her hand.

"My imagination, I guess. I thought I heard something."

Crysta had heard nothing. "A small animal, do you think?"

He smiled. "Probably. I've gone so long without sleep, I must be getting wired. Jumping at shadows."

His hand, callused and warm, tightened around hers. Crysta fell into step with him, acutely aware that the pace he had set was a comfortable one for her.

Touched by his regard, she returned the pressure of his grip. He glanced up from his study of the ground ahead of them, his dark eyes molten and probing. The impact made her miss a step. He hauled back on her hand to keep her from stumbling, which brought her hip into contact with his thigh. Awareness once again crackled between them. She knew he felt it by the sudden tightening around his mouth. This time, though, he didn't increase his pace to put distance between them, and he didn't pretend nothing had happened.

Her heart picked up speed. This was crazy. And to say it was bad timing was an understatement. Sam Barrister wasn't her type, and she wasn't his. An Alaskan lodge owner and a fashion consultant? Ludicrous. So why was she feeling such a strong pull toward him?

Crysta had no answer and no energy to explore her emotions to find one. Derrick was all that mattered. She couldn't lose sight of that.

TODD SHRIVER'S CESSNA was floating up to the island when Sam and Crysta rounded the last bend in the river before reaching the lodge.

"Looks like Shriver brought Riley back with him. I swear, Riley could keep every pilot in the area going with all the flights he makes."

Crysta cupped her hand over her eyes, trying to spot the redheaded warehouse supervisor. "This morning he said he had to go on a beer run."

"He does that frequently."

"Does he have a drinking problem?"

"I'm not sure *drinking* is the word. *Guzzling* might better describe what ails him. At any rate, the luggage restrictions on the pontoon planes make it impossible for him to bring in more than one case of beer per trip, so he quite often runs low and flies back to town for more."

"How can he afford the air fare?"

"His father died recently. I understand he inherited a substantial amount of money."

Crysta wrinkled her nose. "It won't last long."

"Nope, but that's not my business. I give him discounts because he stays here so much and brings so many friends. Maybe Shriver and the other pilots give him special deals, too."

The sound of voices drifted on the air to them. Crysta veered toward the lodge, envisioning a tall glass of water and a thick sandwich. She tried not to think about her upcoming telephone conversation with her mother; some things were better left until you had to face them. No use borrowing trouble, as Ellen would say.

"Hey, Barrister!" a masculine voice called.

Crysta drew up beside Sam, watching as Todd Shriver came toward them, long legs scissoring along the muddy bank. Upon reaching them, the pilot passed an arm over his forehead, laughing and out of breath. "Guess I'm not as young as I used to be."

Looking at him, Crysta tried to catalog his features to decide what it was about him that bothered her. He had an infectious smile, and he was quite friendly. For want of a better explanation, she decided it was not so much his looks, which were above average, but the fact that his face had no character lines. Lines upon the face were like words upon a page; they made a statement. Her tastes ran to men who were a bit older, she decided, with features that bore the marks of their emotions. Laughter, tears. A man or woman had no real depth until they had experienced the heights of happiness and the depths of despair. Evidently Todd still had all of that ahead of him.

"Are any of us as young as we used to be?" Sam flexed his shoulders, making no attempt to hide his own exhaustion. "We've been on a long walk, Todd. Right now, we'd kill for a glass of water. Can it wait until later?"

Todd's grin faded, and he turned his ice-blue gaze on Crysta. "Sure, no problem. Fact is, I'm staying over to do some fishing, so I'll be around longer than usual. Before we took off downriver in the boat, I wanted to offer my condolences to you, Ms. Meyers. I heard about what the searchers found." He shook his head. "A bear—can you believe it? And to Derrick, of all people."

"It can happen to the best," Sam countered, his gaze intent on Shriver's youthful face. "Not often in these parts, though."

"Which makes it all the more a shame. Why here? Why him? I'm really sorry." Todd inclined his head toward Crysta. "You can't know how much."

Crysta noticed that the pilot kept glancing toward the river, as if he was worried that he might miss his fishing expedition. She wanted to accept his condolences graciously, but part of her couldn't. Like Steve Henderson, she found it difficult to accept that other people went on enjoying life when her own was being torn apart. She supposed it was self-centered of her. To Todd Shriver, Derrick had been an acquaintance, nothing more.

"I appreciate your concern," she said. "But let's not forget that his body hasn't been found. I still have hope."

"I don't blame you there. Never give up hope." Shriver flashed a slow smile, calculated, she was sure, to make her pulse escalate. "And like I said before, if you need me to fly you around, it'll only cost you for the fuel." Glancing toward the river, he retreated a step. "Better go before all the boats leave without me."

As Shriver walked off, Crysta gazed after him. More to herself than to Sam, she whispered, "Was I ever that carefree? Right now, the most important thing on his agenda is catching the biggest fish. There's a little-boy quality about him, isn't there?"

"Shriver?" Sam threw her a disbelieving look. "Most of my female guests go cow-eyed when he comes on to them like that."

She shrugged. "Fish, women. To fellows like him, both are candidates for the trophy rack."

Sam laughed, a little uneasily, she thought. "And what a way to go?"

Crysta angled a grin at him. "Looks only run skin-deep. He's a little too young for my taste. Life's still nothing but a big game to him."

Sam's answering grin warmed his dark eyes. Placing a hand on her shoulder, he pressed her into a walk. "He's not a bad fellow. It's nice to know, though, that not all women fall for a pretty face. There's hope for guys like me, after all."

Crysta threw him a sharp glance. Surely a man as handsome as Sam couldn't truly believe himself to be homely. "Do you?" she countered. "Fall for a pretty face, I mean."

He studied her. "Only if it belongs to an especially nice lady."

The response, coupled with the intensity in his eyes, brought a rush of heat to Crysta's cheeks, and she quickly glanced at the ground to hide her discomfiture.

WHILE SAM STOPPED by the kitchen and asked Jangles to bring them a plate of sandwiches, Crysta put in a call to her mother, dreading the moment when she would have to admit that she still had no idea where Derrick was. When her aunt Eva answered and explained that Ellen was asleep, Crysta sagged with relief. Being careful not to mention either of her dreams about Derrick, Crysta updated Eva on the situation.

"I wouldn't mention the bear theory to Mom," Crysta warned. "I'm convinced Derrick's still alive, and hearing that would only upset her. Just tell her I've arrived, and that I'm—" Crysta broke off. "Tell her I'm doing everything possible to find him."

"You worry too much about your mother's health. Sometimes I think she uses that heart condition of hers to manipulate you. One minute she's having an angina attack, and the next she's eating bonbons. I'm four years her senior, you know, and I have a heart condition, too. You don't see me clutching my chest every time things don't go my way."

Crysta stared at the calendar picture of Mount McKinley. Perhaps her mother's heart condition had become a sort of leverage she used to manipulate her children, but Crysta loved her mother too much to take that chance.

A brief silence hummed over the line. Then Eva said, "Crysta, this catastrophe with Derrick isn't your fault, you know. Your voice sounds so strained that I'm beginning to feel more worried about you than I am about him."

"I'm fine, Aunt Eva."

"Are you?"

Crysta shoved her hair from her eyes, acutely aware of the loving censure in the other woman's voice and the static on the phone line. "I'm positive. Listen, Aunt Eva, the rates on this telephone are astronomical. I really should get off. Will you tell Mom I love her?"

"I'll tell her—as if she could fail to know." Eva sighed. "Don't be too hard on yourself. Do I have your promise on that?"

Crysta smiled in spite of herself. "I'll do my best."

Just as Crysta hung up the phone, Sam and Jangles emerged from the kitchen. Jangles stared at Crysta and said, "Sandwiches are on the way."

"Great. I'm famished," Crysta called to the Indian woman as she and Sam entered his office.

She took a seat by his desk, watching while Sam poured a pot of water into the automatic coffeemaker. Then, he grasped the waist of his shirt and tugged the tails free of his jeans, unfastening the snaps as he strode toward her. "Hope you don't mind, but I've got to shed a layer."

"It is warm in here." Averting her gaze from the ripple of chest muscle revealed by his snug T-shirt, she leaned around to open the right drawer of his desk, pulling Derrick's briefcase out. Glancing down at the wastebasket, she frowned. "The salmon is gone."

"Jangles must have dumped it."

"Efficient lady, Jangles."

"Do I detect some animosity?"

"Did you notice that look she gave me a second ago? She's against my being here, and I can't understand why."

"Like I said, it could be superstitious nonsense. Don't read too much into it."

"She didn't even mention the fish. That seems suspicious to me."

Sam smiled. "Crysta, the only place at this lodge where a salmon is out of the ordinary is in my bed. Why would she mention something so commonplace?"

Crysta realized he was right and sighed. "I guess maybe I'm looking for things because she isn't very friendly."

Sam nodded, bracing an arm on the desk to lean over her while she began leafing through the papers in Derrick's briefcase. Crysta had seen most of the documents that afternoon when she had come in here snooping, and hopelessness filled her. "Have you any idea what we're supposed to be looking for, Sam?"

He sighed and eased around her to claim the captain's chair behind the desk. Shuffling through the papers on his blotter, he located the stack of records he had been studying earlier when Crysta had burst in so unexpectedly, brandishing the salmon. "I wish I did. Something out of the ordinary."

She scanned an invoice. An idea struck her. "What if they're buying inferior material? There's big money in that."

"Skimming from the budget, you mean?" Sam shook his head. "I thought of that and called a contractor friend of mine in Anchorage. I gave him a quick rundown on the purchase orders. He said it sounded as if the company was ordering from reputable firms, up to code and getting more than enough stuff. When skimming occurs, a contractor generally buys from a disreputable outfit, using lower-grade materials or less than is required by law."

Crysta groaned and tossed down the invoice. "Then what *are* we looking for, Sam? This isn't a solution, it's a time waster. Wouldn't it be more expedient to return downriver and search the area around the attack site for signs of Derrick?"

"Do you think the searchers haven't done that?"

Crysta knew they must have. "But he can't have gotten far. Not if he was wounded."

Sam's expression grew grim. "If your dream is an accurate account, his attackers must have removed him from the area."

"You're a good tracker, aren't you?"

"Jim, the search coordinator, is a far better tracker than I. If there was a trail out there to follow, he would have spotted it. There is no sign, none at all, that anything but a bear was in the vicinity."

Suddenly it occurred to Crysta just how much faith in her Sam was exercising by even *trying* to believe in her story. "There has to be something we can do besides this."

He glanced up from the documents he was scanning. "Maybe, but the briefcase is the most obvious place to start."

Crysta longed to contradict him, but, remembering the map she had studied, she didn't.

Within ten minutes, the coffee had finished perking and Jangles had delivered a plate of delicious steak sandwiches.

After Crysta ate, she began to feel drowsy. Determined to keep working, she poured them each a second mug of coffee and sat back down to study more papers.

She could see what Sam meant about the quantity of merchandise being ordered by Blanchette. She was no expert, but it seemed to her that the construction company bought plenty of everything, especially conduit. And all from reputable firms.

Exhaustion blurred her vision. She blinked and sat up straighter. Seconds later, she shifted in her seat and stretched, the battle to stay awake growing more difficult.

Glancing up from his desk, Sam studied Crysta a moment, biting back a smile. Her head was nodding, and her grip on the sheaf of papers in her lap was growing lax. He returned his gaze to the paper work, wishing she'd go lie down but knowing she'd resist if he suggested it. Because of the long hours of daylight in Alaska during the summer months, Sam was used to operating on little if any sleep. Crysta wasn't, especially not after the strenuous walk she'd just been on.

Moments later, a soft snore interrupted Sam's concentration. He looked up to see that Crysta had slumped sideways in her chair. Her head lolled on her shoulder. Sam watched her for a moment, smiling each time he heard the purring noise that feathered past her lips. Not exactly a rafter shaker, but definitely a snore. He decided he liked the sound.

The clock on the wall ticked rhythmically. Every once in a while, the coffeemaker sputtered. Soothed by those sounds and Crysta's soft snore, Sam settled in to work.

SWEAT STREAMED DOWN Crysta's sides to the waistband of her jeans. Her chest felt as if a red-hot coal was buried in it. With a groan, she struggled to open her eyes, wondering why the soft leather cushion of her chair felt so hard and uneven.

She stared into thick gloom. She was no longer in Sam's office but sitting on a fireplace hearth, feeble flames flickering in the grate to one side of her. The room around her was dark with shadows and smelled of smoke, dampness and dust. At one end was a broken window, the remaining glass filmed with grime and draped with cobwebs. Struggling to breathe, she leaned her head back against the rock face of the fireplace and stared at the layers of smoke hovering like cumulus clouds below the exposed rafters of the ceiling.

Sick, so sick. Her body felt afire. She looked down and saw that she held a knife in her hand. Her arm shook as she directed the blade toward the small black hole in her chest. The bullet. If it didn't come out, she'd die of infection.

Pain lashed Crysta as she pressed the tip of the knife into her flesh. Swirls of red blinded her. It took all her courage to sink the knife deeper, and then she had to call upon sheer desperation to probe for the lead. Her body began to shake more violently. Sweat streamed down her face.

Please, God.

The knife tip grated against something metallic, and the pain, already excruciating, amplified, flashing across her left breast. The room began to swirl, slowly at first, then faster. Blackness encroached on her vision until she was seeing the wound in her chest through a tiny peephole that was narrowing at an alarming speed. The lead at last popped free and bounced away across the floor, bloody-black and misshapen.

So weak. The knife slipped from her hand and clattered onto the stone hearth. She knew she mustn't lose consciousness, not yet. Through the tiny sphere of her narrowed vision, Crysta stared at the blood spurting down her belly, keeping time with her heartbeat. The bleeding was good; it would clean the wound. She groped for the knife, found it. Summoning all her remaining strength, she extended her arm, holding the blade over the flames until the steel turned a muted red.

Tightening her grip on the knife handle and clenching her teeth, she withdrew the blade from the heat and slapped the red-hot metal over her wound. Body rigid, she hissed, quivering as the stench of searing flesh turned her stomach.

"CRYSTA! Crysta, honey, wake up."

Crysta swam up toward the light and Sam's voice, frantic for air, for a release from the pain. His face burst through the swirls of blackness, muscles taut with concern, his eyes frightened. She swallowed down another wave of nausea.

"It hurts! It hurts, Sam."

"What, where?"

"My chest—my chest."

Sam's arm encircled her shoulders. Crysta leaned against him, not caring when she felt his other hand tearing at the top buttons of her shirt. Cool air wafted across her collarbone. Warm, callused fingers pressed against the side of her throat. She realized he was checking her pulse.

In one smooth motion, Sam lifted her out of the chair and laid her on the floor. "Be still, honey. Just be still and trust me, okay? I'm trained in first aid. You'll be fine."

Frantic to somehow rid herself of the pain, Crysta clutched at her chest. He clasped her wrists, forcing her arms to her sides. Another wave of nausea washed over her, and she tried to sit up, gagging.

Sam cradled Crysta's shoulders, forcing her to lie back against his arm. Fishing his handkerchief from his back pocket, he wiped her pale face, frightened for her yet uncertain precisely what was wrong.

"It's all right, Crysta. Relax, relax."

She pressed a shaking hand over her left breast. Sam stared at her colorless skin, at the taut pull of her facial muscles, and listened with half an ear to her babbling description of what could only have been a dream. A bullet? A knife? Derrick, wounded and alone, in a ramshackle cabin? Sam could tell by looking at Crysta, by the way she quivered, that the dream she was recounting had been no ordinary nightmare.

With an inexplicable feeling of dread, he drew her hand from her chest and stared at the angry red welt rising on her ivory skin, beginning above the cup of her white bra and angling downward under the lacy cloth. Goose bumps rose on the nape of his neck.

Slowly, she began to quieten. Sam held her, stroking her hair, whispering to her. Her breathing evened out. A quick glance told him that the red imprint on her skin was fading. Questions crowded into his mind. Had she caused the red mark herself, clutching at her chest? Could he have done it while opening her shirt?

"He's alive, Sam. He's alive!" She arched her neck to look up at him. "We have to find him. Soon!"

Sam swallowed, uncertain what to say to her. "Calm down, Crysta. It was just a bad dream, a bad dream."

"No." She shook her head, struggling to escape him. "Not a dream. You have to believe that."

During his military training years ago, Sam had watched films on torture techniques. He knew how powerful the mind was. There were documented cases in which blind-folded prisoners, expecting to be touched with hot steel, had actually developed burns when touched with harmless, frosted metal. Was it possible that the mark on Crysta's chest had been put there by her absolute belief that Derrick had placed a hot knife against his chest? Or was it true that Crysta and Derrick, so genetically similar, shared some strange and incomprehensible mental link that enabled one to feel what the other suffered?

"Please, Sam, listen to me. We're wasting precious time! Maybe if we went to the police we could convince them to do something."

"With what as proof?" he asked gently. "Your dreams, Crysta? Jim Sales is one of the best trackers around. He says Derrick was attacked by a bear, and even I have to admit the evidence points to that. What chance have we of convincing the police otherwise?"

"What if we did an aerial search? We might spot the cabin he's in."

As patiently as he could, Sam once again explained to her that the interior was dotted with abandoned cabins. As versatile as Todd's float-plane was, it couldn't land unless the conditions were ideal. Even if they narrowed their scope and chose only a few cabins to investigate by foot, it would take days, possibly even weeks, to reach them all.

"But what about the helicopter you told me about?" she cried. "A helicopter can land almost anywhere."

"The Huey? Crysta, that was a military chopper, brought in especially for the search." Sam studied her pinched face, wishing that he could make her comprehend how vast Alaska was. "Have you ever seen a map of Alaska superimposed over a map of the lower forty-eight? It's mindboggling how large it is."

"We could rent another helicopter. Surely some pilot would take us up!"

"That'd cost a fortune. We're not talking a few hours, but possibly days. I have some money in savings, but not nearly enough." Sam sighed, his thoughts straying to Tip and the exorbitant costs for his special schooling during the winter months. "I'm sorry, Crysta. I just don't have the resources for something that expensive."

"I don't, either," she admitted in a quavery voice. "But, Sam, we can't just poke around in a briefcase!"

Sam helped her to sit erect. He could see she was becoming frantic and that she wouldn't be satisfied with spending any more time going through Derrick's papers. Her pallor alarmed him. It was fast becoming a toss-up what concerned him most, trying to find out what had happened to Derrick or playing along with Crysta to make this as painless as possible for her. This couldn't be an easy time for her, and with every passing hour Sam's hopes of finding Derrick, alive or dead, diminished.

Smoothing her hair, he said, "Okay, I'll admit that the briefcase may be a dead end. The next place to look is in Anchorage." His gaze locked on hers. "You say you dreamed of walking through a warehouse, right? I think we should fly to town with Todd Shriver and get permission to tour the Blanchette warehouses. Maybe we'll find the building you dreamed of."

"And possibly find a lead?"

She looked so grateful to him that Sam felt a twinge of guilt. He *wanted* to believe in her dreams, but his pragmatic side balked. "Possibly," he offered noncommittally. "Before we leave, though, both of us have to get some rest."

"Rest?"

Sam feathered his thumb across her cheek. Dark shadows formed crescents beneath her eyes, all the more noticeable now because she was so pale. "I'm running on sheer willpower."

"But Derrick— We can't take time to sleep, Sam! Time is running out. Derrick needs me. Don't you understand?"

"We have to get some sleep. I've been operating on short naps for five days. I'm beat. My mind is fuzzy. We'll both be better equipped to find and help Derrick if we're refreshed."

With obvious reluctance, she acquiesced with a nod, her eyes haunted. Sam pushed to his feet and offered her a hand up. When she stood, he gazed down at her for a long moment, fighting off an almost irresistible urge to draw her into his arms.

"Why don't you go down to the sauna and freshen up?" he suggested. "It'll relax you and help you sleep. I promise to set the alarm so we don't sleep long."

Too weary and disheartened to argue, Crysta turned to leave, reasoning that the sooner she got some sleep, the sooner she and Sam could fly into Anchorage. At the door, she stopped and looked back over her shoulder. "You'll tell Todd not to leave without us?"

"I'll have Tip go down and give him the message."

EN ROUTE TO THE SAUNA, Crysta noticed Steve Henderson sitting under a cottonwood, back braced against the trunk, one knee bent to support his arm. He looked so desolate that she veered toward him, uncertain what she could say to comfort him but driven to try. It couldn't be easy watching your little boy slip away, especially when all it might take to save him was a donor match. She could only imagine the frustration he must be feeling, his impotent rage at fate.

About ten feet from him, she called out a hello.

He jumped as if she had stung him. His blue gaze rose to her face. She immediately noted how thin he was, almost wasted, as if he were the one stricken with a grave illness.

"I'm Crysta Meyers, Derrick's sister." Suddenly feeling foolish, Crysta let her gaze trail off into the trees. "I, um, heard about your little boy, Scotty. I just wanted you to know I'll be praying that they line him up with a donor soon."

When he said nothing, Crysta returned her gaze to his ravaged features. He was staring through her, past her, as if he found eye contact with her disconcerting. Crysta realized her arrival was probably an unwelcome intrusion on his solitude, that he had come here to grieve and didn't appreciate her company.

"Why would you care about my son?" he asked in a shaky voice. "Who's he to you?"

The wind whipped her shirt tightly around her torso. She dragged her hair away from her eyes, wishing she hadn't come. Maybe he saw her as a morbid curiosity seeker; he clearly resented her condolences. "I'm sorry, Mr. Henderson. I walked up on impulse. I, um, just wanted to—" She shrugged. "You've heard about my brother. Sometimes I feel as if no one cares but me. I know it must be a thousand times worse for you."

His eyes cleared and seemed to focus on her. "That's life, isn't it? No one else really cares. Your world falls apart, but all around you there's laughter."

"Yes." Crysta swallowed, her throat suddenly dry and burning. "That's life. It's not true of everyone though. Some people *do* care. I just wanted you to know that."

He averted his face and let out a ragged sigh. She noticed that he was clenching and unclenching his fist. She had intended to comfort him, not make matters worse.

"Well . . ." She gestured at the bundle of clothes she carried under one arm. "I was on my way to the sauna. Better get on down there before someone else beats me to it."

With that, Crysta spun and walked off. She could feel Henderson's eyes boring into her back. His hostility unnerved her, yet she couldn't condemn him for it. *"Your world falls apart, but all around you there's laughter."* She knew how the sounds of gaiety hurt when someone you loved might be dying.

It took an effort to put the uncomfortable meeting with Henderson into perspective. She had offered to commiserate with him; he had rejected her. No big deal. She had problems enough of her own. Trudging up onto the sauna steps, she flipped over the sign, then let herself in the door. Sam was right, a good steam bath was what she needed—a nice long one so she could forget her most recent dream and relax enough to once again fall asleep.

STEAM ROSE around Crysta in a thick cloud. She tipped her head back and poured water from the bucket over herself, rinsing off the soap. The heat soothed her aching body. She grabbed her towel off the hook and wrapped it around herself, tucking a corner between her breasts. Giving in to exhaustion, she sank to the steam bench and braced her back against the wall.

A muffled thump came from the anteroom. She cocked her head, peering through the swirling steam. Before coming in, she hadn't looked at the sign to see what side was up. Had the previous sauna occupant forgotten to turn the sign back over when he left? If so, she might have put the Occupied side toward the building, unintentionally inviting company.

"Is someone there?" she called.

No one answered, but Crysta sensed a presence. Why would someone ignore her?

Before she could think of an answer to that unsettling question, a rumble vibrated through the planked flooring. Startled by a noise, Crysta shot up from the bench. It sounded as though the woodpile in the anteroom had collapsed.

Unable to see clearly through the steam, she moved carefully in the general direction of the door. She heard the echo of booted feet crossing the floor in the other room, then a creak of metal as the stove door opened. More thunks, which sounded like lengths of wood being shoved into the fire, brought a relieved smile to her mouth. Someone must be replenishing the wood supply. She remembered seeing Tip carrying wood in here earlier.

"Tip, is that you?" Uncertain exactly where the door was, Crysta stepped closer to the wall, groping with flattened palms. "It's me, Crysta. I forgot to check the sign before I turned it over. I don't mind that you brought in wood, but could you come back in a few minutes to stack it? I'll hurry and get dressed."

No answer. She thought she heard the stove door clank shut. Were the walls of the sauna so thick and airtight that she couldn't be heard? Possibly the ducts from the stove piped sound into the sauna, but not vice versa.

She didn't consider herself overly modest, but she drew the line at communal baths. At any moment, an unsuspecting fisherman might stroll in. She found the door and pressed her palm against it, intending to shove it open a crack and peek out.

It wouldn't budge. For an instant, Crysta thought perhaps the door opened inward, but when she ran her palm along its edge, squinting to see, she couldn't find a pull handle. Her heartbeat accelerated slightly.

"Yoo-hoo? It's me, Crysta Meyers. What happened? Did the woodpile fall?" She pushed harder on the door. It still wouldn't move. Giving a little laugh, she leaned closer. "I think the door is blocked."

No answer. Crysta shoved on the door again, putting all her weight against it this time.

"Hello! Is anyone out there?"

A panicked scream worked its way up her throat. She swallowed it down, moving back a step and lunging forward, hitting the door with her shoulder.

"Tip! Somebody! Answer me!"

The sound of her own voice, muted by the steam, bounced back at her off the moisture-soaked walls. She turned to peer through the roiling mist. Was it her imagination, or was the temperature within the sauna rising? Remembering the sound of wood being shoved into the stove, she turned back to the door, horror washing over her. Had someone deliberately blocked her only exit and built up the fire?

"Oh, my God..."

Crysta clutched her throat. There was no point in letting her imagination run away with her. It was probably a simple case of someone coming in with a load of wood, accidentally knocking over the woodpile and not being able to hear her yelling.

She knew from her occasional visits to the health club in Los Angeles that a healthy person could safely remain in an extremely hot steam bath for at least twenty minutes, and she had only been in here about fifteen. If the wood had toppled, which she felt certain it had, then the person she had heard in the other room had probably gone to get help to restack it.

The thing to do was remain calm and— The thought fragmented. And do what? her mind mocked. Slowly parboil? What if the person who had knocked over the wood didn't realize she was in here and took his time coming back? She could suffocate.

Crysta stumbled along the wall, fanning her foot across the floor and patting the shelves with her palm. Surely there was something in here that she could use for leverage on the door. A crowbar would be nice, though she didn't imagine Sam would leave anything metal in here to rust.

Crysta circled until her knees connected sharply with the end of the steam bench. So much for finding a tool of some kind. Pausing a moment to listen, she forced herself to breathe evenly. The last thing she should do was overreact and exert herself.

Sweat streamed down her body. The air tasted hot and thick as it rolled across her tongue. Too thick to breathe. Had the mysterious wood bearer opened the damper on the stove? Stay calm. She couldn't hear any voices filtering in from outside. If she screamed, would anyone outside be able to hear her?

Crysta moved toward the door. Her knees felt strangely weak and shaky. The extreme heat was already sapping her strength. This couldn't be happening. Someone would come. When she didn't return to the lodge, Sam would surely come down to check on her.

Feeling somewhat reassured, Crysta walked face first into
the door and staggered backward, cupping her hand over
her nose. Stay calm. Sam would come. As nightmarish as
this was, she would laugh about it later. Hot air rises. If
worse came to worse, she could lie on the floor. Her head
already felt light, her body leaden. How much longer did she
have before she succumbed to the heat?

"Help! Someone, help me! I'm in the sauna!"

Crysta screamed again and again. She lost track of what
she said or how many times she called out. She leaned
against the door, trying to work her fingers into the cracks.
If she could find purchase for a grip, perhaps she could open
it against its hinges. Her fingernails tore. Her hands began
to throb.

She had no idea how much time passed. She only knew
that her thoughts were growing disjointed and that every
breath she drew seemed to go about halfway down her
throat and stop there. She sank to her knees, giving way to
panic, clawing frantically at the wood. She had to get out of
here. Frightened now, really frightened, she began to pound
futilely with her fists, screaming until her throat felt raw. No
one responded. In the back of her mind, she realized her
voice was growing weak.

She sank onto her side, pressing her face to the seam of
the threshold, praying that cool air might be seeping in.
"Sam! Sam!" A sob caught in her chest. Dizziness rolled
over her.

Chapter Ten

"Where's Crys?"

At the question, Sam glanced up from his desk, focusing on Tip, who had just wandered into the office. A smear of paint angled across the boy's cheek, and his hair looked as if he had stuck his head in the blender.

"She's taking a nap."

Tip looked perplexed. "Uh-uh. I just knocked on the bedroom door, and she didn't answer. I, um, wanted to show her my painting of Derrick."

Sam dragged his attention from the paper work again, fighting down irritation. He'd been neglecting Tip for days. Who could blame the boy for wanting some attention? "She's probably sound asleep, Tip. She's really tired."

A flush crept up Tip's neck. "She isn't in bed. I peeked."

"You what?"

"I knocked first."

"Tip, you know you shouldn't open a lady's bedroom door. She might have been asleep and out from under the covers. Some people don't wear pajamas. I've explained that to you."

"She wasn't in there." Tip turned a deeper red. "I wouldn't look if she was undressed, Dad."

Sam grinned in spite of himself. "Tip, it's a little hard not to look if a naked lady pops up in front of you. Rules are rules. Don't intrude on Crysta's privacy again. She's probably down at the sauna. When she comes back, I want your promise that you won't open her door again, unless she invites you in."

Tip sighed and rolled his eyes. "I promise." He gave an exaggerated shrug. "I don't see the big deal. I see you, and you see me."

"That's different."

"How come?"

Sam leaned back in his chair, studying his son. He sincerely hoped this wasn't a sign that it was time for a serious discussion about sex. As much as he hoped Tip might one day have a normal life and possibly even marry, Sam was too exhausted today to tackle such a weighty subject. "Ladies are different." Sam made a vague gesture at his body.

Curiosity gleamed in Tip's eyes. "I know *that,* Dad."

Sam sighed. "Anyway, they're extremely..." He paused, searching for a word Tip would understand. "Bashful. Like you are when you show your paintings? They don't like it when fellas barge in uninvited and see them without clothes."

"How come they have their pictures taken naked, then?"

Sam stiffened. "Pardon?"

"You know, like in those magazines."

"What magazines?"

Tip blushed, shrugging. "Just magazines some of the guests bring. You know the kind."

"You never mentioned that some of our guests had pictures of naked ladies, Tip."

"There were only a couple, and I figured you knew."

Sam cleared his throat, fighting down a surge of irritation toward the unnamed men who had shown so little discretion in exposing a young innocent boy to graphic sexual photos. He didn't want Tip's attitudes toward women molded by such trash. "I'd really rather you didn't look at that kind of picture again, Tip."

"Is it bad to look?"

"No, not *bad* exactly. But those types of magazines exploit women, and I disapprove." Sam could see that was over Tip's head. With a sigh, he braced his elbows on the desk and smiled. "I think we need to talk. This afternoon

I'm very busy, and I'm worried about Derrick. But by next week, things should calm down. We'll take a lunch up Antler Slough. How's that sound?''

"Fun." Tip scratched his cheek, frowning when he felt the paint. Wiping his fingers on his shirt, he added, "I won't look at any naked lady pictures again."

"Good." Sam started to scold about the paint smear but decided Jangles would probably scold enough for both of them when she found the shirt in the laundry. Heaving another sigh, Sam waved his hand. "Get out of here, you rapscallion. We'll talk later, okay?"

After the door closed, Sam gave a weary chuckle and cupped his hand over his eyes. Did the complications of parenthood never cease?

FIVE MINUTES LATER, the door to Sam's office crashed open again. Tip stood in the doorway, his face washed of color, his mouth working. Sam could see something was wrong. The last time Tip had made an entrance like this, an extremely hefty guest had fallen out of a boat, and the three men on board couldn't haul her back in.

"Calm down, Tip. Take a deep breath."

Tip gasped for air, his eyes bulging. "Crys—Crys—wood—the door. I—I tried to m-move it, but I was t-taking too long. You g-gotta c-ome. Qu—quick!"

Sam leaped up from his chair. "Crysta? Where is she?"

Tip fought to speak, waving wildly behind him. "The s-sau-sauna."

"Oh, Lord!"

Sam raced from the lodge, Tip riding his heels. It seemed as if it took forever to reach the sauna. Sam lunged up the steps and threw the door wide. The sight that greeted him made his blood run cold. The pile of firewood had toppled, blocking the interior door. Crysta's clothes hung on the wall hook.

She was inside.

Sam began tossing wood out of his path. Tip dived in to help. The fire in the stove was roaring, throwing off so much heat that Sam could scarcely breathe. Due to the amount of wood in his way, it took at least two minutes to clear a swath, every second of which resounded inside Sam's head like the ticking of a time bomb. Hurry, hurry. He kicked aside the last piece of wood, grabbed the door and threw it wide. A wall of steam spilled over him. He stumbled forward, fear clawing at his guts.

"Crysta!" His boot bumped into something soft. Sam dropped to his knees, groping, afraid of what he might find. His hands connected with feverish flesh. "Crysta!"

Lifting her limp body into his arms, Sam stood and shouldered his way past Tip to get outdoors. Tip came running out behind him, holding Crysta's towel. Sam wasn't sure covering her was a good idea. He laid her gently on the ground and pressed his fingertips to her throat, feeling for a pulse. At first he detected nothing. Then he felt a weak flutter.

"Tip, run and soak that towel in the cool water tub. Wet down several and bring them back here. Hurry, son!"

Uncertain if Crysta was breathing, Sam quickly shifted her to a position that would give him access for resuscitation. Relief filled him when he felt her chest rise and fall on its own beneath his hands. Tip returned with the towels. Sam wrung them out over Crysta's body. Steve Henderson came running up.

"Is she—alive?"

"Yes, thank God." Sam scooped Crysta into his arms, grabbing a towel from Tip to cover her. "Steve, go tell Jangles. Hurry. She'll know what to do."

CRYSTA SURFACED to consciousness slowly, aware of the light touch of a man's hand on her hair and the ceaseless timbre of a deep voice. Slitting her eyelids, she peered upward. Sam Barrister's dark face came into focus. Behind him, she saw Tip, worrying his pale bottom lip between his teeth.

Then she remembered.

"Sam!" she cried in a hoarse voice, trying to sit up. Her body felt strangely heavy.

"Whoa..." He caught her shoulders, pressing her back down. "It's over now. You're safe in bed."

"The door—it wouldn't open!" Crysta swallowed, wincing at the fiery rawness of her throat. "I screamed and screamed."

"Tip found you." He cupped his hand over her cheek. "You're one lucky lady. A few more minutes and it would've—" He trailed his thumb along her cheekbone. "Want some water? The doctor says we have to pump fluids down you."

"Doctor?"

"We called the hospital in Anchorage. Luckily, Jangles is a fair nurse. A little unorthodox, but she gets the job done." Sliding an arm under her shoulders, Sam helped her sit partway up and held a glass of cool water to her lips. "Not too fast."

Crysta gulped greedily, sucking air when he withdrew the tumbler. It took all her concentration to lift her arm and swipe the sleeve of the lightweight cotton shirt she wore across her mouth. Judging by the shirt's large proportions, she guessed it to be her host's. Exhausted from the supreme effort it had taken to move, she managed a weak smile. "I feel like I've been run over by a train."

He eased her back onto the pillows. "I can't believe it happened. The wood has been stacked along that wall for years, and it's never fallen like that before."

Crysta closed her eyes for a moment. If she lived to be a hundred, she'd never forget how frightened she had been. She tried to reposition her hips, then abandoned the idea. Her muscles felt as if they were made of cold rubber. She shivered and made a feeble tug at the crisp bed sheet, wondering who had changed the linen. "I'm freezing, Sam. May I have a blanket?"

"Not for a while. The reason you're so cold is that we've been rubbing you down with water, trying to lower your body temperature. If I pile blankets on you, it'll defeat our purpose."

A fleeting image of Sam running wet cloths over her naked body hit Crysta, but for the moment she was far too exhausted to expend energy worrying about it. She shivered again, hugging the sheet closer with arms that felt strangely disconnected from her body. "I'm freezing."

"Your temperature is probably still a little high, and your skin is chilled from the ice water. It's like getting chills with a fever. It'll pass."

"My head hurts. Can you draw the blind?"

He quickly accommodated her, then sat back down on the bed.

Crysta licked her lips, longing for more water but too weak to reach for it. She thought of asking Sam for some, but since she'd just had him draw the blind, she hesitated.

"Someone came in there—with wood, I think," she whispered. "Then the woodpile toppled. I called out, but I guess my voice didn't carry to the anteroom. Whoever it was stoked the fire and left without answering. When I tried to open the door, it was blocked."

Sam took one of her hands in his, examining her torn nails. Glancing over his shoulder at Tip, he said, "Didn't you do your chores this morning, son?"

Tip's eyes widened. "I d-did them."

"Did you forget to restock the sauna's wood supply?"

"N-no. I took two loads in. And I stacked it real nice, j-just like you sh-showed me."

Crysta angled an arm across her forehead, squinting through the gloom at Tip. He looked worried about being blamed for her mishap. The throbbing ache in her temples grew worse. "I saw Tip carrying wood in that direction earlier today. There was plenty when I went in, and the pile was neat as a pin."

Sam's gaze rested solemnly on hers. "There's something you're not saying."

Tension knotted Crysta's stomach. "It's so silly that I hate to bring it up."

"Humor me."

"Well…" She drew her arm down from her forehead. "I sort of panicked, I guess, and while I was trying to get out, the thought occurred to me that someone might have—" She broke off and toyed with the sheet.

Sam glanced over his shoulder at Tip. "Son, go and ask Jangles if she'd mind making Crysta a cup of tea. It might take her chills away."

Tip's brown eyes sharpened. He gave Crysta a curious study. Sam reached out and gave the boy a playful punch on the arm. "Go on, Tip. *Now.*"

After Tip left, Crysta waited for Sam to speak. He raked his fingers through his hair, heaving a tired sigh. "You think someone did it on purpose, don't you?"

"The thought crossed my mind." Crysta pushed up on her elbow to take another drink of water. Wooziness hit her. She blinked, trying to bring the spinning room into focus. With a trembling hand, she reached toward the nightstand. "It was probably silly, but one tends to think all kinds of weird things when something like that happens."

Sam helped her steady the glass and press it to her lips. "I'm not so sure it was silly. While Jangles was sponging you off to get your temperature down, I went to the sauna. The damper on the stove was wide open, and the firebox was completely filled with wood. We never put that much in there."

Crysta's scalp prickled. "You aren't saying—" She let him take the glass. Sinking back against the pillows, she stared at him. "But, Sam, I could have died in there."

"You very nearly did."

Crysta closed her eyes. "It's crazy. Who would want me dead?"

"Maybe no one. It could have been an accident. It's possible your voice didn't carry to the anteroom, just as you said. And given the near-disastrous outcome, I really can't blame someone for not coming forward and admitting he toppled the wood. Maybe I'm jumping at shadows again."

He turned to gaze at the shade-covered window, then, at the sound of footsteps outside, he leaped up and jerked aside the blind.

"Sam, what is it?"

He stepped close to the wall, peering sideways through the glass. "It was Jangles," he said in a thoughtful voice.

"She's going down toward the river, toward the trees. There's a man with her."

"The Indian?" Crysta asked hoarsely.

Sam nodded, a frown pleating his forehead. "If a friend of hers is coming to visit, I wonder why she doesn't just ask him in."

Crysta had no answer to that unless Jangles wanted to keep the man's visits to herself. "A boyfriend, do you think?"

Sam watched them for a moment. Then a halfhearted smile touched his mouth. "I guess. He just hugged her goodbye."

That revelation eased Crysta's mind somewhat. "Maybe she's afraid you'd disapprove."

He sighed and rubbed his forehead. "I'd worry, more than likely. If she gets married and I lose her, I don't know what we'll do without her. It's not easy to find help who's willing to live this far from Anchorage for half the year." Returning to sit beside her, he waved the subject of Jangles aside and said, "Back to more immediate concerns. I want you to be more careful from here on in. Try to stay around people—me, Tip, Jangles. I'd rather be safe than sorry."

"I just went to take a steam bath," she reminded him.

"Next time, I'll go down with you."

Remembering the thick steam, she suppressed a shudder. "It'll be a while before I go back."

"It's going to be a while before you do much of anything. The doctor says you have to rest for twenty-four hours. He wants us to pour at least four gallons of fluid into you."

"Twenty-four hours!" Despite her weakness, Crysta could scarcely bear the thought of being confined to bed that long. "Sam, no! We have to go to Anchorage."

"You're dehydrated."

"So? I'll drink water on the way!" She tried to sit up again and immediately felt dizzy. Sam caught her shoulder to steady her. "I'm not staying in bed an entire day!"

She threw her legs over the edge of the bed and pushed to her feet. A wave of dizziness washed over her, and Sam had to catch her from falling.

"There, you see?" he said. "You're ill, Crysta, and you're going to follow doctor's orders and stay in bed if I have to sit on you." He helped her to lie back down. "Feel fortunate I didn't have you flown in to the Anchorage hospital. If Jangles hadn't assured me she knew how to take care of you, that's what I would have done. Getting trapped in a steam room and losing consciousness is no laughing matter."

Crysta could see by the grim set of his mouth that he wouldn't waver, no matter how she argued. "Then why don't you go?" she cried in a voice thick with frustration. "I can describe the building. Maybe you could find it."

"There are several warehouses, and I'm sure they'd all look pretty much the same to me. Besides, I'm not leaving you." He shot a nervous glance at the window. "Not after finding that stove stoked full and the damper wide open. Prepare yourself for a day of constant company."

"I'll go crazy lying here."

"We'll go through Derrick's papers some more."

"A lot of good that will do Derrick!"

Thoughts of her brother were Crysta's undoing. The tears in her eyes spilled over onto her cheeks, prompting her to avert her face and rub blindly at them with the sleeve of Sam's shirt. She knew Sam was right; she was too weak to go anywhere. Feeling so helpless infuriated her.

"If we run out of papers to go through, I'm a great hand at chess," he offered in a gentle voice.

She groaned.

"Rummy?"

No longer caring if he saw her tears, Crysta turned to look at him. "Bring on the briefcase."

IN ADDITION TO GIVING Sam and Crysta further opportunity to study Derrick's papers, the day's delay, though frustrating, afforded Sam, Crysta and Tip a getting-acquainted time, during which they began to forge strong bonds of friendship. Crysta, with some tactful questioning during one of Tip's absences, discovered that Tip's mother, an ambitious interior decorator who couldn't cope with the hardships of raising a learning-impaired child, had walked out before the boy's second birthday. As much as that knowledge made Crysta's heart ache for Tip, she felt even sorrier for Sam. The pain and disillusionment his wife had caused him still lurked in his eyes when he spoke of her.

When Tip left the bedroom again to make some popcorn, Crysta lay back against the pillows and absently shuffled the deck of cards. "I guess we all have our heartbreaks," she said softly. "It makes you wonder if love is all it's cracked up to be."

"Janet didn't know how to love," Sam replied matter-of-factly. "Doesn't say much for my preferences in women, does it?"

"Maybe the fault lay in her, Sam. You can't beat up on yourself for making one bad call."

"It wasn't just a bad call, not with a child involved." His jaw tensed. "Janet lacked the nurturing qualities you need to be a parent. Somehow, I failed to see that, and my son paid the price. Tip was like a toy to her. She loved to play with him when the mood struck, but her energies were mainly directed toward her career, and when it became apparent that Tip would demand far more time than she could comfortably give him, she walked out."

Crysta couldn't think of anything to say, so she said nothing.

"When I look back on it, I don't know how I could have thought I loved her." He made a feeble gesture and shrugged. "I was young—too young, I guess. She was pretty and vivacious and lighthearted. I didn't see the selfish side of her until she settled into marriage and stopped putting her best foot forward." He looked up, straight into Crysta's eyes. "For Tip's sake, I tried to make the marriage work, and even that turned out to be a mistake. She stayed just long enough for Tip to love her and then disappeared from his life." His eyes grew distant and shadowed. "I never could understand how she could abandon Tip. Me, yes, but not him."

Crysta had no answers. In the short time she had known Tip, she had already lost a piece of her heart to him.

"Those first few weeks after she left, I wanted to go after her and throttle her," Sam admitted raggedly. "Hearing my son cry for her, knowing she was probably out on the town with a bunch of yuppies, not even thinking of him...it made me crazy. Sometimes I'd lie awake imagining how satisfying it would be to strangle her."

After an extremely long silence, Crysta touched his hand. "We all get a little crazy sometimes. If you ever meet Dick, ask him about the condition of the bed sheets I gave him when he moved out."

Some of the seriousness eased from Sam's eyes. "There's a story in there somewhere."

Crysta smothered a smile. To this day, the memory gave her a feeling of satisfaction. "He did say that he wanted to *split* the sheets. Far be it from me not to accommodate him."

Sam shouted with laughter. Crysta grinned.

"The moral is that we all get a little radical if someone pushes the right buttons. For you, it was seeing your son suffer. For me, it was taking a back seat to silk sheets. The fact that he already had a girlfriend had absolutely *nothing* to do with it." She slanted a smile at him. "Well, maybe a little."

He was still smiling, though sadly. "You still loved him?"

"Truthfully?" It was Crysta's turn to shrug. "Yes. The divorce was his decision, not mine, though I didn't fight it. He took exception to the fact that my brother intruded into our lives so much."

She took a deep breath and let it out slowly. "Anyway, live and learn. In this day and age, marriage isn't the be-all and end-all of a woman's existence. My life is full now. My shop is thriving. I have lots of friends. And, living alone as I do, it doesn't matter if I wake up from a dream in the middle of the night, convinced my brother needs me."

Sam studied her thoughtfully. "Is it so bad to be needed?"

The skin across her cheekbones felt tight as she forced a smile. "Only if there's a husband around to come unglued. To Derrick and me, that kind of thing seems normal. Not that it *is*." She swallowed. "My analyst believes our mother brainwashed us, and that because Derrick and I are so convinced our dreams are based in fact, we manipulate events to make them come true."

"And do you believe that?"

"I've tried."

His eyes darkened. "Your analyst's theory sounds like hogwash to me. What's normal anyway? I have a problem with that word."

"Be that as it may, I've spent three years and thousands of dollars on counseling since the divorce, trying for that enviable state." She bent the cards backward and let them rain onto her lap. "What you said about being uniquely me hit home. We can't change what we are, no matter how we might try."

"The right man will come along."

She shook her head. "No man would put up with the intrusions in my life, not Dick or anyone. I was the one who couldn't fit into the mold."

"Crysta, the *right* man would understand about Derrick. Don't sell marriage down the river just because you tried it once and failed."

"You're a fine one to talk. You're not ready to risk getting burned again. I can see it in your eyes."

He gathered the cards from her lap and gave them an expert shuffle, tapping them into line on his bent knee. "I met another woman. About five years ago." He flashed a humorless smile. "That time, I thought I was going into it with my eyes open, choosing a woman who was the opposite from Janet—a homebody, not particularly attractive, more serious in nature." His mouth twisted. "I didn't love her. At that point, I was still convinced my child needed a mother. I liked her, and after the experience with Janet, that seemed more important to me than romance."

"What happened?"

He cut the cards, turning up a three, which seemed to amuse him. "With my usual unerring accuracy, I'd chosen badly. If you want lessons on how to strike out every time you go to bat, just give me a call and I'll give you pointers."

"I've done fine with no help," she inserted with a laugh.

"A few days after I gave her the ring, I saw some notes by her telephone. I asked her what they were about. She hedged and then finally admitted she was checking on boarding schools for Tip. End of relationship."

"There are lots of women who would treasure a son like Tip."

"There are special problems raising a handicapped child. A lifetime of them. It's a rare woman who would take them on when the child wasn't hers. These last few years, I've come to realize Tip is doing fine just as things are. I'm content to remain single."

"Content or merely resigned? Tip's handicap isn't that debilitating. The right woman will love him, Sam."

"Will she? You've no idea how often he's been hurt by people. Here, in this setting, he's shielded. The real world is cruel, and kids like Tip get kicked in the teeth. I can't subject him to another rejection."

"Is that why you get so upset about the idea of him showing his paintings?"

His face tightened. "Is it so wrong for Tip to take joy from his art as a hobby? If I let him enter an art show and some critic lacerates him, he'll never again recapture the magic he feels for painting. Painting is Tip's *life*."

"Living life to its fullest means being shot down sometimes. You're holding Tip back, in the one arena where he can excel. Maybe he will get lacerated by art critics. Most big talents usually are. But then again, maybe he'll set the world on fire. Have you considered that?"

"You sound just like Derrick."

She arched an eyebrow. "My brother and I tend to think alike." Growing quiet, she studied his dark face, remembering his scrapbook of Tip's childhood and her initial feeling that Sam was an exceptional father. "I know you love Tip. More importantly, Tip knows. Let him take his knocks, Sam, and be there for him when he needs support. That's what parents are for."

"You're forgetting that Tip is handicapped."

"So was Beethoven."

A soft knock cut their conversation short. Sam got up to answer the door. Todd Shriver stood framed in the doorway.

"I invited myself in," he explained. "I knocked on the front door, but you didn't hear me. Didn't want to be too loud for fear Ms. Meyers might be asleep." Flashing a grin at Crysta, he added, "I heard about your mishap. Now I see I was worrying over nothing. You look fit as a fiddle."

Crysta raised a delicate eyebrow. "I wish you could convince Sam of that."

"Wise fellow, Sam. After what you've been through, a day's rest is probably a good idea."

"Except that I have far more important things to be doing."

Shriver smiled. "Careful. You don't want to earn yourself the reputation of being a difficult patient."

"Impossible is more like it." Sam settled laughing brown eyes on Crysta. She was relieved to see that he didn't seem angry with her for speaking so candidly about his son. "I'll be glad when we're on our way to Anchorage tomorrow so she'll stop needling me."

"Tip mentioned that you two wanted to fly back with me. Going to have her checked over by a doctor?"

Sam shook his head. "No, actually, we have some other business there. Although, her seeing a doctor isn't a bad idea."

"Bite your tongue, Mr. Shriver. Now see what you've done?" Crysta rolled her eyes. "I'm perfectly fine, I tell you."

Returning to sit on the bed, Sam braced an arm behind him, his side pressing warmly against the sheet that covered Crysta's legs. To the pilot, he said, "It's not a problem, your staying overnight, is it? If so, we could probably hop a flight with someone else.''

Todd rested his shoulder against the door frame. ''I wouldn't hear of it. Tomorrow evening the lodge upriver from here is due for a delivery of gasoline. After I get the plane loaded, I have a bunch of errands I can attend to. Taking you out and bringing you back will work out fine for me.''

''Good,'' Sam said.

Shriver's gaze slid to Crysta. ''Planning to pick up Derrick's personal effects?''

''Um, yes, I suppose I might do that while I'm there.''

''Well, I'm glad to get a chance to help out.''

Sam rose from the bed and moved casually toward the door, effecting Shriver's dismissal without having to suggest it. ''We'll see you first thing in the morning then.''

THE WINDUP CLOCK struck midnight, its steady ticking a comfort to Crysta. Sam had lain with his head on this pillow. Being in his room, warmed by his quilt, she felt far more secure than she probably should have.

She lay staring at the twilight beyond the bedroom window, her thoughts on Derrick. As horrible as her last dream had been, she no longer had the frightening sensation that Derrick was dead. The intermittent communication from him proved he wasn't. Her earlier suspicion that the silence inside her might be due to Derrick's being unconscious now had merit. It was a slender thread of hope, but at least it was hope.

The creaking of the door brought Crysta's gaze around. Sam poked his head into the room, then, upon seeing her awake, stepped inside. In one hand, he held some papers. ''How's the head?''

''Much better.''

He glanced toward the jug of water on the nightstand. ''Looks like you've got the third gallon almost whipped.''

''Almost.''

Crysta checked the buttons on the shirt she wore, feeling suddenly self-conscious. During the endless hours of enforced bed rest, she had been afforded plenty of time to contemplate her state of undress when Sam had rescued her from the sauna.

"You feel up to talking?" he asked.

"Sure." Crysta pushed herself up against the pillows, pulling the sheet high. The mattress sank under Sam's weight as he sat beside her. She noted that his eyes seemed shadowed.

"Jim called a while ago."

Crysta stared at him, knowing what he was going to say. "The blood was Derrick's, wasn't it?"

"Preliminary tests show it's the same type."

She took a deep breath. "It's no more than I expected."

He held the papers aloft. "I think maybe I've found something."

Her heart leaped. "What?"

"Now, don't get your hopes up. It could be nothing."

"*What*, Sam? The suspense is killing me."

He spread the papers out, some on his lap, some on hers. "Invoices for conduit, all marked returned. Some have question marks and notes in the margins in Derrick's handwriting."

"So?"

Sam glanced up. "Crysta, don't return shipment documents for each order strike you as odd?"

"Not particularly. If you order way too much of something, you return it. Why keep your capital tied up in stock?"

He held up a staying hand. "You're thinking small-business practices. Think West Coast corporation a minute. Blanchette has a lot of building sites in Alaska, and several warehouses, so storage space isn't a concern. If you'll need conduit at another site within a few months, does it make good sense to return your surplus? When you reorder, you have more shipment costs. Prices might go up. Double whammy, and not cost effective. You're the retailer. Am I off base in my reasoning?"

Crysta's mind clicked into gear. She sat more erect. "All right, I see your angle. It *doesn't* make sense to rack up extra shipping costs to return something you'll have to reorder soon thereafter.'' She quickly scanned the papers Sam had spread across her lap. "But what's the point, Sam? It may be odd, but why would someone do it?"

"I'm not sure. I only know it struck me as odd when I noticed it, and—" he tapped Derrick's initials on one of the invoices "—I think Derrick may have picked up on it, too. It isn't much to go on, but at least it's something."

Crysta slowly nodded, excitement building within her. Glancing at the clock, she said, "I can hardly wait to leave for Anchorage. Maybe we'll find that warehouse I dreamed of, Sam. Maybe we'll find out what it was Derrick went there about."

"Maybe. At least it's a lead. Which is more than we had."

Gathering up the documents, Sam avoided her gaze, still uncomfortable when she alluded to her dreams. Earlier today, he had, on two occasions, encouraged Crysta to be true to herself. He had insisted that those people who were incapable of accepting her as she was weren't worthy to be her friends, that the *right* man would understand her relationship with Derrick. Now Sam found himself in the unenviable position of wanting to be Crysta's friend—possibly even more—but at the same time, doubting her.

To believe or not to believe, that was the question.

Chapter Eleven

The following day was overcast. After another harrowing flight in Todd Shriver's Cessna, Crysta was eager to leave the Lake Hood Airport in the cab Sam commandeered. She settled back in the seat beside him, fighting down a rush of anxiety as the cab wound its way through the city's streets toward the outskirts of town, where Blanchette's Anchorage offices were located.

Sam seemed as nervous as she, shifting position and glancing through the rear window. When they had nearly reached their destination, she noted his odd behavior and followed his gaze.

"Is something wrong?"

Sam looked a little sheepish. "I thought there was another cab following us. Shadows again. I think it turned off about three blocks back."

Memories of being trapped in the sauna washed over Crysta. She turned forward again and folded her arms, shivering. The smell of new vinyl inside the cab made her feel slightly nauseated. Sam could lay his paranoia off on jumping at shadows all he liked, but that didn't alter the fact that someone might have tried to kill her.

"Cold?"

The weather was oppressive enough without her dragging Sam's spirits down with hers. Hesitant to admit she had shivered with foreboding, she opted to tell a small white lie. "A little chilly."

Sam immediately slipped an arm around her shoulders and drew her against his side. Still feeling a bit self-conscious about his seeing her unclad the previous day, Crysta stiffened at the unexpected familiarity and glanced up. The dark depths of his eyes heated, catching glints of light, warming her.

"Don't," he whispered.

"Don't what?"

He tightened his arm around her and settled himself more comfortably against the door. "You know perfectly well what. The entire incident is a blur to me, and that's the truth."

Crysta, who should have been an old hand at having her thoughts read, felt her cheeks flush. Sam wasn't Derrick, and his perceptiveness made her feel vulnerable. She started to avert her face, but Sam caught her chin so she couldn't.

"I mean it. You're feeling embarrassed over nothing."

Crysta nibbled at her bottom lip, fastening her gaze on his chin, which was far more comfortable than making eye contact with him. "It's silly for me to be embarrassed, at any rate."

"You wouldn't be normal if you weren't," he whispered. "And as I recall, being *normal* is of great importance to you."

His teasing tone sliced through the charged atmosphere, relieving her tension, which, if she was honest, wasn't totally due to embarrassment. There was Derrick's plight, the attempt on her life, the days of ceaseless worry, all of which had her nerves worn raw. His invitation to banter offered her an escape from the serious, no matter how brief, and lured her irresistibly. She slid her gaze to his and flashed a dubious smile.

"You honestly don't remember anything? I'm not at all sure *you're* normal, if that's the case."

It was his turn to grin. "I didn't go stone blind, exactly. I just—" He broke off and chuckled. "Crysta, there's looking at someone, and then there's *looking*. Let's just say that if you stood in a lineup of a dozen women, I couldn't pick you out. Is that any comfort?"

"On the one hand, yes. On the other, though, I'm not sure it's very flattering."

He barked with laughter. The cab pulled up in front of the Blanchette offices just then, and he released her to fish in his jeans pocket for cab fare. Crysta beat him to the draw by pulling some ready cash from the side pocket of her purse.

"Lunch is on me," he grumbled as they exited the cab.

The sky hung low above them, a depressing, heavy gray. Crysta took a deep breath of the salty air. "We're trying to find my brother. I should pay the expenses."

"Correction, we're trying to find my friend. Therefore, I should pay the expenses. Besides, he did get lost while staying at my lodge." Crysta had already come to realize how proud Sam was, but she also knew he didn't have much cash in reserve, and she hated for this trip to become an expense he could ill afford. "Look, you've waived all my lodging costs, so how about if we go halves from now on?"

"Fair enough."

They fell into step with each other, breaking apart to circle a wash of mud. Crysta inclined her head toward the office. "Since I'm Derrick's sister, I'll handle this, okay?"

"Fine by me."

The closer they came to the office, the more tense Crysta felt. What if she couldn't finagle her way into the warehouse? Sam took the steps two at a time, reaching the door to sweep it open for her. Once again in a teasing tone, he said, "I suppose you're the type who insists on paying your share when a man takes you out."

Crysta, grateful for his attempt to keep her spirits rallying, rose to the challenge with what she hoped was an impish grin. "Is that an invitation?"

Sam followed her inside. "I'm old-fashioned when it comes to that. If we go out, I insist on paying."

"How quaint." She aimed her footsteps toward the visitors' information desk, then glanced back over her shoulder. "When?"

"When what?"

"When are we going?"

His eyes lit up with laughter. "When I *ask* you."

"You *are* old-fashioned. I was thinking about asking you."

"I accept."

He slowed his pace, drawing up behind her as she approached the blonde at the desk. Crysta introduced herself. After listening patiently to the receptionist stress how sorry she was to hear about Derrick, Crysta homed in on her purpose for being there.

"I was wondering if my friend, Mr. Barrister, and I could take a tour of the warehouses. I, um . . ." Crysta didn't find it hard to look as if she might burst into tears. "I'd like very much to see where my brother worked. I always planned to come, you see. He wanted me to. And now . . ."

"I understand," the pretty blonde inserted in a kindly voice. "And it's no problem at all. In fact, we issue visitor passes all the time. But, Miss Meyers, Derrick didn't have an office. He traveled from site to site, you see, and carried his paperwork with him. I'm afraid that—"

"No, no, I came in hopes of visiting the warehouses."

"Well, that's no problem at all. Let me make you up a list of addresses. We have maps of each complex, too."

Within moments, Crysta had two visitor passes in her possession, and Sam, exiting the office beside her, was studying the list of warehouses.

"The main warehouse is right here in this complex," he told her as they stepped out onto the porch.

A gust of wind hit Crysta, so strong she nearly lost her footing. Sweeping her hair from her eyes, she leaned into the current and went down the steps. "Point me in the right direction."

"You don't recognize anything?"

Crysta shot him a knowing glance. "I didn't dream about the outside of the warehouse, Sam. The dream started inside, walking down the aisle. If you're going to test me, at least be fair."

"I'm not trying to test you."

"Yes, you are."

"Okay, I am. You've no idea how relieved I'd be to see some tangible proof that there's something to those dreams of yours."

Crysta wondered if that was true. As they rounded the office building and struck off toward the aluminum-sided warehouse, she found herself hoping she could provide Sam with that proof. For some reason that she wasn't quite willing to analyze, it had become extremely important to her that he believe, truly believe, in her dreams.

BLUE-WHITE LIGHT bathed the interior of the building, coming from fluorescent tubes suspended in rows from the lofty rafters. The musty-sweet smell of lumber and the heavy fumes of engine exhaust tainted the sea air that breezed in through the massive bay door. Crysta stopped just inside, scarcely noticing the bright yellow hoister that bucked past them.

"This is it," she whispered.

"You're sure? One warehouse looks like another."

"I'm sure." Crysta moved forward, her skin chilled, her legs oddly numb. "I can't explain, but I know this is it."

Looking into Crysta's eyes, Sam had the uneasy feeling that she was no longer really with him. She struck off walking, not watching where she put her feet, her gaze distant. He hurried to catch up and grasped her arm. A forklift nearby grated its gears and lifted a bundle of shingle siding. Another hoister bounced across the loading zone. Neither driver seemed aware that two visitors had entered the area. Tiers of building supplies peppered the broad expanse of concrete floor.

"Crysta?" Her arm felt brittle under his fingers. His gaze shifted to a crane, which suspended an ominous-looking load of three-foot culvert above their heads. In a place like this, an oblivious person could all too easily become a grease spot on the concrete. "Don't get spacey on me."

She kept walking as if he hadn't spoken. Sam tightened his hold on her, attempting to guide her footsteps. At first she seemed to wander, then he felt her pick up the pace. She was heading toward a center aisle. As they stepped into it,

Sam had the sensation that he had entered a narrow hallway, except, of course, that the walls were rows of packing boxes.

When the end of the aisle came into view, Crysta slowed her steps. "The crates and boxes I saw are gone."

Sam followed her gaze to some empty pallets. Crysta started forward again, scanning the concrete floor. When they came upon a splotch of green paint, her slender body stiffened. He increased the pressure of his grip on her arm, frightened without knowing why, possibly because of the expression on her pale face.

"The paint, Sam! It's here, just as I dreamed it was."

To Sam's discomfiture, Crysta jerked free from his grasp and dropped to her knees by an empty pallet. Lying forward over her thighs, she shoved her arm under the framework. He glanced uneasily behind them. If someone happened along and saw her, Sam had no idea how he would explain her odd behavior.

"It's here, I know it is!"

"Crysta, get up from there. What are you doing?"

Ignoring him, she fanned her arm under the slats of wood. "I have to find it. It'll be proof, don't you see? *Proof*, Sam!"

"Proof of what? What are you looking for?"

"It fell from his buckle! Right here, Sam! By the paint!"

"Crysta, warehouses always have paint spills on the floor."

She gave a cry of triumph and pulled her arm from under the pallet. Scrambling to her feet, she turned to face him, clutching something in her hand. Her eyes bright with unshed tears, she extended her arm toward him and unfurled her fingers. Upon her palm rested a silver dollar. An amateur numismatist, Sam knew by the muted sheen of the coin's finish that it was not only pure silver but also extremely old.

He stepped forward, his pulse accelerating. The 1906 dollar that Derrick had had fashioned into a belt buckle had been a gift from Sam. Finding a silver dollar under a warehouse pallet might be odd yet still explainable, but if that dollar in her hand was a 1906, even Sam would have to admit it was too much to be coincidence. With tense fingers, he lifted the coin from her palm to read the date.

Shifting his gaze from the coin to Crysta's face, Sam saw that her mouth was quivering. "I'm *not* crazy. This is proof, Sam."

Curling his fingers around the coin, Sam stepped toward her, realizing, suddenly, how terribly important finding this coin had been to her. It went beyond providing proof for his benefit; it was proof for herself, a vindication after years of self-doubt. Forgetting about onlookers, not really caring at this point who might see, Sam caught her around the shoulders and hauled her against his chest to give her a comforting hug.

"Of course you're not crazy. I never thought you were."

"You didn't believe me, not completely."

"I had my reservations, but I didn't think, even for an instant, that you were crazy, Crysta."

"Do you believe me now?"

Drawing his arm from around her, Sam opened his hand and stared at the coin once more. "Yes, Crysta, I believe you. No doubts, no reservations."

The tension went out of her, and she leaned against him, pressing her face against his shoulder. "You'll never know how much it means to me to hear you say that."

"I only wish I'd said it earlier," he replied huskily.

She gave a wet little laugh and drew away, tilting her face up to meet his gaze, her own still bright with tears. "You were willing to stand by me, to be my friend, even with the doubts. That's what counts, Sam, more than you'll ever know."

Sam's throat tightened. Her friend? He didn't know when it had happened or why, but his intentions had subtly altered. Friendship with Crysta, as enjoyable as that might be, was no longer all he had in mind. That admission rocked him, and he wasn't yet ready to ask himself just what, exactly, he did have in mind.

Moving away from her, he said, "Well, we hit a dead end in one way." He nodded at the pallet. "No crates, no boxes. That adds up to no leads. Now what?"

Wiping at her cheeks with the sleeve of her jacket, she sniffed and glanced around them. "We check the other warehouses. Maybe the crates and boxes I dreamed about have been moved."

"And if the other warehouses turn up nothing?"

"Then we regroup and try to decide what to do next." A glint of determination crept into her hazel eyes. "From here on in, *defeat* isn't in my vocabulary. We aren't giving up."

"No." Sam flipped the coin into the air, palmed it, and slipped it into his pocket. "Let's go call a cab and hit the next warehouse."

NOTHING.

The word resounded in Crysta's head as she and Sam left the last warehouse. In the center of her chest, an ache began to spread, radiating down into her belly and up into her throat. Three warehouses, and they had found absolutely nothing. Images of Derrick, digging a bullet from his chest, swam in her mind. Her brother was dying out there while she toured warehouses in Anchorage. Never had she felt so frustrated... or so horribly guilty. This was her fault, all of it.

"Crysta?"

Sam's voice tugged her back from the nightmares to reality, which wasn't much better. Even the weather, misty and drab, seemed to spell doom. A car sped past, sending up a spray of water from the gutter. The way her luck was running, Crysta was surprised she hadn't been drenched to the skin.

"If you're going to ask me what we ought to do next, I don't know," she said in a shaky voice. "I'm fresh out of ideas."

He placed a warm, heavy hand on her shoulder. "Look, just because we've struck out so far doesn't mean we should give up. We're on to something here. We have to be."

Crysta glanced up and met his gaze. For several seconds they simply stood there, visually communicating what neither could verbalize. Something indefinable was happening between them, and Crysta sensed they would never totally forget or manage to sever the bonds they were forming today.

But what were those bonds? Friendship? That tag seemed pitifully inadequate. It was more of a melding. Sam had stood by her, following through on only the strength of her dreams, with no proof to motivate him. Because of that, she felt closer to him in some ways than she ever had to anyone, even Derrick.

"No, we can't give up." She took a deep breath and exhaled slowly, shoving her hands deep into her jacket pockets. "Not until there's no hope left. And as long as I'm getting periodic flashes of Derrick, there *is* hope."

For the first time since she had found the silver dollar, it struck Sam what all this meant. Her dreams were a reality. Derrick was still alive. There was a chance that he and Derrick would see one another again. If that happened, Sam vowed that he'd never again part company with his friend when either of them was angry. One couldn't count on tomorrow.

"Let's walk," he suggested. "I think better on the move."

Crysta fell into step beside him, staring down at their feet. Today, Sam had doffed the green rubber boots he usually wore in favor of the high-top leather ones she had seen sitting beside his bed. Jeans, boots, a flannel shirt. Not exactly sophisticated garb, but on Sam, it looked wonderful and right.

As they left the fenced enclosure, a Blanchette truck edged up to an open gate, braked, then spun out in the gravel and merged with the traffic. Crysta watched it travel down the street.

"Probably going to pick up a load at the docks," Sam said.

Crysta gnawed her lip. The truck was now a tiny orange blur, nearly lost to sight. "Sam, that's it!"

He scowled after the truck. "What's it? You've lost me."

"What if those boxes in my dream held something illegal? There were no others in any of the warehouses like them! What if they weren't supposed to be there?"

Clearly perplexed, Sam seemed to consider that angle. "Can you back up and run through that one more time? I'm not following."

Excitement soared within Crysta. "Think, Sam. Someone has been ordering too much conduit and sending the surplus back to Seattle. We've already concluded that doesn't make sense. Derrick agreed, or he wouldn't have made all those notes in the margins of the invoices!"

He nodded. "I follow that much."

"Last night, we couldn't figure out *why* someone would over-order and then return the surplus. We only knew it was odd. Think smuggling, Sam! An illegal commodity. How could you get something illegal out of Alaska and down to Seattle, where it could be marketed in the lower forty-eight?"

His gaze sharpened on hers, and his lips pursed to emit a low whistle. "Inside the conduit crates?"

"Exactly! Order too much, hide the commodity inside the crates of surplus, and return them! If you had someone waiting at the other end in Seattle who could remove the commodity from the crates before it was discovered, you'd have a perfect setup."

"Crysta, you're incredible!" He threw another glance down the street. "How did you get all that by seeing a truck?"

"Because of what you said! Picking up a load at the docks! It could go just the other way, returning stuff to the docks."

He nodded. "Of course. Brilliant of me to bring it up, wasn't it?"

She laughed softly and rolled her eyes. "So now, Mr. Brilliant, put on your thinking cap. What could have been in those smaller boxes that I dreamed of?"

"Something illegal?"

"Sam, this is serious."

"I'm being serious. Something illegal. The problem is, I don't have an inkling what. I'll leave it to you. You're the one on a roll."

Crysta pressed her back against the tall chain-link fence. "I haven't an inkling, either." She stared at a crack in the concrete. "So let's play what if."

He took a spot beside her, his arm pressing against her shoulder. "What if?"

"Yeah, what if. It goes like this. What if Derrick noticed the surplus of conduit, discovered it was being returned and came up with the same idea that I did, that someone was using the returned crates to transport an illegal commodity?"

"Then he'd try to figure out what the commodity was."

"How?"

"I imagine he'd come to the warehouse and open the crates that were about to be returned."

"And what if, when he came, he saw some smaller boxes, stacked near the crates, that didn't belong in the warehouse?"

Sam nodded. "If it were me, I'd open one."

"And when you were about to, what if the culprits came?"

Sam, clearly warming to the game, glanced down at her. "I don't know about you, but I'd run like a scalded dog."

"And what if, while you were running, your silver-dollar buckle came loose from your belt? You couldn't risk going back for it."

"I'd pray the culprits didn't find it, because if they did, they'd recognize it and realize I might be on to them."

"And if they did find it?"

"They'd be edgy." Sam met her gaze, his mouth tightening. "Depending on the size of their operation and the money they stood to lose, not to mention the prison sentence they might face, they'd weigh their options. If the costs would be steep on all counts, they'd get rid of me so I couldn't squeal."

"And what if, after they got rid of you, your sister flew to Alaska, asking questions and not accepting that you were dead?"

Sam's eyes took on a shimmer of anger. "They might try to scare her off with a gaffed salmon in her bed. If that failed, they might try to kill her, making it look like an accident."

"More than that, they'd probably decide to bring their operation to a halt for a while. Wouldn't you? Think of it, Sam. You're missing. Your sister is stirring up suspicion. They wouldn't dare continue as usual."

He threw a quick glance over his shoulder at the warehouse. "They'd stop the smuggling operation until things cooled off and hide the evidence someplace."

"And the *last* place they'd hide it would be in one of the company warehouses!"

Sam frowned again and stroked his chin. "It wouldn't be easy to hide a lot of boxes. You couldn't very well bring them home—neighbors and guests might notice. You'd have to find someplace where storing a bunch of stuff wouldn't raise suspicion."

"Someplace dry, probably, and locked up, so no one could stumble across the evidence."

Sam nodded. After a long moment, he snapped his fingers and pushed away from the fence. "Come on! We've got some phone calls to make."

"To whom?"

"Public storage!"

Crysta caught his arm, pulling him to a stop. "Sam, we can't just start calling public storage places. What will we do, ask if anyone's unloaded a lot of boxes in one of their units recently?"

"Not just anyone, Riley O'Keefe."

"Riley? What makes you suspect Riley?"

"Number one, I don't like him. Number two, he's spending money like it's water. Number three, he's a warehouse supervisor. He could be responsible for placing orders or be in cahoots with someone in purchasing. Add that up, and you've got a logical place to start."

Chapter Twelve

From a nearby public phone booth, Sam called several public storage companies, impersonating Riley O'Keefe. With an adroitness Crysta couldn't help but admire, he told each clerk that he had lost the keys to his storage unit and, unable to get inside, was wondering if he couldn't beg an extra set. The first phone calls ended with the clerks trying to find his file and informing him that he must have mistakenly called the wrong place of business.

Just when Crysta was beginning to fear his plan would turn up nothing, Sam connected with a man who recognized O'Keefe's name. From what Crysta could glean from the conversation at her end, spare keys were, as a safeguard for customers, unavailable. If Sam's were lost, he would have to call a locksmith.

With a low laugh, Sam said, "You know, now that I think of it, I tossed out my copy of the rental agreement, since the number of my unit was on the key. I'll need it if I'm going to bring out a locksmith. Could you look it up for me?"

After a short wait, Sam thanked the clerk and hung up the phone. Turning in the restrictive confines of the phone booth, he graced her with a discouraged smile. "Well, I found O'Keefe's storage company, but it doesn't look like an easy entry into his unit is in the cards. A locksmith would demand identification to be sure he wasn't accessing someone else's unit."

Mind racing, Crysta stared at the phone book dangling from its chain. "Is *easy* a key word in that prognosis? Or are we at a dead end?"

Sam, clearly agitated, smoothed his windblown black hair with his palm, his brows drawn together in a thoughtful scowl. "We're so close. We can't let one little hurdle stop us."

Crysta's lips felt like rubber. "Sam, the only way into that storage unit is breaking and entering. That's illegal. We could get into serious trouble if we were caught, as in *jail*."

His gaze slid to hers. A long silence fell over them. Then, with a challenging grin, he said, "Maybe we can be roomies. Are you game?"

Crysta stared up at him, not quite able to believe that this man, so practical and analytical up to now, was suddenly willing to throw caution to the wind. "What about Tip?"

"We're not talking a life sentence here, Crysta. Jangles would take care of Tip. Right now, Derrick's life is hanging by a thread. I have to think of him."

Her throat felt suddenly tight. "Tip needs you, Sam. I don't want you doing something you may regret later."

His eyes darkened with emotion. "I can't let the possibility of a stint in jail stop me. Derrick might die. It won't be easy on Tip if I have to be away from him, but he'll survive it. The way I see it, I don't have a choice."

Crysta remembered all the times she had suspected Sam of being involved in Derrick's disappearance. She wished she could go back and undo that, but she couldn't. "Well, in that case, I can't think of anyone I'd rather have as a cellmate."

"Do you realize what all this means? Your what-if-game led us right to Riley. We're inches away from finding out what's going on. Once we do, we'll know who's involved and be able to question them. That means we could be inches away from finding Derrick."

Crysta couldn't contain a soft cry of joy. "Oh, Sam, how will I ever thank you?"

"For what?"

"For coming here with me, even though I had no proof to substantiate my dreams."

Sam gave a low laugh and, catching her totally unprepared, encircled her waist with one arm, hauling her against him. "The important thing is, we came! We're almost home free, Crysta!"

He ran his hand up the curve of her back. A shock zigzagged through her. Sam's grin faded, cuing her that what he had intended to be a quick, innocently affectionate hug had suddenly turned dangerous. She could feel his heart picking up speed.

Dropping her head back, she stared up at him with surprise on the one hand and a feeling of inevitability on the other. Since their forced embrace yesterday after nearly falling into the slough, both of them had been becoming increasingly attuned to the other. This was a natural, spontaneous culmination of that phenomenon.

"This is crazy," he whispered in a gravelly voice.

Before Crysta could agree, he lowered his head and touched his lips to hers in a shy, tentative caress. Then his arm tightened, pulling her more snugly against the hard contours of his body, destroying all illusion of separateness. The pressure of his arm forced her breath from her lungs, and, by necessity, her lips parted to release it, affording him a taste of her mouth and her a taste of his.

Crysta had been kissed many times and had long since come to the conclusion that kisses were, by their very nature, pretty much the same. Years before, she had abandoned any hope of breathless surrender and starbursts. A nice fantasy, but such things didn't happen in real life. Not to her.

Being so convinced of that, it was with considerable alarm that she realized she couldn't feel her sneakers touching the ground. For a moment she wondered if Sam, being so lofty, had plucked her off her feet. Then she realized that, though her eyes were open, she was losing her grasp on her sense of place. The phone booth began to swirl around her. The world had diminished to encompass only one thing: Sam Barrister. His mouth, deliciously sweet and hungry. His arms, like velvet chains. His body, hard and demanding, making hers throb with longing in every deep, dark, secret place she had.

Coming up for air, Sam skidded his lips across her cheek, tasting her skin, his breath hot and quick. "I can't believe this," he rasped.

Crysta blinked, becoming aware of her surroundings by degrees. More than a little dazed, she pressed her cheek against his chest, listening to the wild beat of his heart as she looked through the glass wall of the booth—directly into the bemused face of an elderly man who stood outside, patiently waiting to place a call.

"Sam?"

"Don't say it. I'm sorry. I don't know what came over me. You must think—"

"Sam, there's a man staring at us." Crysta tried to disentangle herself from his arms.

Sam finally registered what she said and dropped his arms from around her, reaching for the booth door to effect their escape. The man outside winked at her and grinned.

"Sorry," Sam called.

"No problem. Most entertaining wait I've had in a long time." The old man tapped his cane merrily as he walked into the phone booth.

After putting several feet between themselves and their inadvertent voyeur, both Crysta and Sam blushed. Sam turned up the collar of his shirt and lengthened his stride. Crysta hurried to keep up, glad that the wind was tossing her hair around, hiding her face.

"Do you realize that I'm going to be forty-two years old next month? *Forty-two!*" Sam raked his fingers through his hair, looking so agitated that Crysta had to smile. "I can't *believe* I did that."

She shrugged, pretending an unconcern she was far from feeling. "We've both been in a pressure cooker for days. You let the lid off, that's all."

He slid questioning eyes to hers. "*Is* that all?"

The directness of his gaze made her cheeks grow warmer. "For now, it has to be. Until Derrick's found, Sam, I don't have the emotional energy for anything more."

He returned his attention to the sidewalk, his jaw muscle working. "I'm sorry I stepped over the line like that."

"No harm done."

The words echoed in Crysta's mind as they proceeded down the street. Though she would never admit it, she wasn't entirely sure she had emerged from the embrace unscathed. Sam Barrister could prove dangerous to the safe, comfortable world she had created for herself since her divorce.

AFTER THROWING his jacket over the barbed wire above them to protect them from injury, Sam made a stirrup out of his interlocked fingers and braced a shoulder against the six-foot chain-link fence that encircled the public storage yard. Grabbing the fencing, Crysta placed her foot in the cradle of his hands and pushed up, her heart skipping when Sam shoved her skyward so she could throw her other leg over the slanted guard of barbed wire at the top. Crysta felt so conspicuous that she cringed.

"You aren't supposed to do things like this until it's dark."

"We can't wait for darkness, Crysta. This is Alaska, remember? Waiting until after hours was the best I could manage."

In an attempt to dispel her nervousness, Crysta said, "I almost wish Todd Shriver had botched this idea by saying he couldn't wait for us. I've just discovered I have vertigo."

"Just fall in the right direction and land on your feet."

"That's helpful of you. You'd sing a different tune if it was your fanny planted up here."

She thought she heard him laugh and was pleased that he wasn't the type of person who clung to relentless grimness in sticky situations. Over the years, Crysta had found that a well-timed joke could make unpleasant circumstances a little easier to handle.

"Did Derrick ever mention to you that he wanted you and I to get together?" Sam called softly up to her.

Precariously straddling the wire fence, Crysta registered the question with puzzlement. "How on earth is that significant right now?"

"I was just thinking that he was right—we make a great team," he called back in a teasing tone.

At the moment, teamwork was the furthest thing from Crysta's mind. A sharp steel prong was biting through his jacket into her bottom. She gazed at the ground, which seemed a lot farther down on her side than it had on Sam's. To divert herself from the very real possibility that she might twist an ankle while jumping, she opted to focus on something unlikely. "What if they have Dobermans guarding the yard?"

"You read too many mysteries. Just jump."

"I do not." Crysta swallowed. Heights had always bothered her.

"If there are dogs, I'll hop over and play Tarzan. *Jump*, Crysta. If I try to come over while you're hanging up there, that barbed wire will cut you to pieces."

"It already is."

As carefully as she could, Crysta swung her other leg over and pushed off, suddenly airborne. An instant later, her flight came to an abrupt end when she hit the ground.

"I said to land on your *feet!* Are you all right?"

Crysta scrambled up, brushing dirt off her jeans. "So far. Hurry, would you?" She glanced over her shoulder, lowering her voice. "Someone's going to see us."

He chuckled. "You just don't want to be supper for a pack of Dobermans without me."

With amazing agility for so large a man, Sam scaled the fence. Never touching his torso to the barbed wire, he braced hand and foot on the top string and vaulted, landing beside her with far more grace than she had displayed. He tugged his jacket down from the top of the fence and pulled it on.

He flashed her a grin. "Jealous?"

"Since fence-climbing isn't on my list of necessary accomplishments, no. I only resent the fact that you didn't become a human pincushion up there." She fell into step beside him, rubbing the back of her leg. "That stuff is wicked."

His expression turned serious. "Are you okay?"

Crysta threw a worried glance at the fence. "I was until I looked up and saw that barbed wire from this side. How will we ever get out over that guard?"

"I'll find something for us to stand on."

As they rounded the corner of a storage building, they were confronted by a bounding, snarling Rottweiler, fangs gleaming. The dog, which at a quick guess weighed at least a hundred and fifty pounds, spotted them and came to a fast halt, swinging his massive head and snapping the air. Crysta's legs turned to water.

"Get behind me. Move slowly," Sam commanded in a smooth, silky voice.

Crysta was too frightened to move. Sam settled the matter by stepping forward and sideways, putting himself between her and the dog. Then, to Crysta's absolute horror, her protector sank to his knees, commanding her to do likewise. If she was going to be eaten alive, she wanted to die running.

"I said get down," Sam whispered. "Put your palms on your knees. It's a nonthreatening position."

Shaking, Crysta dropped as if someone had dealt a blow to the backs of her legs. The Rottweiler tipped his head and threw one ear forward, clearly perplexed. After studying them a moment, he licked a string of foamy slobber from his chops and sat down, whining in bewilderment.

"Good dog," Sam praised him gently. Very slowly, he lifted his arm, hand dangling at the wrist. "Come here, boy. Let's get to know each other, hm? Come on."

The Rottweiler snarled. Crysta's skin prickled. What if there was more than one dog? She longed to look behind them but was too scared.

"Speak to him," Sam ordered.

Crysta's throat closed off. Working her mouth, all she could manage was a squeaky "Hello, doggie."

The Rottweiler barked, a deep, soul-shaking bark that made Crysta jerk. Then, as if he had looked them over to his satisfaction and judged them to be trustworthy, the dog stood and slowly approached, twisting his hindquarters about in what Crysta presumed was an attempt to wag his bobbed tail. Upon reaching Sam, the animal lowered his head and whined, bringing his nose up under Sam's palm. Sam visibly relaxed and smiled, accommodating the dog by scratching him behind his floppy ears.

"Some watchdog you are," he said with a laugh.

"Some Tarzan you are," Crysta inserted. "Down on your knees."

She placed a shaky hand on the Rottweiler's squared head, smiling in spite of herself. "Aren't you a nice doggie."

The creature responded by bathing her face with kisses. Crysta reared back, trying to protect her mouth. The dog butted her, and she nearly toppled. Sam grinned and rose to his feet.

"It seems to be your day to be attacked by overzealous males," he observed dryly. Grabbing the dog by the collar, he offered Crysta a hand up. "Come on, we've got a storage building to break into."

The Rottweiler accompanied them through the rows of buildings as if it were his role to play guide. Crysta, giddy with relief, had to laugh at how friendly he was. "You can tell he's used to having people come in here during the day."

Sam threw the dog a measuring glance. "His looks are enough to scare most people off. It really isn't necessary for him to be vicious."

When they reached Riley O'Keefe's storage building, they found themselves faced with a new problem. Studying the door, Sam said, "We need a crowbar to bust the lock."

With that, he left Crysta to wait by the building with the dog. Several minutes later, he returned with a crowbar.

"Talk about luck. Where did you find it?"

Sam quirked an eyebrow. "Would you believe it was lying on the office porch?" He inserted the tip of the crowbar under the edge of the garage-style door. "Remind me never to store my stuff here." Sam heaved downward, and on his third try, something inside the door gave a loud pop. An instant later, he shoved the portal up on its runners.

Giving the crowbar a toss, he flashed her a grin. "How's *that* for Tarzan?"

"You're getting there." Crysta stepped into the enclosure, squinting to see. Boxes, several rows deep, lined all three walls. Each container was about two feet long and over a foot wide. Recalling boxes exactly like these in her first dream, Crysta related that information to Sam and grinned with delight. "Pay dirt."

Wasting no time, Sam stepped around her and seized the taped lid of a box, ripping it open. Rising on tiptoe, Crysta peered inside. Small round tins gleamed up at her in the dim light. "What is it?"

Sam swore under his breath. "Canned salmon!"

With the explanation, he unended the box, dumping cans and cardboard dividers on the concrete floor. Using the toe of his boot to scatter them even more, he swore again.

"Nothing! Can you believe it? Nothing but canned salmon."

Crysta dropped to one knee, seizing a can. "Let me have your knife. Let's open a few and check what's inside."

Sam pulled his knife from its scabbard and took the can. Jabbing the lid with the blade tip, he cut around the rim in a rocking motion. Peeling back the lid, he said in a dry voice, "Surprise, surprise—salmon."

Unwilling to give up so easily, Crysta busied herself opening more boxes while Sam checked the contents of several other cans. In the end, their findings were the same. The boxes in Riley's storage building held nothing but canned salmon, which was not, by any stretch of the imagination, an illegal commodity.

When it became apparent that their visit to the public storage unit had proven a dead end, Sam glanced at his watch. "Shriver's expecting us back at the airport in forty minutes. We'd better close down and get out of here."

Working in tandem, they returned the tins of salmon to the boxes, discarding the few they had opened in a garbage can outside. When the evidence of their visit had been erased, they left the storage area, and Sam drew the door closed.

"With any luck, they won't know the lock's been broken until Riley makes another visit," Crysta said.

To her relief, Sam found an empty oil drum outside one of the buildings so they could stand on it and climb back over the fence. Once they had gained the other side, Crysta poked her fingers through the chain-link to bid the friendly Rottweiler goodbye.

DURING THE ROUGH FLIGHT back to Cottonwood Bend, Crysta's spirits plummeted and gave way to a numbing sense of defeat. Time was running out for Derrick. All her and Sam's efforts had gotten them nowhere. She had to think of something, fast, or her brother was going to die.

Shriver seemed intent on guiding the small aircraft through pockets of turbulence, a result of the inclement weather. Stomach knotted with anxiety, she softly quizzed Sam about small cabins near the lodge where her brother might have gone to hide.

With a preoccupied expression on his dark face, Sam turned to look at her. "There were several, like I told you, most of them miles from the river near small lakes."

"Could we check some of them out?"

Sam's expression altered to one of exasperation. "I suppose we could ride double on the all terrain four-wheeler and go to one tomorrow. We'd have to go partway on foot, so it would probably involve an overnight stay. We'd be wasting two days, which we can ill afford to lose."

"In other words, no."

His eyes held hers with unwavering intensity. "Crysta, it's your brother. I won't say no. But understand that if we pick out a cabin and go there, it's a crapshoot. Do you want to take a gamble, knowing how precious time is?"

"Well, it's better than doing nothing. I'm out of ideas. Aren't you?"

"For the moment. That doesn't mean I'm not thinking about it, or that something won't come to me. Let me regroup."

Crysta leaned away from him to gaze forlornly out the window. The endless sweeps of landscape she saw only served to depress her. Sam was right, and she knew it. They couldn't help Derrick by wandering aimlessly around out there.

Crysta's silence afforded Sam a chance to think. Pressing his knees against the seat in front of him, he leaned back, closed his eyes and carefully reviewed their day. Up until he had opened that box of canned salmon in the public storage unit, he had been certain Riley O'Keefe was their man. Now he was no longer so sure. Canned salmon? The amounts Riley had stockpiled boggled Sam's mind, but, like it or not, canned salmon was in no way suspicious. Maybe Riley was selling the damned stuff, making spending money on the side.

Had Sam aimed his suspicions at the wrong man? It was a possibility he couldn't ignore. Which would mean that he and Crysta had wasted an entire day. Maybe picking out one cabin at a time and investigating it wasn't so impractical an idea.

WHEN THE PLANE pulled up to the island, Crysta followed Sam out onto the wing, silently accepting his hand as she made the jump to dry land. Turning to Shriver, she expressed her thanks to him for allowing them to ride free of charge. Then she struck off along the footbridge. When she reached shore, she veered toward the trees.

Halfway there, Sam caught up with her. "Can we talk a sec?"

The last thing Crysta needed was company. At the moment, what she really needed was privacy. "What about?"

He drew up beside her. "I want to apologize. If you want to check out a cabin or two, let's do it."

Perilously close to tears, Crysta wandered off a few feet toward the trees. Over her shoulder she said, "No, Sam. You're right. It'd be a crapshoot, at best. I'm sorry that I keep circling back to that idea, but when I run out of things to do, I start to feel frantic, you know?"

"I know."

She glanced over her shoulder at him, wishing he hadn't followed her. There were times when something hurt so badly, one's only alternative was to weep; this was one of those times for her.

"I, um, think I'll take a little walk."

"I'd really rather you didn't," he said in a gentle voice. "After what happened yesterday in the sauna, I'm not sure it's safe."

The gentle whispering of the cottonwood leaves beckoned to her. She wanted to weave her way through the shadows and lose herself. "But, Sam, right now I need to be alone."

He stepped around so he could see her face. "Are you so upset you can't even talk about it?"

Trying to keep her features carefully blank, she ignored his question. "I'll stay within shouting distance of the lodge."

"Crysta, come here." As he spoke, he clasped her arm and pulled her toward him. "This is no time for you to be alone."

"Yes, it is. Please go, Sam."

He drew her against him, looping an arm around her shoulders and cupping a hand to the side of her face.

"Don't," she whispered. "I don't want company right now."

"I know." Pressing her face against his chest, he hunched his shoulders around her. "There's a problem with that, though. I can't walk off and leave you."

"I'm going to cry," she squeaked, "and when I cry, it's not a pretty sight. I never have figured out how some women manage it without turning red and getting all puffy."

He ran his fingers into her hair and rested his cheek atop
her head. "Do you always try to joke when you're upset or
frightened?"

"The alternative is worse."

"I'll risk it."

"I don't want you to see me like this."

"I'll wring out my shirt afterward and never tell a soul."

A sob caught in Crysta's throat. Leaning against him, she
lost her battle to control her tears. They rushed from her
eyes, streaming down her cheeks in hot rivers. "Oh, God,
Sam, I'm afraid for him. Time is running out. I can feel it."

"We'll find him. If he's lasted this long, Crysta, he can
hang on another day or two."

"What about infection? Or blood loss? Not to mention
food and water. No one can hang on forever."

"We'll find him."

"Maybe not in time, though." A tremor shook her. "I
need to call my mother, but what can I say to her? He's
alive, Mom, but I can't find him? Prepare yourself for the
worst?"

Sam's guts wrenched at the pain he heard in her voice.
Closing his eyes, he tightened his hold on her. Her hair,
thick and vibrant, slid over the back of his wrist like warm
silk.

"Have you ever wished you could just run away from
who you are?" she asked in a tremulous voice. "My mom
will never understand my not being able to find him. Never.
She'll think I haven't tried, that I'm blocking him out!"

"Why in heaven would she think that? You love Derrick.
Anyone can see that."

"Because…" Going tense, she made fists in his shirt and
pressed closer to him. "Oh, Sam, because I've tried to do
just that. God forgive me, I've tried to do just that."

Suddenly, it was brought home to Sam just how difficult
Crysta's life had been. A telepathic link. To an onlooker, it
sounded almost fun, being able to communicate with
someone without words, receiving messages long distance,
seeing images. But it hadn't been fun for her. Nor for Derrick. And now, the telepathic link between them had turned

Derrick's disappearance, which would have been horrible for anyone, into a nightmare. Crysta felt responsible for finding her brother in a way other people couldn't comprehend. If he died out there, it was possible she might never recover from it.

"I guess we all wish we could be someone else sometimes," he whispered raggedly. "But in the end, we're stuck with being ourselves. All you can do is your best, Crysta. No one can expect more than that from you—not your mother, not Derrick and not you. Don't set yourself up for a big fall in this."

"I should be able to *find* him. Can't you understand that? I should be able to see where he is, and I can't."

Sam grasped her shoulders and set her a step away from him so he could look into her eyes. He wondered if he was plunging in way over his head, but the pain in her expression made him take the leap, anyway. "Can you tap into Derrick's thoughts at will?"

"No, but—"

"You listen to me, okay? You're asking things of yourself that other people wouldn't even consider—all because you have a gift? You can only see snatches, not the entire picture. It's unreasonable to blame yourself."

She gazed up at him with injured, tear-bright eyes, her pale face streaked with wetness. Sam winced when he realized how stern he sounded. She needed a good listener, not a lecture.

"Come on, let's go sit down for a while."

Taking her by the hand, he led her to a nearby stand of cottonwood. Picking a grassy spot, he sat down, bracing his back against a silvered trunk, pulling her down beside him. She withdrew her hand from his, looping her arms around her knees. The anguish in her face made him long to wrap his arms around her.

"Talk to me, Crysta," he said softly. "You know what I'm hearing in your voice? Guilt. Layer upon layer of guilt. Why? There's more to this than your not being able to find Derrick, isn't there? Something you're not saying."

She took a moment to answer. When she did, she turned haunted eyes on him. "You're Derrick's friend. You'll never forgive me if I tell you."

"Try me."

With a soft moan, she dropped her head onto her knees. "All right, you want to hear the real truth, Sam? As much as I love my brother, there's a part of me that—"

She began to shake. Sam saw her throat go taut, but the words she was trying to say wouldn't come.

"You hate him just a little, don't you?" he asked her.

She swallowed and lifted her head. "I don't *hate* Derrick. But there's a part of me that resents what he's done to my life." She swiped at her cheek with her sleeve and sniffed. "For a while there I really believed I had escaped him. I was beginning to buy into the analyst's theory—that it was all nonsense that our mother had drilled into our heads. That all I had to do was ignore the dreams, and they would go away."

"Was that what you wanted, for it to be nonsense?"

She fastened bewildered eyes on him. "Yes. Do you remember what I said to you, about marriage not being the be-all and end-all of my existence? It was a lie, Sam. I wanted children, a family. For as long as I can remember, that was what I wanted more than anything. Derrick stole that chance from me."

"Did he, Crysta? Or was it simply that you fell in love with the wrong man?" Before she could protest, he held up a hand. "Oh, I know, it isn't easy to admit. Loving the wrong person hurts like hell, and it isn't easy to face. I think I know that better than almost anyone. But it happens."

"You don't understand. It wasn't Dick's fault."

"Make me understand, then. From what I've been hearing, the guy sounds like a selfish jerk."

"He wasn't, though. No one would put up with what he did. My getting constant flashes of Derrick? You've no idea...."

"Tell me."

"Sometimes, the flashes come at difficult moments." She pushed her hair from her eyes, then plucked a piece of grass.

"It wasn't so bad the first couple of years of our marriage. I'd get flashes of Derrick, sometimes, but I never saw anything alarming. Then he broke up with Eileen." She paused and licked her lips. "Derrick went off the deep end for a while. He started drinking. He had terrible mood swings. And my emotional balance went on the roller-coaster ride with him. Once, Dick and I had just gone to bed, and right—" her face went crimson "—in the middle of everything, I got a flash of Derrick breaking a whiskey bottle against the sink. He put the jagged edge to his wrist. I jumped up and left Dick with his face planted in the pillow. At that time, Derrick only lived a few blocks away, and I felt I had to go to him. Dick was furious."

"Furious?" A surge of anger shot through Sam. "Surely he could understand that you had to get up. What were you supposed to do, let Derrick slash his wrists?"

"You have to remember that Dick didn't believe in my gleanings. He thought the entire thing was baloney. He wanted me to put Derrick out of my mind, out of my life."

"And when you couldn't?"

Another flush crept up her neck. "He accused us of—" She broke off and averted her gaze. "He started feeling jealous. To him our relationship went beyond the acceptable, and he began to suspect that perhaps there was something unhealthy going on."

"Something incestuous, you mean?"

"Yes."

"And how does that relate to your feeling that your mother will hold you to blame for all this?"

"Dick insisted that I choose between him and Derrick, never understanding that I *had* no choice." Fresh tears filled her eyes. "I loved Dick, so I tried. I stopped seeing Derrick. I even stopped seeing my mom. But the dreams still came, the flashes still came, and Dick just kept getting more and more paranoid. Then Derrick had the car wreck. I woke up in the middle of the night and started packing. Thirty minutes later, I was on my way out the door to the airport. That was it as far as Dick was concerned. Soon after, he walked out on me."

Sam tipped his head back, staring at the canopy of leaves that shimmered above them. "Taking his exit when you needed him the most."

"What man wouldn't have? That's why I continued the counseling. I realized I would never be able to lead a normal life unless I somehow grew separate from Derrick." She closed her eyes, worrying her bottom lip between her teeth. "I wanted to be free of him. And now I am."

The pictures came clear for Sam. "And your mother knows you wanted to be free."

"Yes. But worse than that, *I* know it."

"Crysta." Sam finally gave in to his urge and wrapped his arms around her. "Honey, you can't wish someone gone. Besides, what you were really wishing for wasn't Derrick's disappearance, just a chance to have what other people have—love and kids and a normal home life. It's not wrong to want those things."

"It's my fault I can't connect with him!" she cried. "Can you understand that? I tried and tried for so long not to feel anything from him, and now, when his life depends on it, I can't! Don't you see? My mother will never forgive me, and I don't blame her."

Sam did see, with a clarity that cut clear through him. He also saw that there were no words that could possibly soothe her. Barring Derrick's rescue, Sam wasn't sure anything ever could. If Derrick returned, he and Crysta needed to talk this out and toss away the emotional garbage both of them were lugging around. But what if Derrick didn't return?

The sound of a snapping twig caught Sam's attention, and he glanced over his shoulder to see Todd Shriver approaching through the trees.

"She okay?" the pilot called. "Not an easy trip for her, huh?"

"She'll be fine," Sam replied. "Right now, she just needs to be alone."

Shriver nodded in understanding and immediately retraced his footsteps. Sam sighed and tucked in his chin to study the top of Crysta's bent head. He had no easy answers for her. He only knew that he had come to care about this woman he held in his arms, that he shared in her pain. Suddenly, he had a double stake riding on his finding Derrick alive: his own peace of mind, and Crysta's.

Chapter Thirteen

Firelight danced upon the knotty-pine walls of Sam's living room, bright and cheerful, in direct contrast to Crysta's somber mood. The blackout shades were drawn, casting the room into shadow, giving her a much-needed feeling of privacy. Sam had thoughtfully left her here alone for a while, taking Tip with him, so she could regain her equilibrium before she called her mother.

She wandered listlessly, stopping to gaze at framed snapshots of Tip and Sam, sometimes managing a smile because the camera had caught them clowning. Tip was a very lucky boy, she decided, to have a father like Sam. Very lucky, indeed. In every photo, Sam's unconditional love for his son shone through in his expression.

Setting her jaw, Crysta left the apartment to use the mobile phone, almost wishing that the thing wouldn't be working properly so she could put off this necessary chore. No such luck. The call went through without a hitch.

"Have you got news?" Ellen cried.

Crysta glanced up at the sound of a bell jingling and saw Steve Henderson coming through the front door of the lodge. He veered to the right to take a seat at one of the dining tables. As always, he looked sad and troubled.

"No, Mom. Not much news, at any rate. Derrick is alive, though. I'm certain of that much. You mustn't worry."

"He's contacted you again then?"

Crysta's throat tightened. "Yes . . . a couple of times."

"Oh, Crysta, darling, you can't know how glad I am to hear you say that. These last few years, I didn't know what had gotten into you. All that nonsense about distancing yourself from your brother and living your own life." She gave a relieved laugh. "Where *is* he? I've been worried sick."

Crysta leaned against the counter and tightened her grip on the phone. "I haven't figured out exactly where he is, not yet."

"What do you mean, not yet?"

"He's all right, Mom. And I'll find him. Alaska covers a lot of territory. These things take time."

"But you said he contacted you."

"He did. But the pictures aren't—" Crysta closed her eyes. "I'm just getting blips. Not enough to pinpoint his location."

"Have you *tried?*"

"Of course I've tried. How can you ask that?" Crysta pushed away from the counter, struggling for calm. She mustn't lose her temper with her mother. "I'll find him, Mom, I promise."

"Oh, darling, I know you will. Just knowing he's alive is a great relief." Ellen grew quiet for a moment. "I've been so worried—about Derrick *and* about you."

"Me? I'm fine, Mom, really."

The rest of the conversation passed in a blur for Crysta, the only reality the fact that she had promised her mother something she might not be able to deliver. *"I'll find him, Mom, I promise."* The same old trap was closing in around her.

After hanging up, Crysta returned to the apartment. With the promise still ringing in her ears, she sat on the sofa and stared sightlessly into the fire, trying to clear her mind.

Derrick? Can you hear me? Silence bounced back at her. She pressed a trembling hand over her eyes, remembering all the times she had gotten flashes of Derrick. Now, when his life depended on her, she saw nothing, heard nothing.

What had she done? Dear God, what had she done?

Less than an hour ago, Crysta had come to the conclusion that some things hurt so badly, tears were the only solution. Now she realized that some pain ran too deep for tears.

She lurched up from the sofa, heading for Tip's gallery. When she opened the door, the sharp, heavy smell of oil paints wafted to her. Stepping into the room, she closed the door and moved slowly toward the easel.

Tip was doing an incredible job of bringing Derrick to life on canvas. Looking into her brother's face, Crysta momentarily lost her sense of identity. He looked so real, Crysta could almost hear him laughing, feel the wind whipping his curly, cinnamon-colored hair. She looked into his eyes. The sensation was very like looking into a mirror. How was it possible to love someone so dearly, yet feel chained to him?

Her gaze trailed to the background of the portrait, taking in the detail Tip had so painstakingly recorded. Incredible. Todd's Cessna was pulled up to the island. The cottonwood trees were blowing in the wind. Near Derrick's feet lay a string of gigantic king salmon.

Sighing, Crysta moved about the room, admiring Tip's work, glad for a distraction from her thoughts. A canvasback duck. A caribou. A wolf. A winding slough surrounded by a sweep of marshy grassland. Crysta had never seen such lifelike paintings.

She paused before a portrait of Todd Shriver, smiling to herself when she noted that Tip had captured to perfection the weakness of the pilot's chin and the inexpressiveness of his eyes. Todd stood on the river island, the Cessna behind him. Tip had recorded every detail, right down to the lace hooks on Todd's boots.

With an odd sensation that she was missing something important, Crysta shifted her attention to the luggage and cargo Tip had painted on the ground near Todd. Her gaze was riveted. Boxes of canned salmon. With building urgency, Crysta shuffled through the other paintings that leaned against the wall, searching for more portraits. She finally found one of Riley O'Keefe, also standing on the island. Once again, Tip had painted boxes of canned salmon sitting near the airplane.

Crysta raced through the apartment and out the lodge door. She spotted Sam down by the footbridge, talking with Gary Nelsen, one of the men from Blanchette who frequently flew in to fish here with O'Keefe.

Trotting down the slope, Crysta called, "Sam! Can I talk to you for a moment?"

"Sure." Bidding Nelsen goodbye, Sam strode up the bank, his dark eyes searching her face. "Is something wrong?"

Crysta could scarcely contain her excitement. "No. In fact, something might finally be going right. Can you come up to the lodge with me? I want to show you something."

SAM STOOD BACK from the painting of O'Keefe, his gaze resting on the boxes of canned salmon, his forehead pleated in a frown. Then he looked at all the other paintings Crysta had dragged out.

"I can't believe I never noticed how much canned salmon came and went around here," Sam murmured.

"Kind of fishy, isn't it?"

Sam's gaze flew to hers. "You think Derrick intended that comment as a double entendre?"

"I'm certain of it." Crysta raised an eyebrow. "He has a twisted sense of humor sometimes. I'm convinced something more than fish is being hauled around in those boxes, though."

"I think you're right. It's the perfect cover. Boxes of canned salmon are as common up here as noses on faces. No one would ever question why you had them or what was in them."

"Look at this picture." Crysta hauled a painting over in front of him. "It's of Jangles, but look at the background, Sam. Todd Shriver's climbing down from the Cessna. From the looks of it, he's just brought in a load of supplies."

"He could be getting ready to leave with a load."

"No. Look at the water behind the plane, Sam." Crysta touched a fingertip to the V-shaped wake that foamed behind the Cessna's tail. "He had just landed."

"You're right," Sam whispered. "You've got quite an eye for detail, lady."

Crysta laughed. "Me? Tip's the one with the eye for detail. His paintings are like photographs. That happens with the handicapped sometimes, you know. It's as if God compensates for their shortcomings in other areas by giving them some special talent. With Tip, it's a photographic memory and the ability to reproduce it." She trailed her finger to the cargo door of the Cessna. "Look inside, Sam."

Sam leaned forward. "Canned salmon."

"Exactly."

Sam straightened and scratched his temple, looking perplexed. "Salmon comes in, then it goes out. I think I must be slow on the uptake, here. It doesn't make sense to me. First we suspected that an illegal commodity was being transported inside the conduit crates. Now we're guessing that they're using these boxes of fish up at this end to smuggle something out? Are you saying—" His voice broke off. "That something illegal is slipping right past me?"

She flashed an excited smile. "Sam, think about it! You just admitted that you never noticed how much canned salmon came and went. The reason you never noticed is because everyone who visits Alaska is hauling it around! It's the perfect cover, absolutely perfect. Riley brings a few boxes to Cottonwood Bend, puts whatever it is he's smuggling inside the boxes, and then flies them back out again to Anchorage to the warehouse. After business hours, he moves the illegal commodity from the canned salmon boxes into the crates of conduit, which are about to be returned to Seattle!"

Sam whistled, his eyes taking on a glint. "No pilot would pay any attention to canned salmon. He'd haul the stuff around, no questions asked."

"Exactly!"

Sam took another long look at each painting. "Okay, I can buy it. I think you're on to something, Crysta, I really do. Now all we have to do is figure out what in hell he's smuggling. I can't very well call in the cops without evidence."

Crysta threw up her hands. "I'm drawing a blank on that. I've tried and tried to think what, but I can't imagine. Why can't we just waylay Riley before he takes off on the plane next time and open the boxes?"

"He's not planning to leave again until tomorrow. Time, right now, is something we're running short on." A distant expression crept into his eyes. "That night when Derrick came into my office, he was really upset. 'I'll hang the creeps'—that's what he said. Whatever it is that's being taken out of here, it's something he felt so passionately about that he risked his own neck. Secondly, if Riley's smuggling it in those boxes, it has to be relatively small."

"Drugs, maybe? Derrick would be livid about that."

Sam shook his head. "Look at it from a practical angle. It's too remote here for drug running. That usually occurs along the Coast, near a big city for ease of distribution, or along the Mexican border. And, if you're thinking of a lab, the chemicals needed would be far too bulky to be hidden among cans of fish."

"Then what?"

"I'm thinking maybe it could be animal hides. Derrick can really get angry about poaching, especially up here. The thought that the wildlife might be depleted infuriated him."

"Do hides bring that much money?"

Sam sighed. "I suppose you could turn a tidy profit, but not nearly enough to make it cost-effective when it would take so many trips to transport them. Not only that, but a sizable animal hide probably wouldn't fit in a box that size, not if you left in any cans as camouflage."

"What, then?"

Sam looped an arm around her shoulders. "Let's have a cup of coffee. I'm drawing a blank. Sometimes if I just let a problem rest, the answer will come to me out of the blue."

While Sam went for the coffee, Crysta tossed another log onto the fire. When he returned, they sat together on the sofa, shoulders inches apart, taking reflective sips from their steaming mugs as they gazed into the flames.

"I can't think what they could be smuggling that would bring enough money to bother with," Sam muttered.

Crysta leaned forward to set her mug on the coffee table. "There has to be something. We're just overlooking it." She turned toward him. "Oh, Sam, we're not going to find him in time, are we? After all we've done, we're still going to fail."

Looking into her eyes, Sam could see how frantic she felt. After placing his mug beside hers on the table, he ran his hand under her hair and curled his fingers around the nape of her neck. Her skin there felt as soft as down. Drawing her toward him, he leaned back against the cushions, pulling her head to his shoulder. "I don't know, Crysta. I just don't know."

Pressing his cheek against her silken hair, he gazed into the fire, his heart twisting because he couldn't ease the pain in hers. Closing his eyes, Sam moved his arm down to encircle her back, slipping his hand between her arm and her side. Beneath his fingertips, he could feel the fragile ladder of her ribs. Whoa, this was not the time to let physical desire cloud his thinking. Above all else, Sam was a practical man. But, practical or not, dammit, he wanted her.

The realization struck him like a blow. Worse, wanting wasn't even sufficient to describe the emotions roiling within him. He wanted her, yes, but in a way he had never wanted any other woman. So much that he trembled. So much that he felt frightened. There was a rightness between them, a magical sweetness. Holding her like this filled the emptiness within him, made him feel complete in a way he had never experienced. So perfect...yet so impossible.

Sam came as a package deal, saddled with a troublesome man-child who would never mature to adulthood. Loving Tip as he did, he harbored no resentment and didn't feel in the least put upon that Tip needed so much attention. But he couldn't expect a woman who was not Tip's natural mother to be so charitable. Especially not Crysta, who had her own life in Los Angeles, a busy, fast-paced life that precluded mothering a handicapped boy.

Sam's first duty lay with his son. He couldn't allow himself to forget that, even for an instant. And yet he had needs, needs he had ignored for far too long. Was it so wrong to steal a magic moment with this very special woman?

He shifted his hand so the pads of his knuckles grazed the soft swell of Crysta's breast. An ache rose up his throat. Making love to her right now would be insanity. One taste, and he might never be able to get enough.

To his surprise, she turned in the circle of his arm and tipped her head back, her eyelashes casting shadows over her cheeks, her lips parted. "Sam?"

Sam responded to the question in her voice by lowering his head. Crazy, so crazy. But he couldn't stop himself. Just one sweet kiss. Surely God would grant him that much—one kiss to be remembered during the long, cold, empty winter nights to come. One kiss to last him a lifetime. His lips touched hers, so lightly, so gently, but the electricity was there again just the same. Two-twenty, with no ground, and he knew he was a goner.

She tasted like toffee, her mouth warm and sugary from the coffee, her lips moist. Sweet, so incredibly, wonderfully, impossibly sweet. Sam, usually so responsible, forgot everything—that the door wasn't locked, that Tip might walk in. His mind went blank, automatic pilot kicked in, and before he knew it, he had pulled her down beside him on the sofa.

At five foot ten, Crysta fit his body the way a woman should. He wasn't even aware that the sofa wasn't long enough. If Sam had feet, he couldn't feel them. She moaned and let her head fall back over his arm. Sam accepted the invitation and feathered his mouth along the graceful slope of her neck to her collarbone. And then lower.

The top buttons on her shirt opened as if he had magic in his fingertips. His heart slamming, he peeled the cloth back and trailed kisses down her chest to the shimmering mounds of her breasts, breasts that seemed to beg for his lips to explore them above the lacy edge of her bra. Her skin was as flawless and as creamy-white as ivory, silken, warm, vibrant.

Sam stiffened, his hand frozen on her breast, his mind stunned. *Ivory!*

Crysta heard Sam curse, and her eyes flew open. He was suspended above her, his body rigid, his eyes filled with what could only be described as disbelief.

"Sam?"

He shot up from the sofa and smoothed his hair, staring down at her. "Ivory, Crysta." He barked with incredulous laughter. "Your skin is as flawless as *ivory*."

It wasn't a very original line, and Sam's delivery needed work, but Crysta accepted the compliment with as much grace as she could muster. Quickly buttoning her shirt, she said, "Thank you . . . I think."

"*Ivory*, Crysta! That's it, don't you see? That's what they're smuggling! I can't believe I was so dense! It's been making all the headlines recently. Walrus tusks. There have been several killing fields discovered, some on the islands, several up north!"

"Ivory?" Crysta sat up, trying to gather her shattered composure. Then what Sam was saying began to register, and excitement coursed through her. "Ivory! Of course! They could make a mint on that!"

"A mint? A head mount brings over a thousand dollars! One head mount, Crysta. Have you any idea how many they may have smuggled out of here? And that's only for starters. Scrimshaw would bring astronomical amounts. Have you any idea how much one small piece costs? Once they had the ivory in the States, they could commission someone to work it into scrimshaw, then launder it somehow onto the open market."

"Wh-what's a head mount?"

"The front portion of the walrus's skull, with the tusks still attached."

Crysta recalled the magazine cover she had seen with its gory pictures of the beheaded walrus corpses littering a lonely beach. A feeling of revulsion swept over her. And something elusive tugged at her memory.

"That *bastard!* He's slaughtering walrus! No wonder Derrick was so upset!"

Crysta pressed her fingers to her temples, her senses still reeling. She swallowed and closed her eyes. "Wait, Sam. We're not near the coastline. There are no walrus around here."

"Of course not! He's flying them in. It's perfect, Crysta. He hits a beach, slaughters the animals, hacks off the heads and transports them here to be cleaned. He'd have to clean them before taking them to the warehouse in Anchorage. If he didn't, the smell coming from those conduit crates would bowl a person over. And what better place to do it than someplace near Cottonwood Bend? Daily flights out, lodging, isolation!"

"So he cleans them somewhere around here, hides them in the canned salmon boxes, then brings them to the lodge to be flown out to Anchorage? But, Sam, a walrus head with tusks wouldn't fit in a box two feet long."

"It would if you removed the tusks. You can dismantle a head mount, then put it back together."

"And if the mounts were concealed inside the canned salmon boxes, the pilots hauling the ivory would never even realize what they were hauling!" Crysta pushed up from the sofa. "Sam, you're a genius! It fits perfectly! Derrick must have discovered what Riley was doing!"

"And probably followed him."

She held up a hand. "Wait, we're forgetting something. In my dream, I saw three men. He must have helpers."

"That goes without saying. No one could do something on this scale without help. There's probably more than just three men involved. We've already deduced that there must be a contact in Seattle. Then there would have to be at least two or three guys working at the killing fields." Sam's excited grin faded. "Crysta, from here on in, this can only get more and more dangerous. Until Riley's caught redhanded with some boxes that contain ivory, we don't have enough evidence to go to the police. I'm not so sure I want you involved."

"Oh, no, you don't! Questioning Riley is my only hope of ever finding out where Derrick may be. I want to be damned sure the man's caught. I'm in on this to the end, Sam."

His eyes darkened. "I don't want you getting hurt."

"And I don't want you hurt, either. We've done well so far as a team. Let's not rock the boat."

"We have, haven't we?" he whispered, his expression far more eloquent than the words he spoke. After a long, emotion-packed moment, his mouth quirked in a sad smile. "I'm sorry about—" His gaze shot to the sofa. "Not very chivalrous of me, popping up that way."

Crysta laughed softly. "No, it wasn't. But given the reason, I'll reserve judgment until next time."

Would there be a next time? Sam wanted that more than he could admit, but part of him knew that both of them would be better off if the occasion never again rose. Crysta had her own set of problems; she didn't need to take on his.

"Well." Sam wandered over to the fire, not quite able to look her in the eye. "All that's left is for us to unearth the ivory. If we can find the cleaning location, there should be enough evidence there for us to go to the police. Then we can have the searchers brought back in."

Crysta could scarcely contain her excitement. "If we need them. If I see anything familiar at the cleaning location— something I've seen in my dreams—I might be able to find Derrick myself."

Sam glanced up, a grin touching his mouth. Despite the fact that time was running out for him and Crysta, this was a major triumph; a moment for joy. He would share in that with her and worry about tomorrow later.

"The quickest way to find a possible cleaning location would be from the air. It's probably convenient to the river, for ease of transport by pontoon plane."

"Todd's still here. Do you think he'd take us up?"

"I'm sure he would." Sam strode across the room to her and clamped a hand on her shoulder. Guiding her toward the door, he grabbed her windbreaker off the chair and handed it to her. "Let's go commandeer ourselves an airplane, shall we?"

Just as Sam reached for the doorknob, Tip burst in. "Where are you going, Dad? It's almost bedtime."

"Crysta and I have some things we have to do," Sam replied gently.

Tip looked crestfallen. "I thought maybe we could read to each other for a while. I bet Crysta likes to read."

"As a matter of fact, I do."

Guilt stabbed Sam. He had been ignoring Tip for days, and it bothered him to be leaving the boy alone again. Tip often had nightmares and sought Sam out for reassurance. "I'm sorry, son. Maybe we can read before bedtime tomorrow night."

Tip's gaze slid to Crysta. "Will you r-read with us? The book we're d-doing now is really good. It's about buried treasure."

Crysta took Tip's hand and gave it a warm squeeze. "You know, Tip, if we find Derrick, he might be ill or hurt. If he is, he'll have to be taken to a hospital. Since I'm his sister, I'll want to go with him. I may not be here tomorrow night."

Tip's face fell. "You won't come back, will you?"

Crysta hesitated, but only for an instant. "And never see you again? Not on your life, kiddo. We're fast friends, remember?"

Tip's mouth arched in a reluctant grin. "For real?"

"Of course, for real. For always, Tip. I'll come back. Maybe with Derrick. Wouldn't that be fun? We could make popcorn, and all of us could read together."

"I'd like that. W-would you like that, Dad?"

Sam couldn't say how much. "Hey, Tip, how about if I ask Jangles to stay with you tonight? I bet she'd enjoy some company."

"Okay." Tip brightened visibly. "Maybe we can make popcorn."

After leaving the apartment, Sam glanced at Crysta. "I have to talk with Jangles. Mind waiting a few minutes?"

As anxious as Crysta was for them to be on their way, she
knew Sam had other obligations, as well. "Not at all. We'll
both feel better if we know Tip's all right."

The sincerity Sam saw reflected in Crysta's gaze made his
stomach tighten. Was it remotely possible that maybe, just
maybe, he'd finally found a woman who wouldn't resent
Tip? As he hurried through the lodge to find Jangles, Sam
cautioned himself against reading too much into Crysta's
behavior. She might sing a different tune entirely when faced
with a lifetime of making allowances for Tip.

Bitter memories washed over Sam. He couldn't let Tip be
hurt again. Setting himself up for a big fall was one thing,
but putting Tip through another rejection would be criminal.

Chapter Fourteen

The Cessna circled, rattling and shaking as it lost altitude. Crysta pressed her face against the window, scanning the landscape below. The sunken roof of a cabin came into view. She groped behind her for Sam's hand and gave it a squeeze.

"I don't think that's it," he whispered so Shriver wouldn't overhear. "There's no trail leading from the river, no sign of traffic."

From up front Todd said, "What is it you two are looking for? I'm pretty familiar with the area. Maybe I can help."

Before boarding the plane, Sam and Crysta had decided the less said to anyone about their suspicions, the better. Sam followed through on that feeling now by ignoring Shriver's question. He leaned forward. "Bank to the left, Todd. The place we're looking for should be fairly close to the lodge."

Todd did as instructed. Watching the man's skilled maneuvering of the plane, Sam considered the repercussions Todd or any other pilot might suffer if he were caught smuggling ivory. It would be insane to take that risk. Undoubtedly the pilots involved were blissfully unaware of their illegal cargo. Anger welled within Sam. People who slaughtered walrus obviously didn't have much in the way of conscience. They didn't care who they took down with them.

That thought led Sam back to the most troubling question of all. Who were the culprits? Their uncertainty had been the main reason he and Crysta had decided to reveal as little as possible about their reasons for this air search.

Focusing along the wing, Crysta spotted another cabin. She reached back to jab Sam's shoulder.

"That could be our baby," Sam said softly. "There's a path winding up from the river." In a louder voice, he said, "Circle around, Todd, and swing in low."

Crysta's pulse accelerated. As the plane swooped toward the earth and she got a good frontal view of the cabin, a feeling of déjà vu washed over her.

"Sam!" she whispered, her tone urgent.

He turned to look at her, lifting an eyebrow. "You say yes?"

She gave an emphatic nod.

"Hey, Todd, can you land along this stretch of river?"

Todd took a pass, giving the waterway a thorough study. "It looks good from here. Wanna try her?"

"Yeah, set us down."

AFTER LANDING THE PLANE, Todd insisted on accompanying Sam and Crysta to the cabin even though Sam assured him that they were, at this point along the river, within walking distance of the lodge.

"Hey!" Shriver said, lifting his hands. "Why go off and leave you to walk? I've got nothing better to do."

Even though he preferred that the pilot not come along, Sam could think of no good way to discourage him. Besides, if his and Crysta's suspicions proved correct, Shriver was probably one of the pilots who had been hoodwinked into hauling the illegal cargo. And in that case, it seemed only fair that he be along when Sam and Crysta gathered enough evidence to present to the police.

As the two men struck off walking, Crysta fell in behind them. For some reason she felt uneasy. Was Derrick trying to reach her, perhaps? She tried to clear her mind, but her excitement over finding this cabin made serenity impossible.

About a half mile from the river, Sam stopped and scanned the ground. He looked up and pointed to a thicket of brush. Through the network of green leaves, Crysta spotted something gleaming in the sunlight.

"Four-wheelers!" Sam cried. He and Todd waded into the brush.

"Can you believe it?" Todd pulled back branches to reveal one of the bike-like rough-terrain vehicles. "Who'd leave these here?"

Sam met Crysta's gaze, his own questioning. Since Crysta could think of no way they could conceivably continue this foray without leveling with Shriver, she gave Sam a reluctant nod. Without giving names, Sam explained to the pilot their reason for coming here. He finished by saying, "If we're correct, I'd guess that the smugglers use these all-terrain vehicles to carry the ivory from the river inland."

Shriver gave a low whistle. "Talk about a smooth operation. A plane brings in a load from the killing fields and puts down here on the river. They haul the ivory to this point, load it onto the bikes, and take it to be cleaned. After that, they hide it in boxes of canned salmon, and back onto the bikes it goes! Then from this point they drag it to the lodge, hang around until a pilot is making a flight out and load it up. I can't believe all of us pilots were so dense!"

"You can't blame yourself," Sam replied. "Canned salmon doesn't exactly wave a red flag."

"I suppose not." Todd shook his head, giving the four-wheeler's rear tire an angry kick. "What d'ya say we use these bikes ourselves?"

"No," Sam replied. "There could be someone at the cabin. The noise of the bikes would warn them we're coming."

"That's true." Shriver flashed Crysta a smile. "Looks like we'll have to hoof it."

Once again Crysta fell in behind the men. The trail veered to the right across a meadow and came to a shallow slough. Both Todd and Sam wore the green waterproof boots, but Crysta was in sneakers. Without so much as a word, Sam swept her into his arms to carry her across.

Looking back at Shriver over Sam's shoulder, Crysta watched the pilot step off into the shallow water. Sunlight struck his boots, glistening on the green rubber. A chill of recognition crawled up her spine. Her first dream crystallized in her head. The green rubber boots. Not conclusive, Sam had said. And he was absolutely right. The boots were commonplace up here. But the strange way Todd Shriver tied his laces was not.

Todd didn't lace his boots in a crisscross, like most people, but in a ladder-rung fashion. Tip's painting. While looking at it, Crysta had sensed she was almost, but not quite, grasping something she had overlooked, and she'd begun examining the background. If only she had kept her focus on Todd's boots!

The boots in her dream came flooding back to her. She distinctly remembered now that one pair had been laced horizontally from hook to hook, straight across like ladder rungs. Crysta stiffened.

"What is it? Am I hurting you?" Sam asked, tipping his head back to look at her face. "Crysta, what is it?"

Todd glanced up and halted in the middle of the slough. His gaze met Crysta's. For the first time, Crysta saw expression in those icy orbs. Hostility. She tried to speak, couldn't. Shriver reached into his pocket.

"Sam," Crysta croaked, but she was too late. Shriver withdrew a deadly-looking revolver from his pocket and aimed it squarely at Sam's broad back, a target he couldn't possibly miss at this close range. Sam stepped up onto the bank, still oblivious. "Sam? Oh, God, Sam, Shriver's—"

With a quick pull of his thumb, Shriver clicked the gun off safety. The metallic sound stopped Sam cold.

"Go ahead and finish, Ms. Meyers. 'Shriver's in on it'— isn't that what you meant to say?"

The pilot smiled a nasty smile, all attempt at subterfuge abandoned. Looking at him now, Crysta realized what it was about him that had always nagged at her. It wasn't that his face was boyish and a little too perfect. It was the lack of compassion to be read there.

"I had hoped to avoid this until we reached the cabin," Shriver told them. "It would have been so much more tidy that way." He shrugged. "Oh, well, it just brought things to a head sooner than planned. We'll just keep walking, hm?"

Sam set Crysta on her feet and turned to regard Shriver with glittering eyes. "You weren't an innocent party, after all."

"You're extremely slow at figuring that out. We've been walking on eggshells for two days now, convinced you were only inches away from realizing. Especially after I followed your cab and saw you touring the warehouses. Riley about came unglued when I told him." He shrugged. "Of course, he's been worried from the start, ever since he followed you into the woods that first day—you remember, Sam, when Ms. Meyers tailed you? The time you tackled her. Riley overheard you arguing and started predicting trouble even then."

"So there *was* something behind me!" Crysta cried. "I thought so, but when I stopped and listened, I couldn't hear or see anything."

"It's not hard to hide in this country," Shriver pointed out. Gesturing with the gun, he added, "Let's start walking. When you guys came and asked me to bring you out here, I got word to Riley before we left. We knew it was the beginning of the end, at that point. From the air, we knew you'd see the trail leading to the cleaning location, then get suspicious and want to see it. My partners struck off in this direction as soon as the Cessna lifted off. It's a ways to walk, but as you've already determined, they're used to it. We're all supposed to meet at the cabin to solve the problem you two present. Riley, as always, has some very inventive solutions."

"Partners?" Sam repeated. "Who else is involved?"

Crysta had a sinking feeling that she knew the answer to that question. A picture of Jangles conferring in the woods with a strange man flashed through her mind. In retrospect, Crysta couldn't believe she hadn't connected the Tlingit to the walrus slayings the moment Sam mentioned them. It all fit together now. Jangles, a native of Alaska, was the perfect person to help out up here in a poaching and smuggling operation.

Shriver's mouth twisted at Sam's question. "Who else is none of your business. But you'll know soon enough."

"Why you?" Crysta asked. "For the money?"

"Things like this have a way of getting out of hand, you know? Nice guys, trying to make a little extra cash on the side, and, *kaboom,* the first thing you know, Derrick gets suspicious, Riley gets trigger-happy, and you're in so deep you can't get out. Do you think I ever intended to kill someone? Once Riley pulled that trigger, it was too late to bail out."

Sam tried to reason with the man. "For God's sake, Shriver, you're not in too deep yet. But if Riley shot Derrick, do you think he'll hesitate to kill us? For your part in that, they'll put you in prison and throw away the key."

"I think one count of murder and ivory smuggling is sufficient to do that." Shriver shook his head. "Not this fella. I'm not doing time. The only reason I got into this in the first place was for a little excitement and some extra cash to impress my ex-girlfriend. She dumped me for a guy with more pocket change. I don't think a prison uniform would turn her on, do you? Besides, why should I rot in a cell? It's not my fault that Riley has a quick trigger finger and no conscience."

"If you go through with this, you're crazy!" Crysta cried.

"It's your fault, you stupid broad!" Shriver waded toward them, keeping the gun trained on Crysta. "One move, Barrister, and she's dead, so don't decide to play hero."

Sam stepped back, keeping his hands in plain sight.

"Why is it my fault?" Crysta demanded. If she could keep Shriver talking, maybe she could distract him long enough for Sam to make a move. It always worked in mystery novels, and as far as Crysta could see, stalling was the only chance they had. "I'm a victim in this."

"An extremely nosy victim." He jabbed her in the hip with the gun. "Turn around, both of you, and keep your hands above your heads. Now, start walking! That's good."

Crysta heard a splash as Shriver exited the slough behind them, the squeak of his rubber boots on the grass. Her back tingled. What if he decided to shoot them now?

"I just came here to find my brother," she said shakily.

"Yeah, yeah. Wasn't the salmon we stuck in your bed warning enough? That should have been your cue to get the hell out while the getting was good, but you stuck around."

"I suppose you'll tell me next that it was you who trapped me in the sauna?"

"No, I don't have the stomach for that kind of thing. That was Riley's special touch."

"But how?" Crysta asked. "You and Riley were both out on boats fishing."

"Correction. You thought we were. We landed down-river and walked back upstream."

"You stood by while he trapped a helpless woman inside a sauna and built up the fire?" Sam asked.

"Hey! He wanted to go in first and have a little send-off party—give her something to go out smiling about. At least I drew the line at that. Don't be offended, Ms. Meyers. That isn't to say I wasn't tempted. You've got the nicest set of—"

Sam stopped and turned. "Shriver, say one more word, and, gun or no gun, I'm gonna make you eat those pearly whites."

Shriver kept the gun aimed at Crysta. "I don't think so, since she'd go first. Besides, I was paying her a compliment."

"She can do without that kind of compliment."

"Fine. Just keep walking."

Clenching his teeth, Sam did as he was told. Crysta fell in beside him, so frightened she felt sick, and not just for herself.

"Shriver, please," Crysta pleaded. "Stop this, now, before Riley gets here. Sam has a son to take care of. What will Tip do without his father? *Think* about what you're doing, the lives it will ruin!"

"It's out of my hands. Riley calls the shots. Just keep walking."

It was the longest journey of Crysta's life. At the edge of the meadow, they entered a line of trees, which bordered another clearing. About a hundred yards away, Crysta spotted the cabin. Following the rutted four-wheeler path through the tall grass, she absorbed her surroundings.

Sam glanced down at her, his expression grim. "This is outside the official search area," he told her softly. "That explains why the pilot in the Huey didn't report it. Using the spot where I found Derrick's shredded gear as a center point, the volunteers searched in a radius they could conceivably cover on foot in a day's time. When they widened the circle, they found the faked bear attack site and ended the search."

"Clever, weren't we?" Shriver boasted. "We made damned sure they'd find evidence of the attack before the search area expanded to encompass our cleaning location. We ran a risk, of course. If the pilot in the Huey had taken note of the trail to the cabin and sent anyone to check it out, we'd have been had. Fortunately for us, he was relying mainly on the infrared device in hopes of finding Derrick by detecting a fluctuation in temperature. If he flew over the cabin, there was nothing inside to alert him that it wasn't just another abandoned shack like dozens of others in the region."

About fifty yards from the cabin, they came upon an embankment that plunged sharply to a rushing creek. Crysta missed a step, staring down at the jagged boulders jutting up from the water. She remembered them from her second dream. This was the embankment she had been trying to scale. Sweat broke out on her face. She turned slightly to gaze in the direction that she had fled after climbing up the incline. Derrick was out there somewhere, in a dank cabin by a small lake.

"This is where you threw my brother's body, isn't it?"

Crysta turned on Shriver just in time to see his face register his surprise. "How'd you know that?"

"Just a guess," Crysta replied icily. "Why here, Todd?"

"It was far enough away from where we staged the bear attack that the searchers wouldn't find it. With the trees and boulders, his body wouldn't be visible from the air. As you can see, his remains didn't last long enough to be a concern. That's one nice thing about Mother Nature—she cleans up after you rather quickly. Animals—" He broke off. "Well, you get the picture."

Hatred filled Crysta. Shriver deserved a prison sentence. A long one.

"Is that where we'll end up?" Sam asked. "Food for scavenging animals, Shriver?"

"Actually no. Two more disappearances would arouse suspicion. We can't let nature take its course a second time and risk the authorities finding you. Riley is talking about flying you out over the mud flats outside Anchorage. The beauty of it is, if I fly in low, we can shove you out while you're alive and unharmed. When they find your bodies, it'll look as if you went to show Ms. Meyers the sights and walked out too far." Todd clucked his tongue. "In case you aren't familiar with the mud flats, Ms. Meyers, they can be like quicksand. Not too long back, a man and his wife went out there and got into a bog. A rescue 'copter went in to pull them out. The man didn't make it in one piece. Ripped him clean in half when they tried to lift him."

"I'm a *guide*," Sam reminded him. "Who'll believe I was that stupid?"

"You're in love. Everyone at the lodge has seen the two of you together. Men can make stupid mistakes when they're trying to impress their ladies, right? Of course, we'll be sure that's the story that gets started, just to cinch it."

Acutely conscious of Sam beside her, Crysta walked the rest of the way to the cabin. She was instructed to enter first, so the pilot could keep close watch on Sam. The stench of rancid blubber and rotting fish hit her the moment she stepped inside. She remembered the odor from her first dream, and nausea rolled up her throat. Along one wall, a pile of ghoulish skulls were stacked, five and six deep. And suddenly she remembered what had eluded her earlier—her glimpse of an animal skull in Shriver's Cessna. A quick count revealed at least fifty head mounts here. The collection was worth at least fifty thousand dollars.

Her gaze shifted to a worktable on her right. A glint of silver caught her attention. Derrick's buckle. At one edge of the ornate scrollwork was a jagged hole. As she had suspected, the bullet fired at Derrick had gone through the buckle in his shirt pocket, leaving telltale evidence of foul play, which was why his attackers hadn't left it to be found in the mangled garment.

Shriver grabbed some rope from beneath the table and tossed it at Sam. "Tie her up," he hissed. "And no funny stuff. I want it tight. Mess with me, and I'll kill her."

"And have a bullet wound in her head to make the police suspicious when they haul us out of the mud flats?"

"We can always think of something else," Shriver retorted. "I do have an airplane."

As instructed, Sam bound Crysta's wrists behind her, then tied her feet. As he finished tightening the last knot, Shriver walked up behind him and brought his gun down on Sam's head, evidently deciding the danger he represented outweighed the risk of any suspicious autopsy findings. Sam crashed to the floor, his shoulder hitting Crysta's leg. Unable to keep her balance, Crysta fell backward, crying out Sam's name.

Stowing his gun in his jacket pocket, Shriver made fast work of tying up Sam. When he finished, he straightened and met Crysta's gaze, his own curiously expressionless, as it had always been.

"If it's any comfort at all, I won't let Riley—well, you know. I do draw the line someplace."

Praying that Shriver wouldn't decide to check the rope on her wrists, Crysta snapped, "How noble of you."

He shrugged and turned toward the door. "I'll be outside keeping watch for my partners. You wait here, hm?"

CRYSTA LIFTED Sam's head in her arms, sending up a silent prayer that he wasn't badly injured. Placing a hand alongside his face, she fought back tears. Seeing him like this brought home to her how deeply she had come to care for him these last few days. Very gently, she ran her fingers over the angry red bump rising on his temple. She was no ex pert, but it didn't look like a serious injury. He would probably be all right.

It was up to her to somehow keep him that way.

"Sam? Sam, darling... Oh, please, Sam, wake up and look at me."

His eyelashes fluttered open. His dark eyes wandered as he tried to focus on her. "Crysta? We're untied. How did you—"

"It was a trick I learned from a mystery novel. I held the heels of my hands together, with my wrists twisted. It gives you some slack when you straighten your arms."

He licked his lips. "Mystery novels. I *knew* it. You lied to me."

A joyful laugh bubbled up her throat, and tears trailed down her cheeks. "Can you sit up?"

He tried and failed. Crysta tried to help him, but he weighed so much, she couldn't budge him. "Sam, you *have* to get your wits about you."

He fastened bleary eyes on her. "Did you call me darling?"

"*Sam!*" Crysta caught him by the chin. "Shriver's out there with a gun. Riley will be here any time. Snap out of it."

He passed a hand over his forehead, wincing when he grazed the bruise on his temple. "What in hell did he hit me with?"

"His gun." Time was running out. Crysta knew if she didn't do something, fast, she and Sam were going to die. She pulled her arm from beneath him and pushed to her feet. Glancing around, she spied a pile of stove wood. "You just lie there, okay? Keep your hands behind you like you're still tied up."

He blinked again, trying to focus on her. "What are you going to do?"

"I'm going to get us out of here." She picked up a hunk of wood, glancing out the murky window as she hefted it in her hands. Twilight had fallen, which meant a great deal of time had passed. Enough time for Riley to have nearly reached them. She glanced back at Sam. "You concentrate on coming around."

He tried to shove up on one elbow. "Crysta, don't be crazy. You're no match for Shriver. He has a gun."

She held up the wood. "This will do if I take him by surprise."

Stepping behind the door, Crysta pressed her back to the wall. Glancing at Sam, she took a deep breath and let out a bloodcurdling scream. He jumped. She screamed again. An instant later, they heard footsteps thumping up the porch. The door crashed open.

Crysta lifted the wood. Shriver stepped into view. With all her might, she brought the wood down on his head with a resounding thud. Shriver staggered, fell against the wall, gave his head a shake and focused on her. Crysta stared at him in horrified disbelief.

"You little—"

Whatever it was he meant to say was cut short. Sam came up off the floor, swinging his massive fist in a wide arc that caught the unprepared pilot squarely on the chin. Head hitting the wall with a loud crack, Shriver rolled his eyes and began a slow descent toward the floor, surprise crossing his face as his legs folded beneath him.

Sam, bracing a shoulder on the wall beside the unconscious pilot, sank to the floor with him. "If we get out of this alive, I'm enrolling you in another self-defense class. You should have hit him above the ear, not dead on."

"How was I to know he has a head like brick? Besides, I only wanted to knock him out, not kill him!"

"Charitable of you," he grunted. "Tie him up. Fast. If he comes around, he won't be half as nice as you, believe me."

Crysta leaped into action. The moment she had Shriver bound, she turned her attention to Sam. "Can you stand up?"

Bracing an arm against the wall, Sam rose to his knees and gave his head a shake. From the way his eyes looked, Crysta knew he was in no condition to walk. Raising his face, he tried to focus on her, his full lips a frightening gray.

"Go without me," he rasped.

"*What?*"

"You heard me. It's your only chance, Crysta."

She ran to peer out the window. "I'm not leaving you!"

He licked his lips and managed to plant one boot on the floor in front of him. Propping an arm on his knee, he said, "Just this once, would you listen to me? I'll slow you down. They'll catch us, and if they do, we're both dead. Now go!"

"No!"

A little bit of his color returned. He tipped his head back and riveted her with an irritated gaze, his eyes bleary. "Somehow, I *knew* you'd say that. Until I met you, I never realized how boring other women were."

It hit Crysta then, with the impact of a battering ram, that the blow to Sam's head had literally knocked the sense out of him. She ran across the room and grabbed his arm. "Sam, for heaven's sake, this is no time for—"

"Professions of love?" With her help, he gained his feet, staggering sideways, which carried her with him. "What better time? I might not get a chance later."

Crysta took two steps toward the door, hauling Sam with her. His boot caught on Shriver's bound legs. She stumbled, caught her balance and lurched forward again. "Sam, you have to concentrate. Are you listening to me?"

"I'm not deaf, honey, just dizzy."

She gritted her teeth, holding him up with one arm while she threw the door wide with her other. Feeling his solid body stumbling against hers made her heart twist with fear for him. At least she could run. "Our lives are at stake here!" she grunted, steering him out onto the porch.

"Exactly." He tripped down the steps. "Which is why—" He pulled to a stop and leaned forward, planting his hands on his knees while he hauled in a gigantic draft of fresh air. "There are some things you don't leave for later when you aren't sure there'll *be* a later. You're one hell of a lady, Crysta Meyers. I just want you to know that."

"So now I know." She caught his arm again, scanning the line of nearby trees, heart in throat. Riley might appear at any moment. "Now, let's apply ourselves to making sure we *have* a later, Sam. Can you do that?"

He straightened, looking a little better now that he had some clean air in his lungs. Blinking, he pulled his arm from her grasp to drape it over her shoulders and leaned heavily against her. "I definitely want a later, believe me. If I let Riley kill me, I'll never get to investigate that cute little birthmark on your—"

Crysta gasped. "You said you didn't look!"

"I lied, too."

EN ROUTE BACK to the river, Sam had to lean heavily on Crysta to make it. As they crossed the meadow, Crysta felt like a tortoise carrying a load of cement while engaged in a footrace with a hare. Hopelessness filled her. Fastening her gaze on the line of trees ahead of them, she did the only thing she could think to do: she prayed.

Just as they reached the edge of the tree line, Crysta spotted a flash of movement from the corner of her eye. Red hair, a plaid shirt, blue jeans. She turned her head, fear chilling the sweat on her face. Riley O'Keefe. A tall, slender figure emerged behind him. Steve Henderson? She'd no sooner registered that than a shot rang out and dirt geysered right in front of her feet.

"Sam!"

In response to her cry, Sam shoved her forward, the force of his thrust sending her into a face-first sprawl in the grass. An instant later, his body slammed into the ground beside her. The swampy earth soaked her shirt and jeans. Crysta needed no prodding. When Sam scrambled forward on his belly toward the trees, she was right beside him.

Once under cover, Sam rose to his knees, swayed to get his balance and peered out over the blades of tall grass. His eyes still had a slightly unfocused look, and he was quite pale.

"They're coming this way at a dead run." He jerked his head around, grabbed her roughly by the arm and sprang unsteadily to his feet. Before Crysta realized what he meant to do, he pulled her to a clump of brush and shoved her into the foliage. "You stay put. I mean it, Crysta. Don't so much as breathe, do you understand me? Count to two hundred, then run for the river. They won't be able to track you if you wade in the stream.''

With that, he reeled away and took off through the trees. Regaining her wits, Crysta sprang after him. Though still unsteady on his feet, he had already covered a distance of ten yards. Crysta knew desperation was driving him. She broke into a run to catch up.

''Sam! Come back here!''

As if her voice lent him speed, he scissored his long legs to increase the distance between them. Crysta nearly called his name again, but the sound of other booted feet thrumming on the damp earth stifled her. She dived for cover in some nearby brush, eyes riveted to the clearing. An instant later, Riley and Henderson burst into view. They scarcely paused. A crashing sound made them whirl and run in the direction Sam had gone.

Sam was leading them away from her.

Crysta balled her hands into fists, breathing in shallow little gasps. Sam was in no condition to play hero, not after taking that blow to his head. He wouldn't be able to go far. Riley and Henderson would catch him. And when they did, they would kill him.

With a sob, Crysta shoved her way out of the concealing brush. As she gained her feet, fear swamped her. For an instant she stood rooted. Sam was giving her the chance to survive this. If she revealed herself, Riley surely had a bullet in that gun with her name on it. Was she out of her mind?

Like a reel of film being played out in fast motion, Crysta saw herself as she had been before coming here to Alaska. How empty her life had been. Until meeting Sam and Tip, she had fooled herself into believing that she could be happy as a successful fashion designer. Now she realized how pitifully lonely she had been, and how pitifully lonely she would always be if things continued status quo. Sam thought his gift to her was a chance for survival, but she wanted more from him than that; she wanted another chance to live, really live. If that wasn't in the cards, then what did she have to lose? Far less than Sam did.

Crysta sprang forward into a run. She wouldn't let him die because of her. It had been her persistence that had pushed Riley into this in the first place. Her fault, only hers. Bursting from the cottonwoods into the meadow, Crysta focused on the three figures running along the edge of the trees. Sam was keeping himself in plain sight. She could tell by his flagging pace that the blow he had received was taking its toll.

Once again, Crysta felt as if she were watching a film, this one spun out in slow motion. Riley, skidding to a stop and throwing up his arm to sight his gun on Sam. Steve Henderson braking to a halt behind Riley and shouting something. And Sam— Pain twisted inside Crysta's chest when she saw him stop running and look back over his shoulder in her direction. He was making a target of himself! So she could flee.

Crysta screamed. The sound ripped through the twilight. Riley spun around. She waved her arms so he could see her. "Run, Sam! Run! Don't do it! Please, don't do it!"

A shot rang out. The dirt beside Crysta exploded upward, a tiny clod hitting her thigh. She flinched, and a horrible paralysis gripped her legs. Then she heard Sam roar with anger.

"Go back!" Crysta staggered forward, her eyes riveted on Sam as he charged toward Riley. "Sam, go back!" she sobbed, breaking into a run herself.

From that moment, everything happened in a swirling haze of unreality. Riley turned and leveled his gun at Sam. Steve Henderson roared "No!" and threw himself on Riley's back. The two smugglers crashed to the ground in a roll, both fighting for control of the gun. As Crysta reached them, Sam was coming up on their other side.

"I won't let you kill them!" Steve cried. "Enough is enough, O'Keefe! It's over!"

O'Keefe rolled to the top and brought his left fist crashing down into Henderson's face. "Over? One more haul, you stupid bastard, and we'll be *rich*. I'm not letting you screw it up!"

Sam skirted the struggling men and snagged Crysta's hand, dragging her into a run. Behind them, Crysta heard another sickening thud of a fist against flesh, then a roar of rage rent the air. She hauled back on Sam's hand. "We can't leave Steve, Sam! We can't!"

Pale-faced, Sam pulled her into a run, using the advantage of his greater weight. His palm felt sweaty around her hand, and his fingers didn't grip with their usual strength. Crysta would have known he was perilously close to collapse even if he hadn't been staggering.

"He's on his own!" he cried shakily. "I'm getting you out of here!"

Just as Sam and Crysta reached the trees, a shot rang out, the echo strangely muffled. From the look on Sam's face as he braked and wheeled to look back, Crysta knew the bullet had found a target. She saw Riley O'Keefe staggering to his feet, brandishing the gun over Steve, who writhed on the ground, holding his stomach.

"Oh, God!" she moaned.

Reeling like a drunk, Sam passed a shirt sleeve across his eyes, dragged in a bracing breath, then began running again, hauling her along behind him. "It's them or us, Crysta! Run, sweetheart. Run like you've never run in your life!"

The trees seemed to whiz past Crysta. She tried to focus on the ground, on Sam's churning legs, but everything seemed blurred. Her lungs began to ache. A stitch knifed into her side. Though his pace began to slow a bit, Sam still kept running. Across the second meadow, through the slough, back into the trees.

Sam drew to a stop where the all-terrain vehicles were hidden in the brush. Like a wild man, he descended on one of the red four-wheelers, throwing off the camouflage of branches. Crysta hurried to help, terrified by Sam's waxen pallor and the sheen of sweat on his face. She knew he was going on sheer willpower now, and that he couldn't remain on his feet much longer.

"Dammit!" he cried. "They took the key. I'll have to hotwire it."

"There isn't time. Riley's coming!"

Sam swore again and grabbed her hand. As they broke
into another run, Crysta could see patches of the muddy
river and the Cessna through the trees. She threw a wild
glance over her shoulder, acutely aware that Riley might
appear at any second. They should be going in another direction. He would guess that they'd head toward the all-
terrain vehicles or the river.

Suddenly Sam's grip on her hand lessened, and he staggered. Throwing out an arm, he looped it around a tree,
nearly falling. Giving his head a shake, he tried to use the
tree trunk to right himself. "Crysta . . ." He labored for air.
"I'm finished."

Throwing a fearful glance behind them, Crysta grabbed
his arm. "Lean on me."

"No!" He lifted his head, trying to focus on her. "Go to
the airplane. You saw Todd at the controls."

"I can't *fly* it!" she cried, her voice shrill.

"You can taxi it!" he snarled. "Go, dammit! I hear him
coming!"

Crysta heard the footsteps, too. Fright lent her strength.
Vising an arm around Sam's waist, she pulled him away
from the tree. "I'm not leaving you."

He fell in beside her, the toes of his rubber boots dragging the ground with his every step, his weight pulling her
into a crazy zigzag as she tried to head for the airplane.

The Cessna loomed before her. From behind her, she
heard the report of Riley's gun. She sobbed and hurled
herself into the water, carrying Sam along with her mo-
mentum. He fell forward onto the airplane's pontoon,
throwing up a leg for purchase so he could climb inside.
Crysta jerked open the cabin door and shoved him from
behind. "Hurry, Sam, hurry!"

Half dragging himself, half falling forward because she
was shoving him so hard, Sam rolled into the cabin. Crysta
scrambled in behind him, closed the door and launched
herself over him into the cockpit. As she gained the pilot's
seat, a bullet popped through the cabin door and hit the
windshield.

Crysta's brain kicked into automatic, her hands reacting. She felt Sam's elbow bump her thigh. Just as the engine roared to life, he said, "That's my Crysta. I knew you could do it."

As if on cue, another bullet tore through the cabin door and into the pilot's seat, inches from Crysta's shoulder, barely clearing the top of Sam's head. He bit off a curse. Crysta leaned forward to look out the destroyed door window. Riley was charging toward the plane, trying to aim along the bobbing barrel of his gun.

She threw a terrified look at the controls, at the throttle. What next? She couldn't remember!

"Go!" Sam gasped. "Go for it!"

And Crysta did. She wasn't sure what she touched or what she shoved, but some of it must have been right because the plane lurched forward. The next instant, her feeling of relief was eclipsed by horror. The plane tried to lift off. She screamed. The aircraft banked sharply to the left, the wing diving into the water. Sam fell against her.

"Back off the throttle," he cried in a hoarse voice. "Hold it level. Smooth as melted butter. That's it, honey."

He made it sound as if she were cruising along a six-lane highway in a Porsche. But ahead of them, the river took a sharp twist to the right, and she had no idea how to steer the plane.

"Rudder right!" Sam bellowed. "Rudder right!"

"Rudder what?" she screeched.

Sam groped with one arm, the plane veered, and they were executing the turn. Crysta felt as if she might vomit. The river twisted before them, sure death at the speed they were going. But if she stopped, Riley would be following along the bank, ready to empty his gun into their skulls.

"We're not going to make it, Sam! We're not going to make it!"

"Oh, yes, we are." He grasped her knee and dropped his head into the crook of his arm. "We're a great team, you and I. A great team."

Teamwork got them safely down the river, though Crysta wasn't exactly sure how, given the fact that her partner seemed to be only half aware. But somehow, every time she was ready to throw her arms up to shield her face, Sam was there to take over.

After what seemed a lifetime, they rounded the last bend in the river, and there was the lodge. Crysta aimed for the island.

"Slow down!" Sam barked.

His warning came too late. The Cessna hit the shallows going far too fast and did a belly-skid up onto land, coming to such a jarring stop that both she and Sam were thrown forward against the control panel. The propeller blades thunked into the dirt. The small plane bucked and shuddered. Then, with a cough, the engine died, and an eerie silence blanketed everything.

Crysta, all her muscles watery with fright, oozed downward from the control panel and fell backward. Her landing was softer than it might have been; Sam's chest cushioned the impact.

Dazed, she rolled off him, to be wedged tightly between his body and the seat. He dropped a limp arm around her waist, pressed his forehead to hers and whispered, "Did I tell you you're one hell of a lady?"

Crysta blinked and focused on his dark face, still trying to digest the fact that she had actually maneuvered an airplane along a winding river, that she and Sam, against all odds, were still alive. Though he had come through for her on several occasions, she had, for the most part, guided the plane by herself. "I am, aren't I?" she whispered incredulously.

With a weak laugh, he tipped his head back and closed his eyes, swallowing hard. "We have to get to the lodge. Riley might come, and we have to be ready, just in case. It'll take the cops at least an hour to reach us after we get a call through to them."

Crysta doubted that Riley would approach the lodge. He would realize that they'd be ready for him, and cowards like Riley didn't like bad odds. He would probably try to evade the police in the interior. But with no mode of air transportation out, it would be only a matter of hours before he was

caught. She managed to extricate herself from between Sam
and the seat.

"Can you make it, or should I holler for help?"

He flashed her a tremulous smile. "I think that, together, we can make it through almost anything. Don't
you?"

The question seemed loaded with meaning. Throwing
open the door, Crysta glanced out at the lodge, and suddenly, what had seemed so simple back in the meadow took
on terrifying proportions. Sam was offering her a whole new
world, *his* world. There could be no compromises. This was
Sam and Tip's home; they belonged here. The question was,
did she?

In a shaky voice, she murmured, "Derrick's still out
there, Sam. Right now, I can't get beyond that."

He took her hand and struggled to his feet, crouched so
his head cleared the cabin ceiling. His eyes met hers. "The
moment the cops have hauled Riley and his friends in, it'll
be safe for the searchers to go back out."

"I don't need searchers," she replied with a little more
strength. "I know now where Derrick is. There's a small
lake a few miles north of the cleaning location. There's a
cabin there."

Sam gave a slow nod. "I know the place. The lake's not
large enough for a plane to go in for a landing, and the terrain is too swampy to go in on four-wheelers. We'll have to
walk."

"If Derrick's survived this long," Crysta said softly,
"he'll hold out until we can reach him."

Sam's eyes darkened. "By the time the cops have come in
and cleaned up, I should be recovered enough to go with
you."

As Crysta bore the brunt of his weight to help him from
the plane, she had reason to doubt that.

Chapter Fifteen

Five hours later, Crysta stood on the riverbank below the lodge, her ears buzzing from the sounds of airplane engines as they revved to life. Sunlight warmed her face, a direct contrast to the chill coursing up her spine as she watched the police haul Riley O'Keefe past her toward the footbridge. It would be the last time the redhead walked over to the island and boarded a float-plane.

Riley fixed his fiery blue eyes on her and tried to stop walking. The officer holding the cuff chain between his wrists jerked upward, wrenching the smuggler's arms behind his back.

"Keep walking, friend."

Riley spat in Crysta's direction. "If it weren't for you, I'd be vacationing in the Bahamas next week."

Crysta smiled. "But, Riley, it's hot down there this time of year. You might break a sweat."

"You think I don't know what sweat is?" He ran a hostile gaze the length of her. "It was because I was tired of sweating that I did this! It was my turn at the good life, for once!"

Sensing Sam behind her, Crysta pulled her gaze from the departing smuggler and turned. Her heart caught at the seriousness in Sam's eyes. Though he seemed steady on his feet now, his color still hadn't returned completely to normal. "I've gotten four men to volunteer to go with us to the lake. Jangles has packed them food, I borrowed a stretcher, and we're ready to go."

"Sam, it really isn't necessary for you to go."

"You'll have to hogtie me to keep me from it," was his response.

Crysta pressed her lips together. She knew that Sam was risking a great deal of humiliation should her hunch about Derrick's location prove incorrect. At long last, she had found a man who not only accepted her link with Derrick, but also believed in her dreams.

Sam's gaze shifted to the river island. "Do we have time to go over and see Steve for a minute before they fly him out?"

Wordlessly, Crysta nodded and fell into a walk beside him. A few minutes more would make little difference to the outcome for Derrick. After all, they owed Steve Henderson for their lives.

When they gained the island, Sam hailed the police officers who were preparing to board one of the pontoon planes. After a brief exchange, Sam led her around the plane's wing and into knee-deep water, so they could speak to Steve Henderson where he lay on a stretcher in the already crowded cabin.

"Steve?" Sam said softly.

The thin young man opened his eyes, focused on Sam and Crysta, then managed a weak grin. "So you made it. I'm—" His face contorted, and he clenched his teeth. "I'm sorry, Barrister." He grimaced again. "Never m-meant for anyone to be hurt. Know it was wrong, real wrong, but it seemed a fair enough trade for some money... for Scotty's expenses, not for me."

"The moment I realized you were involved, Steve, I knew why," Sam said softly.

Steve's eyes filled with tears. "They found a marrow match. The wife called last night. He's got a chance, Sam. Shame his old man won't be around to play ball with him again." Closing his eyes, Henderson swallowed. "Stupidest thing I ever did, going after those walrus. First thing I ever poached."

"Jangles told me about the donor match. I'm glad, Steve, really glad." Sam sighed. "I spoke to the police. They know you stopped O'Keefe from killing us. That'll go well for you in court. I also called my lawyer to see if he'd take your case. He's already arranging for bail. All that's left is for you to get that lead out of your gut and regain your strength enough for a flight to Seattle. The lawyer's applying for a waiver, so you can be with Scotty."

"I don't deserve your help, Sam."

"Maybe not, but Scotty does. Besides, the way I see it, your biggest crime was making some bad decisions, and things got out of hand. A judge will agree with me, I think. Scotty has a second chance. I'm going to be there in court to testify—so maybe his father'll get one, too."

Crysta started to say something herself, but before she could, a police officer climbed onto the airplane's wing. "Sorry, folks, but this fella's got to be taken to the hospital."

Sam nodded and drew Crysta away from the wing. Wading through the water and up onto land, Crysta sensed the tension in him. Glancing up, she saw moisture glistening in his eyes. He caught her staring at him and blinked.

"He's a good guy. What was he supposed to do? Let Scotty do without? If it had been me, I'd have gone slaughtering walrus, too, and I detest poachers!"

Crysta couldn't imagine why Sam should be angry with her. At a loss, she lowered her gaze.

"Look, I *know* he was there when Derrick was shot. And I don't blame you if you're ticked at me for going to bat for him."

"I'm not ticked, Sam, not at all. I'm glad."

Sam stopped walking, one foot poised on the bridge. "You are?"

Crysta met his gaze. "Of course. Derrick would be, too. There's no need to defend yourself because you pulled strings to help him. It's obvious he only got involved because of his son and that he later came to regret it. He took a bullet trying to stop Riley from hurting anyone else. That's evidence enough for me."

"Why didn't I do more to help him?"

"You raised all the money you could. That's more than most people do."

"It's a crying shame, that's what it is, and the whole deal makes me feel sick."

Crysta stepped up onto the bridge and slipped an arm around his waist. "Point taken. As soon as we find Derrick, let's get off our duffs and do something about it."

His hip bumped against her as they walked along the bouncing bridge toward shore. "Like what?"

The frustration in his voice made her want to hug him. "I don't know, but we'll think of something. People care, Sam. They'll donate. Scotty Henderson's medical costs will be paid, and he'll get to visit Disneyland."

As they stepped off the bridge, Crysta glanced up to see Jangles and Tip standing on shore, waiting for them. The Indian woman was wringing her skirt with one hand and holding a blue hiking pack with the other, her worried eyes fastened on Crysta.

"I have packed you food," she said softly. "Some special cakes the others don't have. And some very strong coffee, for I know you are tired."

Crysta nodded. "Thank you, Jangles. I appreciate that."

The Tlingit caught her bottom lip between her teeth. After a moment, she whispered, "I have been very bad to you, I think."

Crysta tightened her arm around Sam's waist, recalling all the times she had thought the worst of Jangles. The score seemed pretty even. "Let's put it behind us, Jangles."

"No, you do not understand." She lifted sorrowful eyes to Sam. "Some of my family live up north, near the killing fields where Riley's been slaughtering walrus. Three years ago, some poachers were caught and then set free after serving short sentences. We could not let that happen again."

Sam stiffened. "You knew about the ivory smuggling?"

"I—" Jangles broke off. She slowly nodded. "I watch and listen, like a shadow. Sometimes people forget me, and they whisper their secrets."

Sam made an irritated sound under his breath. Jangles threw a frightened look at Tip. The boy nudged her arm. "Tell him, Jangles. When he g-gets mad, he yells, but then he st-stops."

"You knew about this, Tip?" Sam demanded.

"Not until j-just now. Jangles was c-crying. I asked what was wrong, and sh-she told me."

"There is more," Jangles inserted in a strangled voice. "I knew Derrick had been following Riley downriver."

"I see." Sam's voice rang with bridled fury. Turning the full blast of his gaze on Jangles, he said, "Derrick was my friend. He may be dead. You might have prevented that."

"I was very wrong," Jangles cried. "But I did not think they would hurt him! Until he came up missing, I thought he was in on it. By the time I realized he wasn't, it was too late! That is why I tried to make Crysta leave—before the same happened to her. She was asking questions. I saw her follow you the first day." She made a feeble gesture with her hand. "She wouldn't accept that Derrick was dead, and I knew she'd come to harm if she stayed here and made the poachers nervous."

She moistened her lips and shook her head. "I know I should have told you. But at the time—" She broke off and lifted an imploring gaze. "Try to see as we see, Sam. The whites come here and kill our wildlife. And they go unpunished! We *must* fight back! When I guessed what was going on, I called my brothers. This time, we decided to follow the old law and punish the poachers ourselves."

"Your brothers? I saw you talking to a man in the woods. That was one of them?"

Jangles nodded. "I was afraid you'd grow suspicious if you knew they had come."

"Jangles, the old ways don't work now. It's sheer folly to take the law into your own hands! And I especially resent your doing it here! I asked you, point-blank, if you knew anything, and you refused to answer me!"

"I am fired, I guess," Jangles said shakily. "It is what I deserve."

Sam rolled his eyes. "Jangles, you're a member of our family. You don't *fire* family. You just—" He sighed and glanced at Tip. "You just yell a little and get over being angry." He reached to take the pack from her hand. "This isn't finished. I have to go find Derrick right now, but when all this calms down, you and I are due for a serious talk."

"Yes," Jangles agreed solemnly.

Tip visibly brightened. "You see?" he said, nudging Jangles's arm. "He's already done yelling."

"Tip," Sam said in a warning voice.

As anxious as she was to be gone, Crysta couldn't smother a grin. Sam glanced down at her, his face lined with weariness. In a low voice, he said, "Let's go before I end up strangling them both."

Signaling to the other men, Sam struck off downstream.

"Can I come, Dad?"

"No, Tip, not this time."

"But I could help!" Tip protested.

Sam paused to look over his shoulder at his son. As much as he wanted to say yes, he knew Tip's jabbering would probably drive Crysta half mad by the time they reached their destination. She had enough to contend with right now. "Son, I—"

"Sam?" Crysta touched his arm. She waited for the other four men to walk past them and get out of earshot. "It's safe enough for him to go along, isn't it? Derrick might be—" She broke off and seemed to search for words. "I'd like having my friends with me, just in case. Tip and I, we're kind of—" She shrugged. "If you don't mind, I'd really like him to be there."

A breeze caught Crysta's hair, draping it across her face. Sam stared down at her, searching her veiled eyes.

"Are you sure?" he whispered. "He'll talk your hind leg off."

"And bug me, you mean?" She leaned closer. "Sam, understand something. I like your son. We're *friends*."

Sam slid his gaze to Tip. "Go get your jacket. You'll have to catch up with us. Can you do that?"

Tip was already racing for the lodge, long legs flying. Sam watched him a moment, then looked at Crysta. There was a wealth of emotion in his eyes.

Smiling, Crysta turned to look downstream. Her spirits immediately plummeted. It seemed an eternity ago that she had come here to Alaska to find Derrick. Now, the last leg of her search was about to begin. What lay ahead of her? She broke into a walk, her shoulders stiff with tension. Since her dream of Derrick digging the bullet from his chest, she hadn't dreamed of him again or felt anything. It was possible the silence meant her brother was dead.

She curled her hands into fists. She had once yearned to be free of Derrick. If that thoughtless wish came true, how would she ever manage to live with it?

SEVERAL HOURS LATER, the search party crested a knoll. Below them, the cabin sat on a windswept plane of grassland, stark against the horizon, with a smattering of stunted trees on a slope behind it. Though Crysta had seen similar terrain from the air, it looked vastly different from ground level. *Alaska.* She had the eerie sensation that she and her companions were tiny specks in this vast land, so inconsequential that the wind might, at any moment, sweep them away. She had never seen grass so vibrant a green, rolling forever before her. Ribbons of water cut through the marshes, spilling into countless tiny ponds and lakes.

She focused on the small lake before them. Sam had been right. It wasn't a large enough body of water to land a sea plane on.

"Is this it?" Sam asked, taking her arm.

Crysta nodded. She had seen this place in her last dream, and she knew Derrick had to be here. Suddenly, she was terrified. She wanted to race down the incline, but her feet were anchored to the grass. Tip and the other four men hung back, as if they knew she needed to face this moment alone. "I'm frightened, Sam."

"You know, no matter what we find down there, none of this is your fault." When she started to interrupt, he rushed on. "I've been doing a lot of thinking about what you told me the other night. It isn't wrong to want your own life, Crysta. You have to put this thing with Derrick into its proper perspective.''

"You make it sound so simple, but it isn't."

"I know Derrick loved you. Alive or dead, he'd want you to feel at peace with yourself. Don't go down there with a load of responsibility on your shoulders that isn't and never should have been yours. You've lived your entire life feeling as if it was somehow your responsibility to not only *know* when Derrick was in trouble, but to somehow *save* him. That's crazy. It was wrong of your mother to encourage that kind of thinking."

"Put like that, it even sounds crazy to me." She straightened her shoulders. "On the other hand, though, my mother has been right, too, Sam. During my marriage and after it crumbled, I tried to be someone I wasn't. This experience has taught me that I can't deny what's between Derrick and me, and I can't shove myself into a mold to please other people—I have to build a life that fits around me. Does that make any sense?"

"Perfect sense," he said huskily. "Just don't forget that there may be a man who'd be willing to help you build that life."

She squeezed her eyes closed. "Will you go down with me?"

"Try to lose me."

Crysta struck off down the slope, her hand enveloped in Sam's, their clenched fingers pulsating everywhere their flesh touched. She couldn't breathe. Her legs felt numb.

"If he's dead, I'll never forgive myself," she whispered raggedly. "Crazy or not, it's how I feel."

She wished she could think of the words to make him understand. Then he gave her hand a squeeze, and she knew, without his saying so, that he did understand. She turned to look up at him.

"Crysta?"

The whisper inside her head made Crysta freeze. With a surge of wild hope, she whirled toward the cabin. "Der-

rick?'' Breaking into a run, Crysta tore down the decline,
Sam at her side.

''Derrick!'' She hit the rickety, sagging porch in a leap,
grappling frantically at the door, which hung awry from its
rotted hinges. ''Derrick! Oh, Derrick!''

Bursting inside, Crysta hesitated, blinded by the sudden
dimness. She heard movement to her left, and a voice
rasped, ''It sure took you long enough to get here.''

Crysta flung herself across the room. Peering through the
gloom, she saw her brother lying on a grimy old mattress.
He was thin. His eyes were glazed with fever. But he was
alive. Sweeping aside an array of empty cans on the floor,
she sank to her knees. With a trembling hand, she reached
to touch the blood-soaked bandage around his chest.

''Oh, Derrick, what did he *do* to you?''

With a clammy hand, Derrick grasped her tremulous fingers. ''He shot me—as if you don't already know.'' Heavier footsteps behind Crysta caught Derrick's attention. He
grinned and closed his eyes, clearly exhausted from talking. ''Hey, buddy.''

Sam stepped closer, coming to a stop behind Crysta.
Leaning forward, he pressed a palm to Derrick's glistening
forehead.

''The fever's broken,'' Derrick rasped, lifting his lashes.
''That's why I'm sweatin' like a plow mule. You're too late
to play nursemaid, unless you can find something to brace
my leg. Broken, I think, in a couple of places.'' He licked his
lips. ''You got any fresh water? I made it down to the lake
a couple of times. Don't know if it was the rusty can or the
water, but it tasted like—'' He broke off and smiled. ''The
food left here wasn't much better. If I never see another
Vienna sausage or corn kernel, it'll be too soon. What's the
matter? You guys can't talk, or what?''

Glancing down at the empty cans, it struck Crysta as
hysterically funny that Derrick was actually *complaining*
about his accommodations when she and Sam had been
worrying that he might starve. She started to laugh, and she
couldn't stop. And then she found herself wrapped in her
brother's arms, and her laughter turned to tears.

Aware of his wound, she cried, "Derrick, I'll hurt you!"

"Never. Nothing ever felt so good."

A sob tore up Crysta's throat. Then another. "Oh, Derrick, you'll never know how I felt, not being able to find you."

"I was out of it most of the time. A high fever. Unconscious. I guess that's why you couldn't pick up on me. Crysta, don't do this to yourself. Please."

"But I couldn't *feel* you. I couldn't reach you. All I could think was that it'd be my fault if you died."

"*Your* fault? It was *my* fault, Crysta, not yours." Placing his hand on her hair, he tucked in his chin to look down at her. "Why would you blame yourself for something totally out of your control? How can you possibly take responsibility?"

"I couldn't find you." She sniffed and let out a rush of breath. "For so long, I tried to put a wall between us! And then, when you needed me most, I discovered I had succeeded! Mom tried to warn me I'd regret what I was doing, but I was too selfish to listen. Oh, Derrick, I thought I had lost you."

"Selfish?" Derrick pressed his lips against her hair. "Crysta..." He sighed and hooked a finger under her chin to tip her face back. After studying her for a long moment, he said, "Don't you think it's about time we stopped listening to Mom? If she had her way, we'd be wearing coordinating outfits when we were ninety."

Crysta closed her eyes, smiling at the image that conjured. Pulling from his arms, she wiped her cheeks with the sleeve of her jacket. "Look at me, bawling all over you, and you hurt." She reached to touch the stubble on his chin. "Oh, Derrick, I love you. Do you realize how much?"

"Enough to get me some water?"

"I think I can manage that."

Over the next hour, while Derrick got some much-needed first aid, he told everyone what had happened. Much of it Sam and Crysta already knew, but Tip sat spellbound on the floor by the newly built fire, arms looped around his knees.

"One thing bothers me," Crysta inserted. "The staged bear attack wasn't anywhere near the cleaning location. It was at least five miles closer to the lodge."

"I was tailing them. They must have realized, so they led me several miles downstream, then lost me. I stopped to eat. They crept up on me. I ran back toward Cottonwood Bend, leaving my pack and everything behind."

"I found the place were you stopped to eat," Sam inserted. "There was bear track. The pack was torn apart. The obvious conclusion to draw was that you'd been attacked."

"There's bear track *everywhere* here," Derrick put in.

Sam smiled. "I couldn't believe you had been dumb enough to mess with a grizzly. In my experience, you always head in the other direction if you spot territorial markings."

"Oh, I was dumb. Just wasn't a grizzly I was messing with." Derrick sighed. "I wanted so badly to catch them, find out where they were stashing the ivory. Without proof, I knew they'd get off. Pretty cagey of them, making it look like a bear attacked me."

Sam pieced together the rest of what had happened. "When they shot you, they must have thought you were dead. They hauled you away, somehow covering their tracks, and threw you down an embankment."

"Not immediately. First, they threw me into one of their stinking cleaning sheds. I guess they hadn't figured out what to do with my body. I'm not sure how long I was in there. Several hours, because I regained consciousness when they came in to get me. I tried to play dead, but at that point, of course, they realized I wasn't, because rigor mortis wasn't setting in. Lucky for me, Riley didn't have his gun on him, so they settled for throwing me down onto the rocks, which should have finished me, but, by some miracle, didn't." Derrick gestured at his splint. "That's how I got my leg busted."

Crysta remembered the falling sensation she had experienced in her office at the dress shop, the terrible pain in her chest. "And then you lost consciousness again?"

"Yeah, thank goodness. The pain was—pretty bad. When I came around, I was lying wedged between the rocks. The mud had stopped my wound from bleeding, which was probably all that had saved me from bleeding to death or attracting scavengers. By then, I had lost all track of time. I managed to crawl up the bank. I found a tree limb to use as a crutch and came here." Derrick's eyes drifted closed. "I knew you and Sam would come, Sis. Only a matter of time."

"It's a miracle you're here to tell us about it."

"Not a miracle. The belt buckle you had had made for me impeded the bullet and kept the wound from being fatal. By the way, Sis, did you know it was Sam who had given me the silver dollar we used in the buckle?"

Sam touched her shoulder. "We'd better let Derrick rest for a while. It's going to be rough on him making the trip back."

Crysta rose, pulling the blankets they had brought high on her brother's shoulders. Tenderness welled within her.

She and Sam walked outside and dropped wearily onto the porch step, their gazes fastened on the small lake. Acutely aware of Sam beside her, Crysta registered the scenery and realized how soon she would be leaving it all behind. Her time with Sam had been rife with tension and heartache, but now, perversely, she wished it wouldn't end. They had a few hours left, but it wasn't enough.

"Oh, Sam, it's so beautiful here. Now that I know Derrick's all right, I can really appreciate it."

He didn't look at her. "I guess you'll be going back to Anchorage tonight, and heading to Los Angeles from there. I—wish you could stay. It may be pretty here, but it gets mighty lonely sometimes."

She could scarcely speak around the lump in her throat. "I guess it can get lonely anywhere, even in a crowded place like Los Angeles."

He turned to look at her. "I got the impression you kept pretty busy with your business and friends."

She licked her lips. "Yeah . . . busy."

Her eyes clung to his. Suddenly, she knew what she wanted, more than anything.

He dragged his gaze from hers. "You knew what I was asking there in the plane, right after we beached it. I saw the doubt in your eyes when you looked at the lodge. I guess maybe I was rushing you. I'm sorry." He cleared his throat. "I, um, I was thinking, maybe Tip could show his paintings in Los Angeles. We could visit you while we're there."

She studied his profile. He had listened to her, and he planned to take her advice to heart. He was at last prepared to let Tip take risks.

Footsteps thumped on the porch behind them. "But, Dad, I don't want to see Crysta just on visits!"

Tip's voice made Crysta leap. Sam, more conditioned to the boy's inappropriate timing, turned his head more slowly. Tip planted himself on the step on the other side of Crysta, leaning forward, elbows on his knees, to look at his father.

"That'd be dumb. None of us'd be lonely if we stayed together."

A smile tugged at Crysta's mouth. She turned to look at Sam and found his eyes aching with unvoiced messages. *I love you. Will you stay with us?* With a bit of a shock, she realized that Derrick wasn't the only one with whom she could communicate without words.

Sam's gaze flicked to his son, rested there a moment, then returned to her. "Tip, I think Crysta and I need to take a walk."

"That sounds fun. Can I come?"

Crysta laughed softly and rose from the steps. "Tip, I think you'd better stay here. Your father and I have some talking to do."

Sam jumped off the steps, capturing her shoulders within the circle of his arm. "And don't follow us. If I see even a glimpse of you, I'll snatch you baldheaded."

As they neared the lake, Crysta tipped her head back against Sam's arm and closed her eyes. "The answer is yes."

"I haven't *asked* you yet. I realize you're a woman of the nineties, but can we do this the traditional way?"

She smiled. "All right, but if we're going for traditional, I want you on your knees."

He spun her around and up against his chest, his arm tightening at her waist. "Not *that* traditional. They can see us from the cabin."

She arched an eyebrow at him. "Are you going to ask or not?"

"It won't be easy. Tip demands a great deal of my time. He intrudes at the worst possible moments—*always*. And he may never grow up. Do you understand what I'm saying? It's a lot of responsibility you'll be assuming."

She touched a fingertip to his lips. "Sam, listen to yourself. You sound like a recording of me when I was telling you why Dick left me. When something is right between two people, the external difficulties can be worked out. You have Tip in your life, I have Derrick in mine. I think that makes us a perfect pair."

His mouth curved in a smile, and he nibbled at her fingertip. "You know, six months out of the year, the snow gets so deep up here that we close the lodge and live in Anchorage."

"You do?"

His eyes searched hers. "It wouldn't be inconceivable for us to have two businesses—yours and mine. I've been planning to get my pilot's license. With a double income, we could probably afford a small plane. Our travel costs back and forth during the summer would be minimal. I've never turned my hand to designing clothes, but I'd make a great bookkeeper."

"That's a thought. My partner can handle the shop in Los Angeles, and I could probably use my share of the proceeds to open another shop up here."

"Could you be happy with leaving someone else in charge six months out of the year while we travel back and forth between the lodge and the dress shop?"

"Blissfully. In fact, I may hire a manager full-time and simply oversee things."

"But you'll be giving up so much..."

She placed her hand over his mouth and slowly shook her head. "You're forgetting something. I told you, my life-long dream was to have a family. The business, my life in Los Angeles, was filler. I'd like to stay in the fashion industry, but that isn't the most important thing to me. I'll want plenty of free time to devote to being a mom. I have a feeling that two businesses, Tip and a couple of sets of twins will keep both of us busy. We'll be glad we have a manager for the dress shop."

"A couple of—" His eyes widened. "Twins run in your family?"

"Obviously."

His mouth curved into a grin. *"Twins?"*

"Would that be a problem?"

"A problem." He looked a little dazed. "No, not at all. I *love* kids! I just never considered having more than one at a time. Fortunately, I'm quite a hand at changing diapers."

"Well, then . . ."

His face drew closer to hers. "Derrick will be over the moon when we tell him."

Crysta had a feeling Derrick had already tuned in on the news. "You think so?"

His lips brushed hers. "Positive."

A little breathless, she whispered, "You still haven't asked me."

His mouth claimed hers. Crysta melted against him, closing her eyes. Against the blackness of her eyelids, she saw bright little starbursts. Her heart began to slam. With a moan, she gave herself up to the kiss, her senses reeling. The ground disappeared, and there was only Sam.

Some things could be said without words. Sam asked, and Crysta said yes.

ROMANCE IS A YEARLONG EVENT!

Celebrate the most romantic day of the year with MY VALENTINE! (February)

CRYSTAL CREEK
When you come for a visit Texas-style, you won't want to leave! (March)

Celebrate the joy, excitement and adjustment that comes with being JUST MARRIED! (April)

Go back in time and discover the West as it was meant to be . . . UNTAMED— Maverick Hearts! (July)

LINGERING SHADOWS
New York Times bestselling author Penny Jordan brings you her latest blockbuster. Don't miss it! (August)

BACK BY POPULAR DEMAND!!!
Calloway Corners, involving stories of four sisters coping with family, business and romance! (September)

FRIENDS, FAMILIES, LOVERS
Join us for these heartwarming love stories that evoke memories of family and friends. (October)

Capture the magic and romance of Christmas past with HARLEQUIN HISTORICAL CHRISTMAS STORIES! (November)

WATCH FOR FURTHER DETAILS IN ALL HARLEQUIN BOOKS!

Take 4 bestselling love stories FREE

Plus get a FREE surprise gift!

HARLEQUIN®

I N T R I G U E®

43 Light St.

It looks like a charming old building near the Baltimore waterfront, but inside 43 Light Street lurks danger . . . and romance.

Labeled a "true master of intrigue" by *Rave Reviews*, bestselling author Rebecca York continues her exciting series with #213 HOPSCOTCH, coming to you in February.

Paralegal Noel Emery meets an enigmatic man from her past and gets swept away on a thrilling international adventure—where illusion and reality shift like the images in a deadly kaleidoscope. . . .

"Ms. York ruthlessly boggles the brain and then twists our jangled nerves beyond the breaking point in this electrifying foray into hi-tech skullduggery and sizzling romance!"
—Melinda Helfer, *Romantic Times*

Don't miss Harlequin Intrigue #213 HOPSCOTCH!

HARLEQUIN
HISTORICAL
CHRISTMAS
·STORIES·1992·

Capture the magic and romance of Christmas in the 1800s with HARLEQUIN HISTORICAL CHRISTMAS STORIES 1992, a collection of three stories by celebrated historical authors. The perfect Christmas gift!

Don't miss these heartwarming stories, available in November wherever Harlequin books are sold:

MISS MONTRACHET REQUESTS by Maura Seger
CHRISTMAS BOUNTY by Erin Yorke
A PROMISE KEPT by Bronwyn Williams

Plus, as an added bonus, you can receive a FREE keepsake Christmas ornament. Just collect four proofs of purchase from any November or December 1992 Harlequin or Silhouette series novels, or from any Harlequin or Silhouette Christmas collection, and receive a beautiful dated brass Christmas candle ornament.

Mail this certificate along with four (4) proof-of-purchase coupons plus $1.50 postage and handling (check or money order—do not send cash), payable to Harlequin Books, to: **In the U.S.**: P.O. Box 9057, Buffalo, NY 14269-9057; **In Canada**: P.O. Box 622, Fort Erie, Ontario, L2A 5X3.